IF YOU'VE GOT IT, HAUNT IT

GRIMDALE GRAVEYARD MYSTERIES, BOOK 2

STEFFANIE HOLMES

Cover Design: Covers by Aura

ISBN: 978-1-991099-29-7

❀ Created with Vellum

IF YOU'VE GOT IT, HAUNT IT

Nothing is permanent. Not even death.

I'm Bree Mortimer, and I can bring ghosts back to life.

The hot-as-Hades Roman Centurion in my bedroom is living proof that I can raise the dead. Now all I have to do is stop him swimming naked in the duck pond and trying to stab anyone with a man bun, and my life will be perfect.

Hah. That's a joke. My life is a spooktacular failure. I've got two ghostly lovers who are desperate for me to bring them back, too, but if I don't figure out how to control my new magical powers, there could be grave consequences.

And that's going to be difficult since the only person who can help me was ripped to pieces by a monster who can't possibly be human. Some dark power is after resurrection magic, and if I don't figure out how to stop it, I'm next.

Luckily, with a sword-wielding psychotic ex-ghost, a sarcastic royal rake, a cinnamon roll Victorian gentleman, a sadistic bat, a vampire-slaying bookshop owner, and the village undertaker on my side, I stand a ghost of a chance. Right?

Right?

Bree and her ghostly men are back for another spooky adventure in, *If You've Got It, Haunt It,* book 2 of this darkly humorous cozy fantasy series by bestselling author Steffanie Holmes. If you love a sarcastic heroine, hot, possessive, and slightly unhinged ghostly men, a mystery to solve, and a little kooky, spooky lovin' to set your coffin a rockin', then quit ghouling around and start reading!

JOIN THE NEWSLETTER FOR UPDATES

Want a free bonus scene from Bree's school dance and Bree's playlist? Grab a free copy of *Cabinet of Curiosities* – a Steffanie Holmes compendium of short stories and bonus scenes – when you sign up for updates with the Steffanie Holmes newsletter.

http://www.steffanieholmes.com/newsletter

Every week in my newsletter I talk about the true-life hauntings, strange happenings, crumbling ruins, and creepy facts that inspire my stories. You'll also get newsletter-exclusive bonus scenes and updates. I love to talk to my readers, so come join us for some spooky fun :)

Grimwood
Manor

The Fernsby's
Cottage

Welcome to
GRIMWOOD
B & B

For my dad
Who is my first hero

Bibamus moriendum est.
　　Death is Inevitable;
　　Let's Get Drunk.
　　—Roman aphorism, attributed to Seneca the Elder

PROLOGUE

"What's this stone good for?"

The perky-breasted teenage strumpet interrupts her reading.

Vera hides her scowl with a demure little cough, closes her spell book for the eighth time that hour, and turns to the annoying customer.

I'm in the wrong business. She should have started that goat farm, like she wanted to, but her friend Mabel Ellis over in Argleton insisted that she share her gifts with the world. Mabel isn't good with the word 'no' (which happens to be Vera's favorite word), so before Vera knew it, she'd sold her prized goat, paid for a year's lease on a High Street storefront, and stocked up on tacky dreamcatchers.

That was seven years ago now, and in her time running a New Age store, Vera has encountered approximately three truly gifted magic workers and an infinite number of annoying teenage girls, sulky goths, and sad housewives looking for a magical sign that they should leave their husbands.

"Well? Is it for attracting love? Protection? Deepening

friendship?" the girl prods her impatiently. Behind her, two of the girl's equally annoying friends flip through the fantasy artwork, giggling over the bare-breasted *Lady of the Lake*.

"That orange one? You shove it up your cootchie, dear." Vera turns back to her book, hiding the tug of her smirk behind the page as the girl registers her comment.

"You...what?"

"Oh yes. It's an ancient Druidic practice. Women push those stones up their vah-jay-jay and keep them up their foof for a few hours or overnight. They center your yoni, tighten the muscles in your bajingo, and turn your panty underworld into a salacious tunnel of untold pleasure." Vera pauses for dramatic effect. "Praise the goddess."

Vera loves that humans have created so many silly euphemisms for a woman's anatomy just to avoid saying *cunt* – an ancient word that carries so much true power that uttering it in the company of the wrong spell book can unleash the next apocalypse. She likes to see how many euphemisms she can use before customers back slowly away and stop annoying her.

"Oh, well..." the girl stares down at the stone. "That sounds amazing. I have this new guy and I really want to steal him off his hag of a girlfriend. If my, ah, salacious tunnel is better than hers, then..."

"Say no more, my dear. Just place that stone inside the petals of your abyssal flower and he will be completely under your spell."

"Okay! Thanks." The girl chooses the largest piece of orange moonstone and plonks it on the counter. "How much?"

"Wait, we want some too." Her two friends crowd around, choosing the largest stones and shuffling through the saint cards on the counter before purchasing a few of those, too. Vera charges them double her usual price because she doesn't believe stupidity should be rewarded. The bell tinkles as the girls leave the shop in a giggling gaggle.

Happy yeast infection, you silly girl. Why anyone believes that shoving a porous stone into your abandoned uranium mine of carnal knowledge is a good idea, I'll never know, but I'll happily pay the rent on their ignorance. Praise the Goddess for Goop raising a generation of gullible fools.

"That was mean," says Lottie, folding her arms across her see-through chest as she emerges from behind the Buddhism display.

"I thought it was hilarious." Agnes clutches her stomach, her shoulder still trembling with laughter. "Some people are too silly to exist."

"Hmmmph." Vera nods her agreement and returns to her book. The three witches move toward the back of the store, discussing the various uses of henbane and who they want to win *The Bachelor*, which Vera lets them watch on her TV sometimes. She is used to their chatter by now. They treat the shop as their own personal headquarters, but they are at least far more tolerable than her Living clientele.

Vera checks her watch. Just fifty-six minutes left until closing time. She massages her bad hip and thinks longingly about the herbal tea and pot brownies she has waiting upstairs, when the store bell tinkles again.

A chill runs down her spine.

The temperature in the shop drops by *precisely* six degrees.

"What...what is *that?*" Lottie gasps.

Vera doesn't look up from sorting the saint cards that the girls messed up. She knows exactly what it is.

"I didn't expect to see you so soon," she mutters, placing Saint Ignatius down in front of her. Poor Ignatius, fed to the lions at the Colosseum in front of a roaring crowd. That Christian god certainly liked to put His most loyal servants through some heinous torments.

"You know that I am not here for you," the creature rasps. He moves toward her, his footsteps nearly soundless on the thick Oriental carpets scattered in a patchwork style across the store. Vera sneaks a look at his shoes – shiny black boots paired with white-button gaiters. Old-fashioned.

Hmmmm.

She didn't expect that. They usually send someone more modern. They like things to be efficient. Neat. The old ones never had the tools to be neat.

The creature stops in front of the counter. His presence sucks the air from the room. Vera hears one of the witches gasp.

"I think you should run, Vera," Lottie says slowly. "This fellow looks to be no good."

"Rather dapper, though, don't you think?" Mary adds. "That smart hat and elegant cape..."

"Did you get a new boyfriend, Vera?" Agnes asks in her sharp tone. "You might've told us. If you think we're going to leave so you two can canoodle in peace, you've got another think coming. We've already been banished from loitering around Grimwood Manor and we need a place to conduct our important ghost business—"

The creature lets out a low, terrifying hiss, like a tea kettle boiling over, that shuts Agnes right up.

"If you're not here for me, and you're not going to buy anything, then I have nothing to say to you." Vera shuffles the Saint Agatha cards to the front of the display.

"I am here to deliver a message."

"Do I look like I have ROYAL MAIL stamped on my fore-head?" she snaps.

"You are not the messenger. You are the parchment."

Vera jerks her head up, because if she is truly to die today, then she will stare death in his face.

It is *a rather dapper hat...*

"Oh," she breathes. "They sent *you*. Bringing out the big guns, I see."

And then everything goes black as the monster begins his grisly work.

I

PAX

I have bones.

And *skin*.

I hold my other hand up and tug on my fingernails. I have fingernails, and they feel as though they'll hurt if I pull them out.

I feel *everything*. I feel the weight of my body on my legs, and the soles of my feet digging into the dirt beneath my sandals. I feel a niggling pain in my sword elbow. The wind whips my tunic around my knees, brushing against my verpa as it swells with joy.

Bree's fingers squeeze mine, and the touch is more pure and visceral than anything I've ever known.

I smell the freshness of the woodland and fox piss and someone nearby baking something delicious.

I smell *Bree*. Her pear and almond scent, tinged with smoke and sadness.

"Pax?" Bree cries. Her voice is pure music to my ears.

My ears! I tug on them. They're real!

The gods have chosen me. They have saved me!

I am alive.

My heart bursts with a joy that I have only known when I was stabbing Druids, or the night Edward and Ambrose and I took Bree to bed. I wrench my hand from hers and take off into the wood, hooting with delight because I can run! My legs wobble at first before they remember what it is they are supposed to do.

I skip and I jump and I roll in the dirt. I laugh until my throat hurts. Tree branches scrape my skin, leaving little scratches that hurt. One of them even bleeds. I'm *bleeding*.

"By Mars' saintly scrotum, I'm bleeding!" I yell.

"Are you okay? Pax, where are you?"

I slow to a stop, and I grab the hem of my tunic and linen undershirt and flip them up. Underneath, my tackle is still intact, and for the first time in nearly two thousand years, it is... intact. I can no longer see through my verpa onto the ground below. I grab my verpa and give it an experimental stroke.

The sensation of touch...it's indescribable. Even the other night, with all we were able to do with Bree's crystal, it didn't feel like this. This exquisite. This *real*.

I forget about running now. I haven't had a proper wank in nearly two thousand years.

"Pax, where are you? Did you hurt yourself?" Bree crashes through the trees. Her eyes widen as she sees me. "You're alive again, and this is the first thing you can think of doing?"

"No," I growl, dropping my hands from my verpa. I move toward her like a lion stalking a fawn, closing the space between us. I slide my hand behind her neck, around her silken hair, and pull her to me. "*This* is the first thing I wish to do."

And I crush my lips to hers.

2

BREE

Pax's lips are warm. He tastes of cool summer wine and blood and vengeance. He tastes like all my darkest dreams come true.

He tastes *real*.

His fingers tangle in my hair, crushing my head to his. His other arm wraps around my body, his muscles so thick and strong that he could snap me in half if he wanted to. But that is the thing about Pax – even though he's a terrifying monster of a ghost, I've never for a moment believed that he could hurt me. He's always protected me.

Except he's not a ghost anymore.

And that hunger in his eyes is *all* man.

All mine.

"Little Bree Mortimer," he whispers as he walks me backward, his bulk overpowering me. "All grown up now."

He backs me up until I'm leaning against the trunk of a tree. A silver cord extends between us still, although now it's wrapped in a pale, ethereal blue light.

I realize that we've run in a large circle and we're right back where we started, in the clearing with the gnarled old oak, the

19

crumpled altar, and his open grave. I don't know if we should do this here, with Pax's bones watching over us, but then his hands are all over me and his teeth scrape my neck and I do not give one single fuck about a grave.

Pax is alive.

Alive.

And the way he touches me...

He fists my t-shirt in his huge hand and tears it down the middle. I'm not wearing a bra underneath, and his whole face lights up like it's Roman Christmas.

Pax bends down and take a nipple in his mouth. He's gentle at first, his tongue swirling in a slow circle that drives me wild. But I should know that my soldier can't be soft for long. He bites down a little, but it only makes me howl with want.

The public path is only a little further down the gully. Anyone could walk by and see us. I don't care. *I don't care.* I care about nothing but his hands on me, his tongue and lips devouring me, making me his.

He groans as he grinds against me, his cock – verpa – hard as a sword and very, very real. I remember how big it was in my mouth, how good it tasted, and I don't want to wait another moment. My heart clenches and my belly aches, and I want him inside me, *now.*

"I want to do what we couldn't do last night." Pax slams my back against the oak. Instinctively, I lift my legs and lock my ankles behind him. The skirt I'm wearing rides up over my thighs. There's only the thin scrap of my panties between us.

"Good. Because I'm dying for Roman cock inside me."

It's a poor choice of words, especially since *dying* is exactly what brought us here, to this moment of desperation in the woods. But I think all Pax hears is the need in my voice.

With a roar, he tears off my panties.

The cool air kisses my naked pussy. A needy sound escapes

me as he lifts my thighs, angling me just so. The mossy side of the tree cushions my back as he pushes my legs higher and thrusts inside me in one long stroke.

It hurts *so good*. It's been a long time since I've had sex. The last was a fellow hiking guide in New Zealand, and I crawled into his sleeping bag one night while we were alone in a cabin... only we weren't really alone. The ghosts of two hikers who'd accidentally eaten poisonous mushrooms wouldn't shut up and I couldn't get in the mood, so I just left him with blue balls and went outside to smoke some weed.

But Pax, he feels like he's made for me. His 'verpa' hits all the right places, stretching me until I feel like I'm being impaled. Like he'll drive all the way through me, up into my heart.

Who am I kidding? He's already there.

"You are exquisite," he breathes.

His gaze collides with mine, his baby blue eyes swimming with hunger and something like worship. Pax bends toward me, cupping the back of my neck with his huge hand and squeezing a little, not enough to hurt or to cut off air, but enough that I feel the rough thrill of his possession in my belly as he pounds into me.

I can't think. I'm being fucked into oblivion. Is this how I'm going to die, up against a tree with my pelvis ground into dust by the best sex of my life?

What a way to go.

Birth control? STIs? Can you even get pregnant by a centuries-old Roman centurion? That's tomorrow's problem.

I squeeze my legs together, bringing him closer still, driving him deeper. Pax's teeth scrape my bottom lip. I taste blood. I claw at his shoulders as the pleasure climbs inside me, the bees swarming, the queen desperate to feed and fuck.

Pax thrusts his other arm between us, pressing the pad of

his thumb into my clit, rubbing it so hard that it's on the edge of hurting. But I'm so close to the edge that it tips me over.

I throw my head back as I come. The woods go dark. I lose my fucking *vision*. I'm a star gone supernova, a black hole sucking in everything in its path, existing only in an explosion of pleasure.

Slowly, my vision comes back, and I return to my body to find my knees have given out completely and the only thing keeping me from sliding into the dirt is Pax's strong arms. He grunts, his features rapt as he possesses my body the way he has always possessed my heart.

"I could leave this world happy," Pax whispers, "now that I've seen you come like that on my cock."

"What about you?" I ask.

"Oh, woman, I'm right on the edge."

He thrusts so hard and deep I know I'm going to be sore tomorrow. His face twists, and he comes with a roar. A war cry. A warrior doing battle with his own demons for my body, and emerging triumphant.

We lay against the tree, panting, sweat pouring from our bodies. Pax's sweat smells sweet. What must it be like to sweat for the first time since the Roman Empire?

"For someone who hasn't fucked for two thousand years," I whisper, "you're a quick study."

Pax steps back, his tree-trunk legs shaking a little as he holds my waist and makes sure I can stand under my own weight. "Some things you do not forget, no matter how much time has passed."

"Pax, fuck. What do we—"

"Bree, where are you?" a familiar voice calls behind us, making me leap into Pax's arms. "What's going on?"

Oh, shit. We've been spotted.

3
BREE

The voice shudders in my chest.

"That's Ambrose," I whisper.

Pax grunts, nuzzling my neck. I shove him away and start scrambling to pull down my skirt.

"He can't see you," Pax says.

"That's not the point." My shirt is ruined, so I tie the two ends together so it at least covers my tits just as Ambrose floats into the clearing.

"Bree, are you here? I can smell you. Where's Pax? I can't sense him. Is he off on a Druid hunt? Sometimes I wish there really was a Druid left for him to hunt. It would make life rather interesting—"

"Watch out!" I yell, but I'm too late. Ambrose yelps as he topples into the grave.

Pax and I run to the edge of the hole and peer inside. Ambrose turns in circles at the bottom. "What is this? Bree, why is there a giant hole here?"

"Get out of there," Pax demands. "Stop dancing on my ribcage."

I turn to Pax in surprise. "You can see him?"

He nods.

Interesting. So Pax the human can also see ghosts. Or, at the very least, one ghost in particular.

"Pax?" Ambrose's confusion deepens. "Is that you? I can hear you, but I can't sense your ghost anywhere..."

"Ambrose, take my hand. You need to come out of there." I lean over the side and thrust my hand down to him. Ambrose's fingers brush mine, sending that now familiar jolt of heat through me. He uses his sense of me to guide himself to the wall and float back to the surface.

(Don't ask me how a ghost can fall into a hole when they technically float. The answer is always ghost mojo, okay?)

"That was hilarious. You fell on my bones." Pax whacks Ambrose across the shoulders. His arm goes right through him. "In Ancient Rome, you would be crucified for that."

"Bree, what's going on?" Ambrose shudders as he rubs his shoulders. The shadow beneath his lip darkens. "When you touched me right now, it *hurt*. And what's this big hole doing here?"

"It's..." I suck in a deep breath. *I guess we're doing this.* "It's Pax's grave."

"You found his dusty old bones?" Ambrose gasps.

"Yeah."

"And it's an actual grave? His men gave him a proper Roman burial? So does this mean he crossed over?"

"I'm right here, Ambrose," Pax folds his arms.

"There's his voice again, almost as if he's still here with us. I guess he always will be, in our hearts."

"He *is* still with us." The delicious ache between my thighs is evidence of that.

I open my mouth to explain, but Pax being Pax decides that a demonstration will get the point across more succinctly. He thrusts his arm through the center of

Ambrose's chest. Ambrose yelps and staggers back, clutching at his belly.

"That was horrible. It was like being run over by a wine-soaked steamroller. Bree, have you been bathing in wine or something? Owwwww, why did you do that? It hurts *so bad*."

"I didn't do it," I say. "Pax did."

I don't understand any of this." Ambrose's eyes widen. "Pax can't put his arm through me like that. And if you found Pax's grave, then he should have crossed over. Does this mean that this wasn't Pax's unfinished business after all? Do we have to perform some Ancient Roman ritual to appease his gods? Can I help? I do so love a ritual."

"No ritual needed," Pax says. "Bree brought me back to life."

Ambrose laughs, then winces as he rubs his stomach again. "Sure, Pax. Bree made you not a ghost anymore. That's a thing that she can do."

"Apparently, it is," I say.

"Wait, he's *alive?*" Ambrose's eyes widen as he takes it in. "Pax, the Roman centurion, is *alive*."

"Very much so."

"Bree and I just fu—" Pax mumbles as I clamp my hand over his mouth.

"I don't know how this happened," I say quickly, not yet ready for Ambrose to find out about that part. "I found the grave a few days ago, and I've been tormented by the idea of losing him, so I didn't say anything to any of you. I brought Pax here today to say goodbye. When I showed the grave to him, this silvery cord surrounded both of us. I touched his hand, and suddenly his fingers were curling into mine."

"This is...Bree, it's amazing." Ambrose's fingers find mine, and he squeezes. His whole face breaks out into a smile. "We always knew you were special, but this is incredible. You brought Pax back to life."

"I'm sure it's got nothing to do with me. It's probably one of those coins or amulets in the grave or something. I gave Pax the coin his soldiers left him to pay the ferryman." I turn to Pax. "Maybe he didn't get sufficient payment and spat you back out."

"Could you do it for me?" Ambrose hops with excitement. "Can you bring me back, too? Pax, hand me that coin."

"Ambrose, no. I don't know *what* I did. That's just the problem!" I throw up my arms. "I don't think this has anything to do with me. I can't recreate it if I don't understand it. I don't want to accidentally hurt you."

Or send you away where I can't follow.

"That's okay. We can figure this out. We have to get Pax back to the house. Edward's going to be pissed when he sees this." Ambrose is practically jumping up and down with excitement. Pax has lost interest in our conversation and is entranced by a ladybug crawling over his fingers. "No matter what you say, I know you made this happen. Somehow, you brought Pax back to life. Maybe you can bring all of us back, and we can be together."

4

BREE

"When you said on the phone that you had something to show me," Dani hugs the doorframe for dear life, "I did *not* expect a seven-foot Roman centurion to be standing in your living room. Hi, Pax. You're taller than I expected."

"Dani? You are flesh and blood, like me." Pax runs at her, arms open, and lifts her off the ground in an enormous bear hug. "You are a friend of Bree, and therefore, a friend of Pax. I swear by Jupiter's jangling gonads to protect you with my sword and to run your enemies through or crucify them or feed them to lions, whichever is your preference."

"That's, er...great," Dani gasps out. "But for now, can you let me go? I can't breathe."

Pax lets Dani go, and she drops to a heap on the floor. She picks herself up, dusts off her overalls with little grim reapers on them (they're cute. I need to ask her where she got them), and slumps down onto the uncomfortable sofa.

From Pax's chest, the silver cord wreathed in blue curls around the room before entering my chest. *Why is it still there, if he's alive? Why is it coloured blue?*

"Bree, what's going on? Either you hired a very convincing actor from that Shakespeare troupe in Argleton, or that really is Pax. As a living, breathing, human..."

"Yes," I say in a small voice. "It's Pax."

"But how? I like to consider myself kind of an expert on death, and I can tell you that people who died two thousand years ago don't suddenly start walking around and sampling the liquor collection."

Pax makes a sheepish face as he throws back his head and glugs a generous mouthful of amaretto straight from the bottle. "Tastes like Druid scrotum." He wipes his mouth. "It is delicious. Can we get scones? I'm starving. I haven't eaten since the pre-battle feast."

"None of this makes sense. How can he even be alive if his bones are literally sitting on a table in Alice's museum right now?" Dani continues.

"I don't know." I throw myself down in the chaise lounge. Edward yelps as I land on top of him before sliding through him and plopping down on the cushions. My body flushes with intense heat, and the room shimmers and changes briefly, becoming darker, lit by candlelight and filled with sweet-scented opium smoke, before the vision fades. *Another memory that doesn't belong to me.* "Sorry, Edward. I didn't see you there."

"Story of my life," Edward mutters. Ambrose was right – he is not taking this well. Pouty, sulky Edward is annoyed that he's not the one alive right now, as if I should have known that as royalty, he rightfully deserved to be brought back first.

As if I needed even more problems, I'd have to appease Sulky Edward at some point. But I don't know what to offer him that would make up for the fact that he's still a ghost and Pax is very much alive.

I press my thighs together, urging myself to stay focused on

Dani and not get distracted by memories of what happened in the woods.

I fail.

"You'd better find out what's going on, and fast," Dani is saying. "Because Pax can't stay here."

"Why not?" I don't like the finality in her tone.

"Because he's a Roman soldier! He thinks that the proper way to deal with criminals is to feed them to lions!"

"And Christians!" Pax's face lights up. "Don't forget Christians. Lions love Christians. Taste like chicken."

Dani shoots me a look that says *Exactly*. "He doesn't belong in our time, and this isn't a quirky rom-com where you have to teach him the ways of modern life while we all laugh hilariously at his mishaps. Pax is going to get mad when the pub doesn't stock Roman ale or whatever and stab someone, and then we're all going to be in trouble. I don't want my best friend shipped off to Bedlam because she can raise the dead, but that's what's going to happen if you don't send him to where he belongs—"

"I don't want to go to Elysium." Pax flexes his arm muscles, and a flutter of heat burns through my stomach. "I don't want to be a ghost again. I want to stay here. With Bree. I want to make love to her again."

"You..." Dani's eyes are about to pop out of her head. "You fucked him?"

"Well..."

"*Bree!*"

I grin sheepishly. "Look at him! I'm surprised I've been able to resist this long."

My gaze darts to the other two ghosts, and my elation turns cold. Edward's cool expression freezes my blood. Ambrose's face has fallen completely.

I think about all of us together in my bed the other night – how beautiful it was when the three of them worked together to make me come over and over. And how gutted we all were when we discovered that ghost dick isn't strong enough to allow us to go all the way.

But now, Pax and I share an experience that they can't replicate. Yet another thing that death deprives them of.

I didn't want them to find out like this.

Fuck, everything is such a mess.

Dani flops back in her chair. "Are you sure you're feeling okay? You're not coming down with something? That's the only explanation for why you're acting so strangely. I mean, a psychotic Roman centurion comes back to life in modern-day Grimdale and the first thing you do is *fuck* him. Did you use protection? Do you even need protection? Are you gonna have little ghost babies? Does that mean you've messed with the universe on like, a cosmic level?"

"I don't *knooooow*," I moan.

"It was the best sex ever," Pax thumps his chest. "There will be many babies. I was as virile as the god Jupiter, and Bree's *cunnus* wrapped around me so tight that she squeezed me dry—"

"*Do* shut up," Edward snaps.

Dani is laughing now, and my face burns with heat.

"This is all very exciting. I'm sure we can figure out how this happened," Ambrose says. "My good friend Charles Dickens once said that facts alone are wanted in life. We should plant nothing else, and root out everything else..."

"My root would like to be inside Bree again," Pax growls.

Poor Ambrose blushes, but he can't hide his enthusiasm. I know exactly what he's thinking – that if we can get to the bottom of what happened to Pax, then maybe he could be brought back to life, too. I want that, more than anything, except that...

...except that I'm *terrified*. I'm frightened that I might be responsible for this, that I might be even more of a freak than I thought, and that I have no understanding of what I am or how to control this power. Or it might have nothing to do with me at all, which means that some other force brought Pax back to life for reasons that aren't clear and could be nefarious.

Either way, my instinct is to run out of the room and keep running until I hit ocean. But that's been my solution to everything strange and unexplained in my life. I ran from Grimdale five years ago, and look where it got me. So even though my feet itch and my palms are slick with sweat, I remain rooted in my chair. For now.

"Ambrose says we should approach this scientifically," I say, trying to keep my voice calm. "The way we did when we tested the moldavite crystal."

"That's a good idea." Dani pulls out her phone. "I'll start a file. My first question...how do we scientifically study something that's not scientifically possible?"

"I guess we begin with what we know about ghosts."

"Bree's ghost rules. Got it." Dani smiles. She and I have been talking about ghost rules ever since I told her that I could see the restless dead. "We know that ghosts can alter the temperature, and that they usually hang around either the place where they died, or somewhere important to them."

Ambrose paces excitedly in front of the fireplace...and a little bit inside the fireplace. "We know that when we complete our unfinished business, we're supposed to cross over. That's what happened to Albert. And the actress ghost. And that cat who got run over chasing the mouse across the street, remember? The mouse died a week later and they chased each other into the light..."

"I remember the cat. That was sad," I say, my gut twisting as I realize that I'm going to have to come clean. "So...there's something I haven't told you all."

I describe how I've been seeing the silver cords stretching from ghosts for a while now, and what happened with the actress and Albert, how I felt their silver cords snap. And how the same thing was going to happen to Pax, but then he grabbed my hand and didn't let go.

Dani's mouth hangs open.

"I knew it!" Ambrose cries. "I knew you were the one who brought Pax to life!"

"Does this mean that if Brianna touches us while we complete our unfinished business, we'll become Living again?" Edward peers up at Pax with a new interest. "Because I have a *lot* of unfinished business. And most of it involves doing sinful, wanton things to Brianna's body—"

"Gross, I heard that," Dani says to the space slightly to the left of Edward's head. "But the prince might be onto something. I propose an experiment: we find a ghost who's about to cross over and have Bree touch them and see if this brings them back—"

"Um, are you all forgetting something?"

"I'd like to forget that you had Pax's prick inside you, but that's neither here nor there," Edward says.

"I don't want to forget it!" Pax booms. "I want to do it again, right now."

He lunges for me, but I duck under his arm and raise my hands. They all stop and watch me.

"You're forgetting that I have *no idea* what I did to Pax, or why it worked with him and not with Albert. I can't just do it again! What if I accidentally send someone away who's not yet ready to go? What if I hurt someone Living—"

"We don't know that until we try," Ambrose says. "I know you won't hurt anyone—"

"I can't take the risk." I shove my trembling hands into my pockets.

Dani studies my face until I can't bear her eyes on me, and I have to look away.

"You know," Dani begins. "We've never looked into why you *can* see ghosts when no one else can. We assumed it was because you had that near-death experience. But maybe there is something more. Maybe there is something special about *you*, Bree, and the moldavite brings it out."

"We all know Brianna is special," Edward points out, rather huffily. I remember what he told me, that he thought I could see or sense the ghosts even before my accident. This certainly makes me think Dani could be right – that there was something more to my ability to see ghosts than my childhood bump on the head.

I don't want to think about that. At all.

"Beyond her general wonderfulness, Bree is not just seeing into the world of ghosts anymore," Ambrose says. "She can influence us. Through her, we can influence the Living world."

"There is no one else who can do what Bree does," Pax says.

"Are you sure about that?" Dani asks.

The ghosts and Pax exchange a look. I know exactly what they're thinking.

They don't want Dani's questions to scare me.

They don't want me to run away again.

I square my shoulders. *It's okay. I'm okay. No matter how scary things get, I'm not running again. I have the ghosts, and Dani, and Mina and Quoth. I'm not alone. I don't have to be the freak.*

"I was a ghost for over two thousand years, and Bree's the only Living who's ever been able to talk to me," Pax says. "Or do all those other things to me, like that thing with her tongue—"

"Okay, I've heard enough about that." Dani plasters her hands over her ears and glares at Pax. "Besides, the ghost mojo has kept you tethered to the house, correct?"

"Yes. Until Bree got the stone, I could only walk along the

path in the woods and to the main road of the village. It was tough for one soldier to patrol, but I managed it. What of it?"

"You don't have a large sample size, do you?" Dani jots something down on her phone. "Somewhere else in the world, there could be someone who has the same powers as Bree."

"I've been all over the world," I say. "And I've met a lot of the world's ghosts. But I've never met another Living who could talk to them."

But maybe they were trying to hide. Maybe they were trying to drown out the voices with weed and booze and terrible dubstep music.

After all, that's exactly what I was doing.

From the look on Dani's face, she's come to the same conclusion. "What about that crazy old woman who owns the Basic Witch shop? Ever since she gave you that stone, something's been different with the ghosts. Do you think that she knows?"

"And she looked *right at me,*" Edward points to his fathomless obsidian eyes. "As if she could see me."

"She didn't say anything about seeing ghosts," I say. "And you'd think that if two of us lived in the same village, we'd have noticed each other chatting up lampposts."

"I'm surprised she didn't fall to her knees to worship my handsome visage," Edward continues. "But perhaps she was too overcome—"

"I think we should talk to her," Ambrose interrupts, which is honestly the only way to deal with Edward.

"She doesn't know anything," I say. "She's just a crazy old woman."

And all of this started before I visited the shop. It's been going on since the moment I stepped foot back in Grimwood Manor...

"I've been able to hear Edward since she gave you that stone," Dani points out. "That doesn't sound crazy to me."

It's less crazy than me bringing a Roman soldier back from the dead and fucking him in the woods.

I cross and uncross my legs.

Dani throws up her hands. "Look, I don't know how any of this works. I learned nothing at embalming school about the scientific effects of ghost mojo. But it sounds like that woman at Basic Witch knows something, and I think you owe it to your newly corporeal friend to check it out."

"Yes!" Pax thrusts his sword into the air, narrowly missing the chandelier. "We go to the old woman and find out how to make our friends mortal, too!"

"Yes, fine, you're right," I grumble. "We'll go first thing tomorrow."

"No," Pax declares, rubbing his stomach. "We will go now, after the Bake Off judging. I am hungry and I haven't eaten anything in two thousand years. First, we fortify ourselves with scones, then we get answers."

5

BREE

"This is a scone?" Pax stuffs it into his mouth. "By Jupiter's juicy testicles, it tastes like happiness."

Watching his face, I know I made the right decision by stopping at Albert's wake on the way to Basic Witch. The village decided to turn the Bake Off into an impromptu memorial for Albert. Most of the village has turned out for it, and all the bakers had donated their leftover desserts to the cause. It's nice to see just how much Albert was loved, even if he's no longer here to see it himself.

"Can I get you anything else?" Maggie asks as she sets down a steaming hot steak and kidney pie. She must've gone straight to her kitchen the moment we said goodbye. "Any friend of Bree is a friend of mine, especially since she tells me that you were instrumental in clearing my name. The police have told me that Linda admitted to killing my dear Albert, and she was even going to feed me a poisoned cupcake! All so she could win the Bake Off. Can you imagine?"

"I would slay a whole army for your baking," Pax says, his mouth full of scone crumbs.

"Of course, dear." Maggie pats him indulgently on the

shoulder. "And I heard from Alice Agincourt that you desperately needed her help to put that nasty real estate agent and her husband behind bars. She's a bright girl, is our Alice."

I groan. Trust Alice to present my sleuthing in a way that made her look good.

It is true though – thanks to Alice's testimony about Pax's grave, Annabel and Kieran are in deep trouble. Annabel and Kieran weren't guilty of Albert's murder, but they had stolen hundreds of artifacts over the years. When presented with my evidence, they broke down and admitted all of it, and even gave the police the address of the lock-up where they stored their loot, and their Cayman Island bank account.

I now even have answers about the clues that led us astray – the bath products kit was a hobby of Annabel's, and the belladonna leaves in the rubbish bin were stuck on the bottom of Kieran's boots after he got back from a metal detecting trip. Annabel made him scrape them off so he wouldn't track foliage through the office.

"Enough of this chitchat," Pax booms, rubbing his stomach through his leather armour. "More baking!"

"Ah, I do love a man with a healthy appetite," Maggie grins. "We have a wide selection of English baking available. I was even able to whip up a batch of my award-winning scones and bring them down in time for the judging. Nothing like a spot of baking to celebrate my newfound freedom. Or I could cut you a piece of Mr. Graham's sticky date pudding, or there is this Victoria sponge—"

"Yes." Pax holds out his plate. "All the cakes."

"I think I'll just grab a coffee," I sigh. "And I can cut Pax's cakes. You shouldn't be serving up during Albert's memorial. You'll have to excuse my friend's manners. He's...a foreigner and he doesn't understand our customs."

"A foreigner? Oh, how exciting," Maggie coos. "That

explains the outfit he's wearing. It's not often we get people from Scotland in the area. And don't you mind me – I love seeing people enjoying good food. Albert would be so happy you're here. I'll go cut you a nice big slice of sponge, dearie."

"And some lemon cake!" Pax booms, his mouth filled with scone crumbs.

When Pax is so full of baking that he can hardly move, we say goodbye to Dani and Maggie and head over to Basic Witch. I glance around the bustling village green, searching for the three witches. For once, I'm interested to hear what they have to say when they see what's happened to Pax.

Odd. I can't see them anywhere. They don't normally miss a big village event like this. Mary should be skipping from stall to stall, shoving her face into every cake and flan on display. Agnes should be stroking Walpurgis and yelling insults at everyone, and Lottie should be dangling her feet happily in the duck pond or trying to get a peek up the breeches of the Morris dancing troupe.

But I have enough to worry about now without wondering what Important Ghost Business (IGB for short – it's whatever ghosts are doing when you can't find them) the three of them are up to. I'm on a mission to figure out what's happened to Pax and why I seem to be able to suddenly bring ghosts back to life.

And even though I'm terrified of what the truth is, I *need* to know. And I have my ghosts and my centurion with me. I can handle whatever the old woman has to tell me.

It's late in the day, but I'm relieved to see the shop is still open. Most of the High Street businesses have set up stalls outside to take advantage of the foot traffic, but I notice Basic Witch is as quiet as ever.

Despite their business relationship, I hadn't seen the old hag at Albert's memorial, so I assumed she must still be inside.

"I can't believe I'm back here," I mutter as I step around the orc statue and grab the handle. "This place gives me the creeps."

"Maybe so," Ambrose says. "But if anyone will know about your newfound ability to raise the dead, it's the creepy old bird."

"True. Hello?" I call out as I step inside. The shop's bell tinkles. "Strange old lady? Are you here? I'd like to talk to you..."

"You probably shouldn't call her the strange old lady if you want her to help you," Ambrose suggests. "Just an idea."

I hold up my finger to my lips and listen. The shop is quiet. *Too* quiet. There's no Deepak Chopra music on in the background, no chatter of teenagers hunched over the sex magick section, no burbling from the Buddhist fountain.

I approach the counter, my stomach sinking as an ominous chill skitters down my spine. The saint card stand has been knocked over. Bright-coloured cards showing various Christian saints are scattered across the floor.

"Old woman?" I call out, my heart leaping into my throat. *I wish I'd thought to ask her name.* "Is anyone here?"

"Brianna." Edward floats across the shop and points at something behind the counter. His face is even paler than usual.

"What? What did you see?" I take Ambrose's hand and cross the shop. There, behind the counter, is the old woman.

She's lying on the ground, her black skirts twisted around her gnarled legs.

She's not moving.

"Oh, no. Are you okay? Don't worry, we're here now. We're

going to call an ambulance." I bend down and pick up her hand to feel for her pulse.

But her skin is ice cold.

And that's when I notice the horrific mess.

Bile rises in my throat.

The old witch isn't just dead, she's...*defiled*.

Someone has ripped her open and spread her organs around her body, like some kind of macabre decoration.

"Oh no," I groan. "Not again."

Not another murder.

6

BREE

*A*nother murder in Grimdale. And this time, it could be connected to the very strange magic that hums in my veins.

Pax draws his sword and skulks around the shop. "Come out, come out, wherever you are, murderer. I promise I won't hurt you. I just want to introduce you to my good friend, Mr. Gladius. He'll be so glad to see you."

"Just a hint," Edward says. "Most murderers don't come when called, like lost puppies."

"Get it?" Pax chortles as he lifts the lid on a large Chinese urn. "'Glad' to see him? Because a Roman sword is called a gladius—"

"Take that!" an angry voice cries from inside the urn.

I gasp as a figure leaps from the urn. A fuzzy black shape hurtles through the air toward me, yowling as its tiny, furry legs spin wildly.

I reach out to catch Walpurgis, but the terrified ghost cat falls straight through my hands before dropping silently to the floor, landing on all four legs.

The see-through figure floats out of the urn and stands in

front of me, her familiar features narrowed with concern, her eyes wide with fear. She's followed by two equally-familiar ghosts. They hold each other and tremble.

"It's about time you got here," Agnes scolds us. "We've been hiding inside that urn for *hours*."

"I can't believe you threw your cat at me!" I bend down and pat Walpurgis on the head. He plonks down on his arse and starts licking between his toes, his harrowing flight already long forgotten.

"We thought you were the beast, come back to finish the job!"

I narrow my eyes at them. "And you decided to sacrifice Walpurgis so you three could escape?"

"We were hoping Walpurgis would unleash those devilish powers witch's familiars are supposed to possess," Agnes snaps. "You know, the powers that are the very reason we were all burned at the stake—"

"I know you're bitter about that, but can we focus on the situation at hand?" I point to the spindly, blood-speckled legs poking out from behind the counter. "The old witch is dead."

"I'll have you know that I look exceptionally young for my age," Agnes says.

"Don't mind her," Lottie adds. "She gets even more snarky when she's afraid."

"And our friend's name is Vera," says Mary. She stares down at the pool of blood widening around Vera's body and wipes a ghostly tear from her eye. "She didn't deserve this."

"Your friend?" I narrow my eyes. "Wait a second, do you mean that Vera could *see* you?"

"Of course." Agnes puffs out her chest. "A real witch always recognises her kind, even when her kind have been dead for centuries."

Anger bubbles in my chest. "You mean all these years, you

knew there was another person in Grimdale who could see ghosts, and you never thought to tell me?"

"You never asked, dear." Agnes sniffs the incense.

"You were ignoring us when Vera moved to the village," Mary adds. "We thought you wouldn't want to know."

"Plus, Vera told us not to tell a soul," Lottie finishes. "And we always keep our promises. A witch is only as good as her word."

"We come here to sit with her sometimes," Mary says somberly. "She hates customers almost as much as your friend Mina's boyfriend Heathcliff. It was nice to hang out with someone who shared our love of turning cheating husbands into toads. Plus, Vera makes – er, *made* – a mean pot brownie. They were so strong that even sniffing them made me feel stoned."

I look between the three of them, trying to compute the fact that they'd kept Vera's abilities a secret from me. I shove my hand in my pocket, gripping the moldavite that Vera gave me. Now that I had the power to touch them, I had half a mind to knock their heads together and make them see how it felt to be left out of important things.

But that's not fair. As much as the news that Vera was like me is *freaking me the fuck out* right now, this is not about me. It's about Vera's corpse lying on the shop floor, and finding the person who ripped her apart.

"So the three of you were inside the shop when this happened?" I ask. "What did you see?"

"It was horrible," Mary shudders. "We were hanging out by the window, minding everyone's business, and we were just talking about heading across to the tent to sniff some scones when *he* burst through the door."

"Who?"

"The beastly creature," Mary makes a face.

49

"He wore a spiffy top hat and cape, and wielded a long, sharp blade. And he had eyes like the devil's own ballsacks," adds Lottie.

"All red and fiery." Mary hugs herself.

"I don't know who he was. Or rather, *what* he was," Agnes snaps. "But he's not human."

That's exactly what I'm afraid of.

"But not a ghost, either?" Edward wrinkles his nose as he nudges the toe of Vera's shoe with his toe. His foot goes right through hers. "Even with Bree's stone, a ghost wouldn't have the power to do this, right?"

"Not any kind of ghost I've ever met before," says Agnes.

"Can someone describe the body to me?" Ambrose asks.

"Why?" Edward scoffs. "Want to write about it in your new book?"

Ambrose's see-through face flushes red. "Of course not. I couldn't bear writing another book after the publisher lost mine forever. But something about this murder feels rather familiar. I can't quite place my finger on it. I thought some details might help."

Something niggles in the back of my head, too. Vera is murdered days after she gave me the moldavite and hinted that she knew something about my power. Now I discover that she can see ghosts like me. And from what the witches describe, her killer is not entirely human.

This is all connected. I know it is.

"I can tell you everything you want later, Ambrose. Right now, we have to call the police." I turn away from the body, not wanting to look any closer. As I move toward the door, I pull out my mobile phone. "The shop's still open. We have to keep anyone else from entering so they don't contaminate the scene."

"Haven't we already contaminated it?" Edward frowns. "Or

rather, you and Pax have contaminated it, since Ambrose and I don't have DNA."

"You're right. And Wilson isn't exactly going to be thrilled to discover I'm the center of another grisly murder. I'm not exactly doing cartwheels myself. So please, let's do this right."

I turn away from Vera as Edward hovers over her and describes her injuries in salacious details for Ambrose, and make the call. When it's done, I click off my phone and force myself to look back at the grisly scene. I have to swallow several times to keep from throwing up.

Look at this scientifically, Bree, I tell myself, wishing Dani were here. I steel myself as I crouch down next to Vera's body. *You're looking for a clue about what happened.*

I can't see any clues – just a lot of blood and...organs on the outside when they should be on the inside. Vera wears orthopedic shoes, grey stockings, a brown corduroy skirt, and a blue jumper. Her hands are clenched into fists at her sides, and there are no visible bruises on her arms as if she didn't even fight back. Saint cards are scattered across the floor, and the stand lies broken in front of the counter. They must have knocked it over during the struggle.

Or maybe she wasn't given the chance to fight back.

"I'm no expert in modern investigations," Edward says. "Although I did watch that *Midsomer Murders* marathon with Sylvie, and I'm pretty sure you're not supposed to touch the crime scene."

"I'm not going to touch." My stomach churns as I lean forward and inspect the wound as close as I dare. "I just need...I don't know what I need, but the police are going to be here any minute, and once they arrive I'll never get another look at her. They're not going to be looking for...for signs of a magical beast in a top hat."

"Like what, a parchment that says 'The Bogeyman Was Here'?" Edward asks.

"It's good to know that even in a dire emergency, you retain your sense of humour," I shoot back.

But just in case, I check her hands for a note. My heart skips as I see something clutched in her fingers.

I bend down and slide it free, holding it up to the light. It's a saint card, the image partially obscured by splatters of blood. It shows a man wrapped in a white cloth emerging from a cave, his hands raised to the sky in prayer, while several other people crowd around him and a woman reverently reaches up to touch his face.

I haven't spent a lot of time studying Catholic saints, so I have no idea what I'm looking at, but as I peer at the image, the prickling on the back of my neck becomes a full-fledged chill.

I make a snap decision. I shove the card into my purse.

"I'm pretty sure *Midsomer Murders* was quite explicit about not taking things from a crime scene," Edward points out.

"This card is meant for me," I say. I don't know how I know that's true, but I feel it in my gut.

Somehow, Vera knew I'd be the one to find her, and in her dying moments, she grabbed this saint card as a message for me.

But what does it mean?

7

BREE

"Well, well, well, if it isn't Bree Mortimer at the scene of another crime," Wilson says as she enters the shop. Detective Hayes follows her in, licking cream from one of Maggie's famous scones from his fingers.

"Can't a man enjoy the Bake Off in peace?" Hayes mutters to himself as he steps around the Buddha fountain to inspect the scene. "We already spent the morning processing the last killer, and you've already got a fresh one for us."

I can't believe that only hours ago, we 'haunted' Linda into confessing to Albert's murder. Between then and now I had watched Albert cross over, brought Pax to life, fucked my Roman centurion against a tree, ate my bodyweight in scones, discovered another corpse, and learned that the witches had been hiding the truth about Vera's powers from me for literally *years*.

It feels like this day has gone on for ten years. Or at least, ten chapters.

"I don't wander around the village, hunting for crimes to embroil myself in," I snap. I need a drink. And chocolate. A mountain of chocolate. A literal continent of chocolate.

"Could've fooled me." Wilson's lips smack together as she takes in Vera's body. "Shit. This is bad, Guv. We never had a murder this brutal in Argleton, and that place is murder-central."

"We just came in to look at Maggie's candles and found her like this—"

"Who's *we?*"

Pax pounds his fist against his chest. I squeeze his hand. "Me and my...er, friend, Pax."

Now is sooooo not the time to feel nervous about using the 'boyfriend' word, Bree.

I can't help it. I haven't called anyone my boyfriend since... well, since *ever*. The Spanish tour guide in Greece liked to call me his girlfriend, but I always avoided the topic. And then he cheated on me with a Polish surfing instructor, so I guess it didn't mean all that much to him, either.

'Boyfriend' means a connection. A commitment. A rope tying me in one place, with one person. What does it mean when you have feelings for three guys but only one of them is corporeal?

What does it mean if you're terrified that this wonderful thing between you and these guys that you may or may not have feelings for could be torn away at any moment?

Not ready to face that thought, I turn my attention back to

the current situation. Wilson frowns at Pax. "Why is he dressed like a Roman soldier?"

I clamp a hand over Pax's mouth before he can explain. "Because we're going to a fancy dress party tonight, okay? Maybe worry a little bit less about Pax's outfit and a little more about the eviscerated woman on the floor."

"I'm doing my job, Ms. Mortimer. Have you touched the body or otherwise contaminated the crime scene in any way?" Wilson's tone is accusatory.

The saint card burns a hole in my purse. "I held up her hand to check her pulse, but after that, I backed away quickly. I haven't touched anything else...not that I can remember. Neither has Pax."

The lie tastes like acid on my tongue. But I know I'm doing the right thing. The police won't look for a supernatural explanation and I'm not going to tell them that three ghostly witnesses saw a demonic monster kill Vera. That saint card is our only clue about who *really* did this.

"I touched that urn," Pax corrects me. "I was checking that monster wasn't still skulking in the shadows like a no-good Druid—"

"You touched this urn? And what's that sword?" Wilson fixes on the gladius clutched in Pax's fist. "You're holding a *sword* and this woman has been stabbed and cut."

"It's a prop for the costume party," I say.

"The blade looks sharp."

"Pax is a... Roman re-enactor. He's nuts about historical accuracy."

Pax nods along, his expression implying he has no idea what I'm talking about. "I have enormous nuts. They are quite majestic. I can show you if you like—"

"That's fine." Hayes waves him off with an irritated glance at Wilson. "Have a little empathy. Can't you see that the poor girl is in shock? Bag the weapon and take their statements and let them go and have a cup of tea."

"Sorry, sir." Wilson smarts. "It's just that I saw Bree hanging around with Mina Wilde at the Shakespeare festival, and this is the second murder in Grimdale where she's found the body. *And* her boyfriend is waving a blade around."

"He's not my boyfriend—"

"Being friends with someone is not a crime," Hayes wags his finger at me. "But don't you let Mina or those men of hers fill your head with tales of their amateur sleuthing, young lady. They may have got lucky a time or two, but you need to leave this work to the professionals."

It's my most fervent wish that I never, ever see another dead body again. Especially not any that have been so brutally...eviscerated.

"Speaking of professionals," Wilson shakes out an evidence bag and holds it out to Pax. "I'm going to need you to relinquish that blade."

"Never!" Pax cradles his sword to his chest like it's a newborn baby. "A soldier's sword is an extension of his body. He should never be parted from it."

"And it's quite a nice extension, too." Lottie licks her ghost lips. "Long, with a decent girth—"

I shoot her a look over Pax's shoulder, and she shuts up.

"I know you don't like it," I whisper to Pax. "But Sergeant Wilson really does need you to give it to her. She'll take good care of it and return it later. They're going to test it to make sure it wasn't used to stab Vera."

"Can she tell whose blood is on it?" Pax stares at the blade in wonder. "Because I have slain many hundreds of Druids, but I always wipe the blade down with Pericles Perfect Shiny Sword Formula—"

"Hand it over, Pax."

Pax expression shifts when he sees how serious I am. He

strides across the shop and drops the blade into the evidence bag. When he steps back, he reaches down to his leather belt, as if to rest his hand on the hilt the way he often does. Only it's not there. He winces.

"Thank you for your cooperation," Wilson says in a voice that doesn't sound appreciative at all. "The officer outside will take your statements, and we'll call you if we need anything further. And we *will* call."

As the ghosts follow us out of the shop, I hear Mary whisper, "With her sunny personality, that woman should be a weather witch."

"Some people just need to be hugged," Agnes says back. "In the face. With a chair."

THE POLICE VEHICLES and arrival of the SOCO team attract the attention of the villagers enjoying Albert's memorial. Maggie comes over, surrounded by a gaggle of her elderly friends. I sit down on the bench outside and drop my head between my legs, doing my best to answer Officer Shrive's questions without letting anything supernatural slip. As soon as I extract Pax and myself from Officer Shrive, Maggie wraps me in her arms.

"I'm so sorry, Maggie. I know she was your friend."

"Oh, Vera wasn't anyone's friend," Maggie says lightly.

"That's not true!" Mary cries. "Vera loved us hanging out in the shop. She looked after us. She always said that I was like a lighthouse in a desert."

"She means that you're bright but not useful, dear," Agnes says.

I try not to smile. *Vera certainly was a character. I wish I'd had the chance to know her.* "I've heard that Vera had the tact of a bowling ball."

"She only offered to sell my candles and soaps because, in her words, 'the idiots in this town will buy anything if it's filled with twigs and sold by a warty old witch'," Maggie says. "She was an excellent baker. Delicious brownies. I could never get her to enter them in the Bake Off, though."

That's probably a good thing.

"What happened to her?" Maggie asks. "You said she's been murdered? Was it gory? She wasn't *violated*, was she?"

"I don't know what I'm allowed to say," I tell her. "The police will inform everyone. But it wasn't very nice—"

"She was stabbed to death!" Pax declares. "Very messy, not precise like a Roman centurion would do it. This is the work of a barbarian, possibly with Druidic ancestry—"

"I see you're squiring this handsome fellow around the village." Maggie looks Pax over again with interest. She elbows me in the arm. "Bree, I see you have done well for yourself, my dear. Very, very well."

As Maggie and her friends surround Pax for all the grisly details, I catch the eye of someone approaching me.

"Hi," the medical examiner grins at me as she steps into her sperm suit. "You're Bree, right? I recognised your face from the files on the Albert Fernsby case. I'm Jo, Dani's friend."

"Yup, I'm Bree. Nice to meet you." I offer my hand, but Jo shakes her head, showing me the gloves she's pulled on. "I'm sorry it's not under better circumstances."

"Don't worry about it. My best friend Mina has plenty of experience getting into trouble and inserting herself into the middle of investigations. The Sarge seems convinced you're going to follow in her footsteps."

"I swear that I'm trying not to," I say. If only Jo knew how much that was true. "Any idea what happened in there?"

"I'll know more once I get her back on the slab, but what you saw is pretty much the situation. Someone cut her throat and sliced her open, thankfully in that order. It's ugly and brutal and *bold* of the killer to do this in the middle of the day while the shop was open, with the Bake Off judging going on outside. Anyone could have walked into the shop while he was going about his grisly business."

"I know. It's awful." I shudder.

"In a way, that might be good news. It means this is someone who doesn't care if they get caught, which means that he'll have been sloppy about leaving evidence behind. It means that we'll catch him." Jo points to Maggie and her friends surrounding Officer Shrike, all of them talking like hurtling freight trains as they offer up every minute detail about the Bake Off/Memorial and the people in the village they suspect of foul play. "Someone will have seen the killer entering or leaving the shop, or we'll catch him on CCTV. He will have left clues behind. We'll catch him."

As Jo enters the shop, I slump back down on the bench, hugging myself. Edward stands in front of me, his shirt billowing open as he places one finger beneath my chin, tilting my head up so I have no choice but to meet those remote obsidian eyes of his. I swallow, unsure of how I can be reeling from discovering Vera's mutilated body and still feel the bees buzzing beneath my skin where he touches me.

"You must consider the happy news, Brianna," he says. "If we had not been watching Pax stuff his face with pastries in the Bake Off tent, we might have arrived at the shop just as Vera was attacked, and met the killer ourselves."

Holy ghost-balls, I hadn't even thought of that.

"What you're saying is that eating scones saved our lives?" Pax booms from behind Edward.

"The gods may have deserted us, but the Roman's stomach

has saved us," Edward breathes, his thumb stroking a delicious circle over my chin.

"Good." Pax leans forward and yanks me through Edward, who yelps with indignation. "Because I am hungry again, and we have many more lives to save."

8

AMBROSE

"Don't look at me like I paid any attention in Sunday School," Edward says as Bree describes the saint card to us, for my benefit. "I was too busy trying to figure out how many communion wafers I could hide in my codpiece. Besides, saints are Catholic nonsense. We staunch Protestants don't go in for any of that guff—"

We're floating around Edward's bedroom while Bree gets it ready for the first guests of the season. Pax tried to help, but he pulled the first sheet too hard trying to tuck it in and ended up tearing it in two. So now the three of us watch while Bree straightens and tucks and tell us about the blood-splattered card with the drawing of a man in white, like a ghost...

"It's Lazarus," I say, suddenly remembering.

"What's a Lazarus?" Bree asks.

"I don't know much about him," I admit. I wasn't exactly a keen student of Sunday School, either. "He was a man who died, and Jesus performed a miracle and brought him back to life."

The room falls silent as the news hits. For once, not even Edward has anything to say.

Bree lets out her breath. "Then I'm right – it is a message for me. It has to be. Vera could see ghosts, too. She wanted me to find this card. But I don't understand what it means. She didn't write anything on it. Unless the image itself is the message. I wish we knew more about this Lazarus fellow."

"Maybe you should talk to an expert," I say. "Isn't a priest going to be sleeping in this room?"

"Mussing up my bed with his saintly feet," Edward mumbles. "Brushing his teeth with holy water in *my* sink. Thinking impure thoughts about choir boys in *my* favorite chair for thinking impure thoughts."

"Edward," Bree warns.

"What of it? That's *my* chair. I won't have it sullied with vulgar Catholic daydreams."

Bree sighs. She sounds tired. I kind of wish I remembered what being tired felt like. A lot has happened today, and Bree clearly does not have the patience for Edward's... Edwardness. "If Dani can hear you, then other people might be able to, too. I need you to keep your thoughts about filthy Catholic priests to yourself while our guests are here—"

"Are you serious? I've waited centuries for the opportunity to communicate with Livings. I have so many things I want to say." Edward's voice grows imperious.

"Me too." Pax thumps his chest. "This will be my first time meeting a fellow Roman."

"He's a Roman *Catholic*, Pax," I say. "Not quite the same thing. If I recall, you used to throw men like him to the lions."

"Oh, even better." Pax rubs his hands together with glee. "Are there any lions nearby? We could have a party."

"No parties," Bree says firmly. I hear her fluffing the pillows. "I've still got beds to make and then I'm—"

"The bed is made. If you'll all kindly extricate yourselves

from my presence, I'm going to bed," Edward announces, interrupting Bree.

"But the Great British Bake Off is about to start," Pax says.

"As exciting as it is to watch the finalists make mini Charlotte cakes, which I thought was one of those emo bands teenage Brianna was so fond of, I can see Pax's stalk hardening beneath his tunic and I know exactly how this night is going to end, and I'd rather not be here for it."

He won't?

I don't understand. After the night the four of us had together, where Edward showed me all the ways I can pleasure Bree and made her scream and writhe again and again and again, he does not wish to repeat this? Now that Pax is a human, he can do what we couldn't do. He can be inside her, give her exactly what she is craving. This is what Edward ghosts for, and he doesn't want to be part of it?

I don't understand.

Bree's voice tightens. "Don't be like that, Edward—"

"Goodnight," he says stiffly.

I can't see what's happening, but I sense the mood of the room shift. Why is Edward behaving like this? There is so much between us that has been left unsaid, so many more hours to pleasure Bree before the guests arrive.

And now that we know that she can bring ghosts back to life...Well, *Pax*. But he's a ghost. And not just any ghost – the oldest, largest, toughest ghost in all of Grimdale. And now he's a Living again.

That means there's hope. My whole body fizzes with the hope of it all. I don't think I'll ever be able to climb back into my tiny hideaway at the back of the closet, not with all this hope threatening to burst inside me. Not now that I can *feel* Bree and can make her body do things I never thought possible.

Even after Vera's grisly death, when Bree has been so silent and sullen, I can't keep the spring out of my floating or the smile from consuming my face.

Why is Edward not leaping through the walls? Why is he not gathering Bree in his arms and demanding that she free him next? Because it's all I can think about.

"Okay, Edward." Bree sounds miffed, too. She flicks off the light and slips her hand through mine. My ghost body responds to her touch with a delicious shiver as she helps to guide me out of the room without steering me through any walls. "Come on, Pax, Ambrose. We'll leave the prince to his slumber."

Bree kicks the door shut behind us.

"And you'd better not make any noise!" Edward calls after us. "I'm in a beheading mood."

"Can't cut mine off," Pax shouts back. "I'm a carpet now."

"The word is 'corporeal', Pax," I say helpfully. "It means, 'having or relating to your physical body'."

"My physical body will do horrible things to that ghost if he interrupts the semi-final," Pax mutters.

We move down the staircase in the direction of the guest lounge. Even though Mike and Sylvie have a cozy living room for the family in the west wing of the house, Bree always prefers to hang out in the guest lounge with its ancient carpets and crackling leather Chesterfield and gilded portrait of Edward on the wall.

Bree leads us into the room and settles Pax on the sofa. "I'm exhausted. It's been a strange and wonderful and terrifying day. I'm off to bed, but Pax, you can stay up and watch the Great British Bake Off if you like."

"But I need you to use the buttons...oh, no I don't!" I can hear Pax stomping his feet in the happy little dance he does whenever something exciting happens. "I can use the TV all by myself."

"That's right." Bree yawns. "But I need to get some sleep. So please keep the dancing and yelling to a minimum."

"I cannot make you an oath," Pax says with seriousness. "It's Patisserie Week, and if they eliminate Janusz I will be as angry as the time a Druid kicked me in the plums right before I was going to chop off his head."

"Well, have fun. Or..." Bree's voice trails off. She sounds uncertain. "Maybe you could skip your show, *just this once,* and come to bed with me?"

"I will be outside your window as soon as the winner is announced," Pax says. "That is my duty. I will not shirk it, but first...little Charlotte cakes."

"Pax..." Bree's voice shifts. I hear it – the tremor of her need. And suddenly, it all falls into place – why she's been so quiet all evening. Why she hasn't been as excited to dig into the mystery of Pax's sudden personhood.

Bree's afraid.

She's terrified.

Of course she is. She's just found out that she has unknown powers she can't control, and she now has a very boisterous and very real centurion to wrangle. And just when we had a plan to get answers, she learns that the only other person in the world who shares her power had been brutally murdered.

My hands clench into fists.

Bree doesn't feel safe in Grimdale, and that is terrible. This is her home.

And more than that, this is the most wonderful place on earth, and it's wrong to feel sad here. It's *unfair.*

Throughout all my travels, Grimdale was the place where I loved to return. Back then, the house was owned by my close friends, the Van Wimple family. Ever since my father disowned me, they gave me a bed whenever I needed it.

I would hole up in the room in the turret, the one that

became Bree's childhood bedroom, and I would sit beneath the window with the sun streaming across my face, and I would use my frame and pen to write my memoirs. I spent the evenings in the Van Wimple's drawing room with my friends, laughing over good food and wine and regaling them with tales from my adventures.

And so it seems fitting that when I died, I found myself as a ghost not in the remote Siberian village where I was poisoned, but back at Grimwood Manor again. I didn't get to travel outside the village, which was sad, but I did get to spend many more years with my friends, watching them grow old. And then the house passed to Bree's family, and when her parents turned Grimwood into a B&B, I got to be surrounded by travellers and wild tales again. I never got to participate in the lively recounting of misadventures, but being apart from others has long been my lot in life.

Until Bree.

I love this house, and I love Bree, and I don't want her to feel alone or afraid. But I am still apart from her. I cannot protect her from my side of the Veil. Perhaps with Pax's arms around her and his enormous Roman todger inside her, the Bree I love will once again smile and feel safe.

But I have to get the Roman to understand.

"Pax," I lean in to whisper to him. "I think Bree is trying to ask you to take her in a manly fashion."

"Thank you, Ambrose," Bree whispers, a hint of laughter in her voice.

"I thought you said that you were sleepy," Pax's voice wavers. "Women are confusing."

"I don't know what I want," Bree says, and I think it's the most truthful thing she's said all day. "All I know is that I can't bear to watch you stand sentinel at the end of my bed. I can't sleep alone tonight."

My eyes prick with emotion, because I can hear the need in her voice, and I want so badly to be what she needs right now. But I am a ghost, and Pax is real, and at least one of us can give her what she needs.

And maybe, *maybe,* we will figure out how her magic works, and then I could be with her, too.

Pax doesn't have to be told twice. He throws the remote at the moving picture box, but the sound doesn't stop so I'm guessing he missed. Thankfully, nothing shattered. I tap my stick and move across the room, and call upon my newly formed ghost powers to touch the button and turn it off. Between Bree's powers, the moldavite stone, and Sylvie's meditation app, I'm thrilled with my newfound ability to interact with the world around me once more.

It takes a gargantuan effort, but I manage to turn off the moving picture box. I whirl around, but Pax and Bree aren't paying any attention to my feat. I can't see what they're doing, obviously, but I hear Bree's faint, pleading moan, and I sense the air thicken and tremble with wanton promise.

"Ambrose, you may have the lounge. I will take Bree to her room now," Pax grunts. I hear Bree squeal with joy as he hoists her into his arms. I try to stamp down the envy snake coiling in my gut. My fingers itch with the desire to touch Bree, to slide my fingers over her skin and explore the terrain of her body, over and over and over.

"Can I...can I stay with you?" The words tumble from me before I can consider them. "I want to...to listen, to feel, as much as I can."

"Yes, you must stay!" Pax's voice shimmers with delight. Whether he's fighting or fucking, Pax believes everything is better with friends.

"Are you sure, Ambrose?" Bree's fingers graze mine, the

touch lighting my ghostly veins alight. "I don't want you to be hurt because of what Pax can do and you can't—"

"The only things in life that can hurt us are the things we love," I say to her. "You are worth all the hurt in the world to me."

"Oh, Ambrose." Her voice catches on my name. She leans in, and I sense the moment her body brushes me. The tingles race through my being, and then her lips are on mine.

Her kiss, oh her kiss. It starts slow and gentle, like waves lapping against a distant shore. But like the ocean it swells with the tide, threatening to pull me under, to sweep me away.

I am ready to be swept.

"My turn." Pax tears her away from me. Bree laughs as he marches off with her, down the hall toward her room. He must've thrown her over his shoulder.

"Ambrose, come with us," Bree cries.

I follow their voices as best I can, my cane discarded on the floor of the sitting room. Bree must still have the moldavite stone with her, because I graze the wall and can feel my way along the corridor. I find the doorway to her bedroom and enter.

The bed creaks. Bree calls my name. I float over, excited for what might happen.

"Oops," I murmur as I knock into a vase, and it shatters on the floor.

"Don't worry about it." Bree's voice is a low purr in my belly. "It was an ugly vase. Come here."

I move gently to the side of the bed. My leg brushes her thigh. She's sitting on the edge of the bed, and as I move closer, she parts her legs, notching me between her thighs. Behind her, Pax is crouching on the bed, his bulk making the mattress dent. He runs his hands over her body and kisses along the edge of her neck.

Suddenly, something soft lands on my face, falling half through me, but catching on my strangely more corporeal form. It feels like material. I remove the offending garment. It's Bree's shirt. I breathe it in. It smells of almonds and mulled wine and smoky fireside liaisons.

"Stop sniffing the fabric and get into bed with us," Pax growls.

Bree's fingers try to unbutton my frock coat but they keep sliding through the buttons. These small, precise movements seem beyond the connection we now have.

I reach up and unbutton it for her, dropping the coat onto the floor and following it with my vest, shirt, trousers, and undergarments.

"You're like a Christmas gift, all wrapped up in layers of finery. Hurry up and unwrap yourself, man," Bree says with a laugh in her voice. "I want to enjoy my present."

Finally, I kick aside my boots and socks and climb up beside her. Bree turns me to her. She leans me back onto the sheets. I can feel the bed beneath me, the soft cotton dragging against my bare, ghostly skin. I cannot describe the sensation except to say that after so many years of feeling so little, of hanging in a dark void where only the tip of my cane could connect with the world, the feeling means *everything*.

But it is nothing compared to the sensation of Bree's lips on mine. She is everything. She is exquisite. I let out a shaky breath, and her tongue slips into my mouth. It sweeps mine, hungry and tender. Her hands grasp my shoulders, warm and thrumming with life. A whimper rises out of her, and it makes my own heart soar...if I even have a heart.

While we kiss, Pax's hands roam over her body. I feel his fingers slide between us, rolling Bree's nipples in his hands until she bites down on my tongue. His hand spreads across her stomach, and she arcs back into him, leaning her head back to expose her neck.

I kiss along her neck, trailing over the delicate skin of her collarbone. My lips tingle from where I sink into her a little, every ghostly nerve of me alight with the sheer taste of her.

I let my fingers float over her, moving in languid circles around Pax, enjoying the way she writhes beneath us. The heat of her, the sensation of her, unfurls something inside me that I have spent days tying up in knots again. That wretched, beautiful hope that I might be able to have more than this, more with her.

Edward is maudlin, I think, because he believes it is better not to hope. Pax finished his ghost business – he learned that he had a proper burial after all, and Bree's magic brought him back to life somehow. But compared to Pax's simple unfinished business, mine is next to impossible. I do not know what it is that has made me remain as a ghost. If it is my desire to see the world and everything in it before I pass over, then I fear I shall remain a ghost for all of time.

But if I can have more nights like this, with Bree, then I am content to remain invisible.

And yet, how fervently I wish...

I graze my fingers between Bree's legs, softly caressing her mound. She moans and thrusts her hips forward, begging for more. But Edward taught me that by being soft when a woman demands force, I can increase her pleasure. So I move my fingers slowly, softly, teasing Bree's entrance, dipping just inside before returning to circle the small nub that never fails to drive her wild.

And she is wild now – her breath laboured, her body shifting beneath me, and the exquisite moans and purrs and curses falling from her lips.

Wild. And exquisite. And for this night at least, mine.

"You are a dream," I whisper as I dance my fingers over her.

"She can't be a dream," Pax growls as he grabs her hips and shifts her, moving his thick thighs beneath her. "In my dreams, she rides me like a Scythian warrior atop a mighty warhorse."

Bree cries out as Pax lowers her back onto him. My fingers are still between her legs, and I feel his gentleman's maypole slide inside her, filling her, stretching her. Bree sighs, her thighs falling open, her hands gripping my shoulders, fingers sinking inside me, kindling stacked against my ghost skin, ready to burn me alive in her flames.

Bree's fingers clench, digging deeper inside me, penetrating me although I cannot penetrate her. She falls forward, her lips brushing mine, so hot and warm. I dance my fingers over her clit, the way Edward showed me, drawing beautiful little mewling sounds from her as Pax thrusts deeper.

Her body jerks with every thrust, her tongue sliding over mine, through mine, the connection between us flickering in and out like a flame desperate to catch.

Want tugs at my body, awakening long-dead senses, stoking the fire inside me with insatiable, toe-curling *envy*.

"Tell me," I say to Pax as he drives himself inside her over and over. "What does it feel like to touch her? To *truly* touch her?"

"She is like silk," he growls, his huge hands brushing over mine as he moves over her skin. What I would give to touch her like that, to feel her truly. A tugging, jerking sensation fills my whole chest, like something has wrapped itself around my heart.

I ignore the discomfort because I want to be with Bree. I swirl my fingers against her, wanting to feel as much as I can when she gives herself over to Pax, when her body succumbs and she comes around that thick Roman member of his. Pax was close now, I could tell by his rapid breath and the way he draws her tighter against him. Bree's lips cling to mine like she needs me to breathe, and it feels so wonderful to be needed, to be wanted, even though I cannot...

I suck in a not-breath as that strange force clamps around my heart.

"Oh," Bree's voice trembles. "Ambrose, the cord..."

But whatever she was trying to say is obliterated by the force of her orgasm. She cries out as she trembles between us, and the thing around my heart pulls *hard*.

I fall forward into her, *through* her, *inside* her. But I do not feel the same pain that I usually feel when I walk through a solid object, that brief but excruciating sense of my ghostly body being ripped apart and remade around something more solid, more real.

Instead, the fire that is Bree consumes me, and I am reborn in her flames – a glowing, reckless burst of starlight. I am inside her. I can feel her organs and bones and veins and sinews. It is the most intimate thing I could ever imagine.

And I *see*.

I *see*.

But I don't understand.

After I went blind, it took around five years for me to stop dreaming with vision, for my memories to rewrite themselves with only four senses. This is the first time since then that I have seen something *inside* my head. It feels like a memory, only it does not belong to me.

Bree's scent swirls around me. I am on the floor of her house, playing with some blocks, and a woman with a pink suitcase kneels down beside me...

And then, the memory shifts. I am riding a red bicycle with bright silver ribbons and a bell that I ring constantly. My dad holds the back of the bike as I ride around and around on Grimwood's driveway. "You're doing awesome, Bree-bug! You're a natural."

I *feel* like a natural. I laugh at the swoosh of the wind in my hair as I pedal faster, so fast my dad can barely keep up. I look up at the house, grinning at the two figures watching from the window.

And then Dad lets go, and I'm flying for real. I'm doing it! I'm riding a bike!

I fly out of the gate and turn on the footpath toward the cemetery. I pedal hard as I ride through the high iron gates. Dad chases after me, laughing. "Careful, Bree-bug. Don't go too fast. You'll wake up the ghosts!"

I fly around the corner of the tallest mausoleum. My laugh dies in my throat as a figure steps out of the shadows, clad in a long, black hood. There's something *wrong* about the person, but I don't know what. A cry freezes in my throat.

The hooded figure steps toward me, raising a hand. I yank the handlebars hard around. My wheel spins but I'm going too fast. The ground rises up to meet me and my dad yells "Get away from her!" and the world explodes with pain—

My heart squeezes, and the same tugging sensation that pulled me into Bree, into this memory that is not mine, shoves me out again. Hard. I jerk backward and fall through the mattress onto the hard floor. My head cracks against the floor, but I'm too shocked by what I saw to focus on the pain.

I crawl out from beneath Bree's bed and clamber back up. Bree's fingers find mine, and she tugs me back into her arms, where I belong. She presses her naked body against mine, and I feel her heart thudding.

"Ambrose," Bree breathes. "You were inside me."

"I was."

"I felt you. I felt you in my bones. And I saw through you."

"He is see-through," Pax reminds her with a growl. He is still inside her. "He is a ghost."

"No, I mean I saw through your eyes. I was in your memories. I was sitting at a desk in my old bedroom, in front of the window, writing furiously with pen and ink and a wooden frame, my hand unable to go as fast as my mind. I felt frantic, desperate to get down the scene before I forgot it, but my heart was light." She leans forward and nuzzles her cheek against mine. "I felt completely at home. And then I came, and the memory was gone."

"And I was in your memories," I breathe, astounded by this strange new power she had shared with me. I don't want to talk about the memory of the bicycle, because I know exactly what happened that day. Edward and I watched it from the window. So I tell her about the woman with the pink suitcase. "It was the day that the manor house opened as a B&B. You were sitting on your playmat in the kitchen, stacking colored blocks into a tower and then gleefully knocking it over, when Mike and Sylvie brought in a beautiful, blue-eyed woman carrying a small pink suitcase. Mike offered to take her bag to her room, and Sylvie got the kettle on, and the woman bent down on the rug and swiped a piece of dirt or something off your forehead. Then she handed you a red block and said that you didn't have to worry, you would always have someone to play with."

"I don't remember that," Bree says, her voice breathy. "I must've been very young."

"You were wearing a diaper, and an adorable pink bib—"

I sense Bree making a face. "Promise me you'll never use the word diaper while we're in bed together ever again."

"I will promise you anything," I say with a happy sigh. "As beautiful as it was to see through your memories for a moment, that wasn't what I meant when I wished to be *inside* you."

"Oh, Ambrose." Bree's fingers glide across my cheek, leaving a trail of starlight behind them. "I wish that so much. If we figure out what's happening with my magic, if we can make sure that I'm not going to hurt anyone, I will find a way to bring you back, too."

Her breath hitches on the words. I know she's afraid of what she is, what she can do. As desperate as she is to close the final gap between us, she is too frightened to attempt to figure out my unfinished business.

I will wait until she is ready. I have waited for a woman like Bree my whole life and for all of my death. I will wait as long as she needs. I will be content with moments like this, with nights like tonight. Any part of her is enough for me.

"You look sad," she says.

I shake my head. "I'm never sad when I'm with you."

"I know you, Ambrose. You crave more. You always want to experience *everything*, and it's killing you to know what Pax has that you don't. I wish I could give it to you, but I can't. Not yet. Not until I know that I won't hurt you. But I can give you something." Bree's fingers trail over my shoulders. She nudges me back. "Lie down," she whispers.

I obey. My back presses into the sheets. With Bree so close to me, I don't fall through this time.

She trails her fingers down my chest. My whole body burns with the wanting that I know she can't fulfill...

But then her warm, soft mouth closes over my member.

Oh, but it is exquisite. Her pear and almond scent closes around me. She slides her lips down my shaft, making me wet, taking me into her until I can feel myself in her throat. The thick coil of need in my stomach unfurls, and all I can feel and smell and sense is *her*.

Bree digs her hands beneath me, forcing me to thrust my hips up, driving me deeper into her mouth. *Oh, her mouth!* It is the most exquisite pleasure! Her tongue is a flicker of fire dancing over my tip. Her lips curl around me, and when she takes me deep it's as if she swallows down every bad thing that's ever happened to me. She moans against me, using her fingers in a fist to stroke and squeeze me. I can't see of course, but I'm certain Pax is using that filthy Roman tongue of his on her clit, and it won't be long now until she falls to pieces again, for me, for *us*.

A deep, keening moan escapes Bree's lips, and she sucks me so hard that she lifts me off the bed. My balls tighten, the knot a living thing inside me. Any moment now, I may, I *may...*

"Ambrose," Pax says suddenly. "I could teach you a Roman trick."

"Sure," I manage to choke out.

I feel Pax's hand reach between my legs. As Bree's mouth closes around my length, Pax strokes his finger beneath me. Bree takes my entire length into her mouth, and he pushes on that piece of skin.

I *see* stars. Bright bursts of light dance inside my eyelids. I am afraid for a moment that I have crossed over, that my body has become dust and starlight. But then the pleasure burns off, and I realize that I am still here, still a ghost, still in bed with Bree and Pax.

"Ambrose," Bree strokes my cheek. "You look shocked. How was that?"

"I..." I wiggle my fingers. They feel all strange and tingly. "I am quite overcome. But was that not messy for you?"

"No, nothing came out. Which is kind of cool, actually. I guess that ghosts don't produce semen. But I tasted...something. I tasted *you* on my tongue. A Mediterranean cocktail with a hint of salt."

Wow. This is amazing.

She's *amazing.*

I turn to Pax. "So, can you teach us any more Roman tricks?"

9

EDWARD

"In vain she waits for votaries at her shrine,
None come, though all at wanting her repine;
Her hand holds forth the register exact,
Of every generous, every friendly act—"

"Ooooooooooh! Pax, oh, oh..."

I stand at the window of my private boudoir, soon to be invaded by a priest, and recite the words of Voltaire, a poet after my own dark, depraved, and anarchistic heart. I get down on one knee and extend my hand, my fingers unfurling beautifully as I shout the next stanza with all the passion boiling in my ghostly veins:

"...Favors in which esteem with friendship vied,
Received not meanly, not conferred with pride:
Such favors as those who confer forget,
And who receive, declare without regret—argh!"

"Ambrose, yes, yes!"

I throw myself down on the bed and go to pull the pillow

over my ears before remembering that I'm a ghost, and my hands fall right through it. Instead, I jam my head through the wall and bite into the electrical cable. The lights flicker and a buzz surges through my body, but all it does is make the sounds from downstairs reverberate inside my ectoplasmic skull.

No matter how loudly I recite my favorite poem, I cannot drown them out. Brianna's screams of ecstasy echo through the walls and pulse inside me, punctuated by the obnoxious grunting of that Roman oaf, Pax, and the exclamations of that traitor Ambrose.

It should be me.

I am the prince. I rightfully own Grimwood Manor. I'm in charge and I have all the brilliant ideas. I should be the one who Brianna brought back to life. It should be *my* scepter that she's bouncing up and down on right now.

"This history of the virtues of mankind, Within a narrow compass is confined;" I mutter to myself as I stare at a mouse running through the internal wall cavity. Electricity hums through my body, and my wretched scepter responds by standing proud and true, throbbing with a need that only Brianna can satiate.

You could march downstairs and join them, a dark voice whispers inside my head. *You are the prince. Demand the worship of your subjects. Take what is your due.*

It could be like that night all over again – the night that I relive every moment I'm with Brianna. Even my most depraved and salacious fantasies cannot live up to how it felt when she kissed me, when my name fell from her lips in a breathy whisper. Even when I was living, no woman has ever made me feel so alive.

But it's never going to be like that again.

Because Pax is alive, and I am not.

Because Ambrose believes we can all be made alive, too, but I cannot.

Because my friends deserve their second chance at happiness with her, but I do not.

I will never be able to be alive again, because I never cared about anything when I was alive enough for it to bind me to this mortal coil.

I have no idea why I'm a ghost, and so I will remain a ghost forever, watching Brianna as she grows old with Pax and Ambrose, as they fuck and wed and fill this house with tiny children whom Pax trains with tiny wooden swords to be a constant annoyance to me. They will have their beautiful life together and I will be the spectre in the walls.

It is what I deserve.

I will be trapped here with their happiness, and it will turn me into the monster I secretly know I am.

My scepter throbs with urgent need. Even though I know it's useless, that one of the punishing horrors of being a ghost is being unable to give yourself climax, I wrap my fist around it and stroke.

Bree's screams reverberate through the walls as the electricity pulses and my fist pumps. Stars dart across my eyes.

What are they doing to her? Is Pax rolling her nipples in his fingers, giving them a little pinch just the way she likes? Is Ambrose kissing her with all his passion and amateurish enthusiasm? Is she writhing with a Roman cock buried inside her while a Victorian adventurer worships at the altar of her body?

It's better this way. Better that she is with them.

My balls contract painfully. My fist pumps harder. *So close, so...*

I come.

I cannot believe it. A wave of pleasure consumes my body. I stare down at my scepter as the engorged purple head twitches and jerks in my fist. Nothing comes out, because I have no live-giving juices left inside me. But my body sags with relief.

The lights in my room flicker again, and blink out.

Great, I've blown a fuse. Bree's going to kill me.

But Bree doesn't seem to notice the power is out and all of Grimwood Manor is in complete darkness. She's still screaming. I extract myself from the wall, float through into Pax's bedroom, and wipe my hands that have touched myself on his pillow, because that is the kind of petty insult I enjoy. I return to the window in my bedroom and listen, my body churning with emotions.

Go to her, the voice whispers.

I refuse.

The history books have described me as many things, but never a good man. I cared only for my art and my fancies. I chased pleasure because I knew that my demons would eventually overcome me. I wanted to be adored by everyone, and to keep the party going so no one of my bohemian friends had the chance to see the real me in the harsh daylight. I did nothing of value or substance unless you count my poetry collection which – if I'm being brutally honest with myself in the darkness – never received the critical acclaim it deserved.

Brianna believes I am a better man. I want to be worthy of her. But it will never be true.

So I stay away.

Ambrose thinks that I am clueless. Poor, selfish Edward. He can't see what's really going on.

Tosh. I see more than a blind adventurer.

I listen to Brianna. Okay, granted, when she goes off on one of her feminism rants, I do tend to tune out a bit. (I thought allowing women the vote might at least make politics spicy. Instead, it's more tedious than ever.)

I listen to every word she says, and I listen to what she does not say.

I know that Brianna is afraid.

She thinks she's going to end up like Vera, sliced up on the floor of a deserted magic shop.

She may not be wrong.

And there is nothing I can do.

I'm *useless.*

I can't slay her enemies. The most I can muster up is a ghostly voice to frighten a couple of vapid strumpets. I can't stop this monster from finding her and ripping her to pieces in front of me.

In fact, my very presence puts her in danger, making it more likely that Brianna might accidentally reveal her powers to this monster.

And I have not Ambrose's wit or charm or intellect. I know nothing about Lazarus. I don't have Pax's psychotic streak. I might've been trained in the princely art of fencing, but I've never had to face an enemy in open battle, unless you count my standoffs with my father across the throne room (which I always lost).

I am nothing more than a distraction to her. A devastatingly beautiful distraction, but still...

I am worse than...

...*useless.*

My father's voice echoes inside my head. I close my eyes, and it's as if he's right here beside me, his voice pounding in my ears.

"Has my vapid, wastrel of a son finally slunk back to court with his tail between his legs? What do you need this time, Edward? Let me guess, you've been kicked out of that expensive painting conservatory for starting a fight, and now you need more of my money to throw away on opium and French women? At least I have one son

with the wit of half an ox. Thank the heavens that I have Henry, so that this country shall never be so cursed to have you as king."

Not like my brother. Not the great Henry, who was adored by everyone at court, who could do no wrong in my father's eyes.

Even after all this time, even knowing that my father died in agony of the pox and my mother was sent off to live in solitude in a dreary Scottish seat, his words still haunt me.

That day, I yelled at him that I didn't care what he thought of me. It was a lie. The last lie I ever told him. I had come to court only to plead the case of my good friend, Charles Villiers, 6th Earl of Dorset. Charles had accrued a substantial gambling debt and was being chased across the countryside by a band of vicious thugs intent on collecting his debt in pounds of flesh. I needed soldiers to protect him, and myself as his companion, since I also owed a small fortune to the same lender.

But my father claimed he could spare no men for our cause. Not a single sword would be raised for the life of his firstborn son. He said that if I were found floating dead in the Thames, he would throw a party. I shouted back that it would be the only pleasure his miserable court would ever see once he had deprived his courtly ladies of the pleasures of my boudoir.

He said that on the night of my conception, he wished that my mother had swallowed his seed. He wished that I had never been born.

After twenty-six years of my father's abuse, his words should have little impact on me. But as his desire to unmake me from the world reverberated from every lofty corner of the throne room, it amplified every memory of his cruelty. He never wanted me. Every time he praised Henry for his horseback riding or his shooting or his other kingly pursuits, it had twisted the knife deeper.

Edward isn't a real prince. Edward doesn't have what it takes to survive at court. Edward has his head in the clouds – he has no mind for war or politics. Edward is too stupid, too sensitive, too lazy, too selfish...

I wanted to please him so badly that I became the man he thought of me. I gave them the excuse he needed to disown me and raise Henry as his heir. I thought once he had what he wanted, he might see some use for me, might take the time to understand my art, to understand me. But he hated me more than ever, and so I fled to Grimdale, to the grand manor I'd purchased there as a country base for my most impure acts. I brought with me all the people who made my life worth living and set them up in the house, starting with Villiers. I thought that if I could not make my father love me, then I would build my own kingdom in this house of sin, and my subjects would love me as their Father of Lust.

A hard lump forms in my throat, even though, strictly speaking, I do not possess a throat.

Nothing has changed. I am still Edward the Disappointment. Edward the Failure.

I cannot make them love me.

They intend to leave me and I cannot blame them.

I am useless to Brianna. It is better that she never knows me, that she never falls for me the way she is obviously falling for Pax and Ambrose.

I will never be worthy of her.

I'm everything that she's afraid of.

I *am* the monster.

I know these truths, but with every moment that passes in Brianna's presence, my resolve weakens. The urge to run downstairs, to throw myself at Brianna's feet and kiss her toes and do all the wanton things to her body that I know she desires threatens to undo me.

I must get further away. Before I forget myself.

Before my beastly heart believes in the impossible.

Before I convince myself that I deserve her.

I stayed away from Brianna once, even though it was agony. I can do it again.

I float out the window, heading for the cemetery. But then I catch a glimpse of my mausoleum, towering over the rest of the graves. The lump in my throat closes. I cannot go there.

I *will* not hide in that effigy to my failures.

Besides, the acoustics out here are even worse. The lights may be out, but Brianna's keening cry pierces the silent night, and it takes every ounce of self-control I possess (which granted is not much) to hold myself back from diving through her window and into bed with them.

Where to go? With Brianna's new powers, we can now move further from Grimdale than ever before. But it fades the further I move away from her. Still, it is worth a try.

I float across the front garden, passing over Mike's zodiac mosaic that Kelly and Leanne trashed. The mosaic marks the spot where I fell to my doom, crashing from the turret window into the cobbles below and stabbing the glass through my buttocks.

As if on cue, the shard prickles. I reach around behind me and absentmindedly pull it out. I toss the shard at Brianna's window, but it vanishes midair. A second later, my arse tingles as a new shard is formed.

I am cursed by my own uselessness.

I float down the street, but I only get to the corner of Grimwood Crescent before the ghost mojo tugs me back to the front garden, right outside their darkened window, just in time to hear Pax command Ambrose to do something *interesting...*

I creep closer, drawn by Brianna's cries. My scepter leaps to attention once more.

Maybe I could just take a little peek.

Just to know what I'm missing...

No.

No.

Bad Edward.

I cannot fall into temptation. One peek at Brianna's champagne eyes hooded with lust and I will be lost again. I will want impossible things. I will begin to believe that I deserve her.

I swallow hard. I back away.

I know what I have to do. The only way to hide from my temptation, to force myself to never bend to my weakness.

I must sit with the evil I have done.

At least there I won't be tormented by the sounds of Brianna's pleasure. Three years ago, Mike spent a whole summer perched up there, laying insulation to help keep the manor warm. It rendered the space practically soundproof, although no less miserable.

I know it well, because I lived there for two miserable years, cowering in terror from a beast of such malevolence that it wouldn't surprise me if he were Vera's murderer. But I must risk facing him.

I am an addict. I need my medicine.

Trembling with terror, I float back up to the master bedroom and slip through the walls. The pain of my body passing through the solid objects is nothing compared to the ache in my heart. I avoid the electrical outlets. If I'm distracted, I'll have time to change my mind.

I slip up the wall cavity and into the attic. The moon shines through one of the tiny dorma windows, dancing long, eldritch shadows over the jumble of old furniture and oddments stashed up here.

"H-h-hello?" I call timidly into the gloom. "Are you up here?"

No reply.

"It's me, Edward. I know you haven't seen me in a while. I promise I'm not here to hurt you. I'm not here to make any of my many threats come true, even though you deserve every single one. I just need to hide here a while."

Maybe he's out, sharpening his claws.

SQUEAK.

My blood runs cold. I'd recognise that squeak anywhere. I jerk into a stack of old vinyl records, which topples through my toes, but the sharp pain is nothing compared with the terror churning inside me.

I peer into the gloomy darkness. "H-h-hello?"

SQUEAK.

"You're here. Of course you're here. This is your home. Ha ha. It's your home and I've come back, uninvited." I swallow. I hold up my hands, trying to steady myself so he can't see me trembling. "I've come seeking sanctuary. I know that I have no right to ask, but it's not for me. It's for her—"

SQUEAAAAAAK.

"Please," I murmur, sinking to my knees. "I promise. I just need to...to see if it's still here. I'll be ever so good, I promise."

Nothing.

I sigh with relief. If I were alive, I would let out a breath I didn't realize I'd been holding, as all women in lascivious novels are wont to do whenever their overwhelming terror subsides. I move quickly through the crowded room. The attic is where each successive owner of the house dumps the previous owners' junk after all the decent furniture is sold. I pass a whole corner dedicated to the ghastly mahogany furniture Ambrose's friends the Van Wimples were so fond of, and some trunks of clothing from Brianna's grandmother.

I find my way to a familiar corner. It's even more grim than I remember. A curtain of spiderwebs hangs from the ceiling, draped like gossamer lace across Bree's old red bicycle and

Mike's StairMaster machine. The old piano that once sat in my drawing room, around which my friends and I gathered for drinking songs on many languid, opium-soaked nights, gathered dust up against the window.

I suck in a deep breath, and plunge my head inside it—

"Ow," I mutter, as my face shoves between the strings like a cheese grater. I'm solid enough that I find the space inside the piano cramped and uncomfortable. But I locate the object quickly. I remember watching from the armoire on the day it was shoved inside, forever rendering my beautiful piano tuneless. Useless, just like me.

I try to pick it up. My fingers close around it, and I can feel the texture of the leather case. I try to tug it out, but I can't draw it back through the wooden piano. I drop it back into its hiding place with a puff of smoke.

Ambrose's manuscript.

He thought it was lost in the fire at his publisher's office. In his death amnesia, he forgot that he made a copy and hid it here, just in case. I don't think he's even considered that his manuscript might be the key to his unfinished business.

Just another way in which I am superior.

I've known it was here for years, of course. I watched Ambrose hide it in the piano before he left for the trip to Russia, from which he returned only in spirit.

He does not know it's here. He does not know that I used to follow him around whenever he visited the Van Wimples. Pax and I were going through another twenty-year stretch of not talking to each other – apparently, one of my poems offended his gods or some such nonsense, so I occupied myself with the liaisons of the Van Wimple's unusual houseguest.

I've never admitted to anyone that I found Ambrose... intriguing. This earnest man with his thirst for knowledge and adventure. This beautiful man who couldn't see the world and yet found more joy in it than anyone I'd ever met. I sat in his room at night and watched him work diligently on his wooden frame, long after the last candle had burned down to a stub. I wondered what it must be like to have a purpose.

In those long two years where we lived in the attic beneath Ozzy's thumb, I felt certain that he would find it.

I squeeze my fingers around it, so tight that my hands fall through the manuscript to caress the crumbling pages within it. It's always been the key to helping him cross over, and now, it's what he needs to become Living, like Pax.

And that's why I've kept it hidden all these years.

Apart from the Roman oaf, Ambrose is my first real friend. And if he finds this manuscript, he will leave me. They will both leave me. They will both be able to be with Brianna.

And I'll be alone. Again.

IO

BREE

My eyes flutter open. Sunlight streams in my window, casting dappled shadows across the furniture. I vaguely remember the power going off last night, but I was too far gone in the arms of two of my best friends to care.

A ghostly hand drapes across the pillow above my head. Ambrose. He floats a little above the rumpled sheets, his azure eyes rimmed in sunlight. "Good morning," he murmurs.

"It is now." I reach up and stroke my fingers along his cheek, loving the warm tingle where my skin meets his ghostly form. We're not quite touching, but in so many ways, it's even better than touching.

Ghost sex is the best sex. I'll fight anyone who says otherwise.

"You were so beautiful last night." Ambrose's fingers explore my skin. I know that whole thing about blind people touching your face to 'see' you is just a silly myth, but Ambrose isn't like most people. He wants to know everything, feel every emotion, experience every facet of humanity. He wants to know

every part of me, even the shape of my nose or the way my ears are just a little bit pointy.

"You were pretty fine yourself." I smile. "I'm glad you enjoyed Pax's Roman tricks."

"I am simply ashamed that I require my friends to teach me these things. I should be the one showing them Victoria's scintillating secrets or explaining the varying uses of a hysteria machine—"

I can't help it. I start to giggle. He looks hurt. "What's so funny?"

"Ambrose, Victorians are famous for being sexually repressed. It's kind of a cliche—"

"Well, then, I am pleased to be here to divest you of these wild lies you have heard about us," he muses. "These sensations are all new to me."

"I know you're a virgin. But didn't you ever..." I gesture to his ghostly crotch area. "You can do a lot by yourself. Sometimes, I prefer it. Much less complicated and messy."

"Heavens no." Ambrose makes a face. "I admit, it has been tempting at times, but I have abstained ever since my physician informed me that masturbation causes insanity."

I snort-laugh. Sometimes I forget that the ghosts aren't aware of all the modern medical advances.

"What? It's true. Self-pollution has been linked to numerous disturbing maladies. And judging by the fact that Edward's love of onanism has driven him to seek his thrills within the electrical currents, it is absolutely *not* something I wish to, er, pursue." He leans forward and presses his lips against my clasped fingers. "I much prefer you as my teacher. I do not know what is expected and what isn't, what is normal and what is taboo. All I know is what feels good, and that's being with you, and with my two closest friends."

"Good. Unfortunately, we can't spend the morning

smashing more puritanical Victorian stereotypes. I've got to get to work."

I sit up and reach for my water, but stop short as I see the shadowed figure at the end of my bed.

Pax stands straight and tall, his eyes fixed on the windows. His hands clench and unclench, clearly he misses his sword.

I sit up. "You didn't stay up all night, did you?"

"It is my duty. The night watch was uneventful, although the magical self-lighting lanterns didn't flicker back in the village until dawn."

So there was a power cut. I hope it was a normal, everyday power cut and not the kind caused by an overexcited royal rake after a few jollies.

Pax yawns.

"Pax, you're human now. You have to sleep...I think?" I furrow my brow at him. "I guess we actually don't know what formally-ghost humans require."

"I require one thing only, and that is your body beneath mine, writhing in ecstasy..."

He yawns again.

"Fine, fine, but how about some breakfast?" I ask. "I'll make a Full English."

"With the tiny circles of golden crunchiness?" Pax perks up.

"Yes, with hash browns. It's not a Full English without hash browns."

Pax skips down the hallway, his Roman sandals slapping against the stone floor. I pull on jeans and a hoodie, and Ambrose walks with me, one ghostly hand threaded through mine, the ball of his walking stick tapping on the ground.

As we cross the foyer, I gaze up at the staircase leading to the master suite. Not a single sound stirs from that direction. "I think Edward is upset with me."

I *know* he is. First, Pax became human and not him, and

then a woman gets murdered and all the attention is on her and not Edward the prince and his quest for mortality. Sometimes I swear, that ghost will drive me to an early grave...but my chest tightens at the thought of him not joining us last night.

"I think perhaps we don't give Edward enough credit," Ambrose says. "He may pretend to be an uncaring wastrel, but I think he feels deeper than we can ever know."

"The only thing Edward feels is jealousy that he's not the center of attention," I say as I push open the kitchen door. "He's—"

"Well, well, well," Edward says tersely as he turns from the stove. "I see we have dragged ourselves out of bed finally."

My words catch in my throat. Edward must've heard what I said about him. He won't meet my eyes as he watches a pot boiling on the stove. Eggshells lie across the counter and crunch under my feet as I step forward.

"Your eggs are almost ready," Edward says conversationally as he moves to the bench and starts slamming an orange against the surface. "The toast is a little charred, as I had a little disagreement with the toaster. But I personally prefer them as scorched as my wretched soul will be once the Devil gets his hands on me. I couldn't get the can of beans open, but I didn't want to wake you lest you think I was trying to be the center of attention—"

"Edward, I—"

My apology dies in my throat as Edward picks up the now profoundly bruised orange in his fist, holds it over an empty glass, grits his teeth, and makes a face that can only be described as a royal prince visiting the privy after an all-night curry and cheese party.

"What are you *doing?*"

"I'm trying to make fresh squeezed orange juice." He grits his teeth. The orange skin splits and two drops fall into the empty glass. "Now that you're in the room, the squeezing is a little easier. You should really employ servants to do this. It is an inefficient use of my time."

"Step aside," Pax cracks his knuckles. "I shall squeeze the orange as I once squeezed the king of the Gaul's brains out through his eye sockets."

"What a delightful mental image." I move to the fridge and pull out the container of orange juice, which I set on the counter beside him. Edward makes a face as he watches me pour juice into the glass. Delicately, he sets down the orange and licks his fingers in a slow, luxurious way that makes my insides all gooey.

"It comes in a box, I see. Everything comes in a box. Does one not need servants for anything in these dark, modern times?" Edward peers into the open carton. "Do tiny servants live inside, stomping on the fruit to get the juice?"

"Oh, yes." I swipe the glass from the counter and take a long sip. "We use a shrink ray on them. Sometimes they get swept into the juice and I accidentally drink one. They stick in your throat something awful."

Edward's mouth twitches. "You are mocking me."

"A little."

"If we were in my father's court, a woman who mocked a royal may find her head on a spike."

"Good thing we're in my house, where the worst that happens is that *someone* shuts the power off to the entire village."

"That was an accident." Edward glances away. "I did not know what came over me. But I saw some servants from the council outside repairing it earlier, so I cannot be blamed for—"

"You should have come to bed with us," I whisper. He darts away, forgetting that he has the orange in his hand. He squeezes it so hard that it squirts right into his eye.

"Ow," he cries. "That actually hurt! I'm a ghost, it's not supposed to hurt. This royal prince demands that my eye stop stinging and Pax stops laughing immediately."

"Not going to happen," Pax chortles. Ambrose tries to hide his smile in his shirt sleeve. He turns toward Edward, his eyes widening as he ponders the same question that I'm dying (pun intended) to ask.

Edward was so grumpy last night, so determined not to enjoy himself with us, and yet here he is, making breakfast.

"For your laughter, Roman, you shall have nothing. Ambrose, I have already set out your favorite," Edward gestures to a plate of burned toast on the table. "Sourdough bread slathered with honey."

"Thank you, old bean," Ambrose says earnestly. "That's very thoughtful of you."

"Twas not a problem, my friend. If we're stuck in this house for the rest of our ghostly days, then we deserve the simple pleasures, don't you think? And I found some flowers to brighten up this dull room. I must say, they are quite lovely, although their loveliness cannot compare with our Brianna."

I can't help the blush that creeps across my cheeks at Edward's flattery. But then I notice the bunch of weeds and a foxglove from the woods are shoved into a vase in the middle of the table, drooping onto the plates.

I grab the plants and toss them out the window.

"Is that what you think of my gift?" Edward clutches his hand over his heart. "Why, Brianna, I am wounded. I have been stabbed through the heart—"

"Bree is no good at stabbing," Pax pipes up as he peers at the boiling pot, which is now emitting a rather noxious smell. "She doesn't understand that it's all in the wrist—"

"I love the flowers very much," I say quickly, the warm feeling inside me bubbling and fizzing with all their antics.

Edward making breakfast for everyone (well, me and Ambrose) and picking flowers is incredibly sweet. And very unlike Edward. "And I especially love that you seem to be back to your usual self. But foxgloves are deadly poisonous, and we shouldn't have them around the food."

"Of course." Edward's jaw tightens. "I knew that."

"What have you cooked for us?" I reach for the pot, bracing myself.

"Eggs with soldiers."

My heart stutters. When I was a little kid, eggs with soldiers were one of my favorites. Pax used to sit across from me while I ate and use my food to explain military formations.

"Edward, that's...that's wonderful. Thank you so much."

"It's hardly worthy of being on Great British Bake Off," Edward mumbles as the egg timer goes off. "But it's something..."

He lifts the lid off the pot. I lean over to see inside and immediately regret it. A huge cloud of black, noxious smoke hits me in the face. I stagger back, clamping my hand over my mouth and nose.

"It smells like the siege of Antioch in here," Pax grumbles as he shoves open a window.

My eyes sting with tears as I shove the lid back on the pot. "Edward, I don't know what you made, but it wasn't eggs."

"I don't understand. I did exactly what your mother always did. I put a pot on to boil and set the egg timer for five minutes." Edward frowns at the timer. "Perhaps it is a Roundhead, out to destroy the monarchy and replace us with eggs—"

"Did you put water in the pot?" I run to the window and fling the entire pot into the garden, slamming the window shut on the horrific smell.

"You're supposed to put water in?"

Edward looks so utterly flummoxed by the idea that to boil

something, one requires water, I can't choose between shouting at him or bursting out laughing. One look at the clock makes my decision for me.

"I'm afraid that thanks to Edward's well-meaning breakfast attempt, I'm not going to have time to clean this all up or make a Full English before I leave for my five-hour shift at the cemetery," I say as I set down food bowls for Moon and Entwhistle. "After that, I have a meeting with the Friends of Grimdale Cemetery Society, and then I have to greet the guests and make sure they're all settled in, and they don't think it's strange that Pax is dressed in Roman garb because I have to wait until tomorrow to meet Mina, who's kindly agreed to spend her day off shopping for clothes for Pax."

"I have clothes," Pax tugs on his leather armour. "Proper Roman attire. My mother says I am the picture of manhood."

"Yes, I'm sure if this was AD100, you'd be on the cover of Vogue. But in case you haven't noticed, we're not in the ancient world any longer. Men these days tend to wear pants."

"Pffft. Trousers." Pax makes a face. "Only barbarians wear trousers. Real men need their tackle dangling free. Edward agrees."

"He does," Edward says, clutching his codpiece.

"Edward agrees because he died with his breeches open and a shard of glass sticking out of his arse. I'm not sure I'd use him as an example," I say as I turn toward the pantry. "A couple of these muesli bars will have to do for breakfast, and—"

"I am still hungry," Pax thumps his fist against his breast. "Edward's siege breakfast reminds me of home, but it was not a nutritionally-balanced meal for a growing soldier."

"Yes, of course you are." I'd forgotten that I had to actually feed him. I'm still not used to Pax being human. I search through the pantry for something he might like. "Here. You can have these Walkers Salt and Vinegar crisps, and this can of tuna. You put your thumb through this tab and pull to open it."

"Delicious." Pax smacks his lips. "You put those in your lunch box and we will eat once we arrive at the cemetery."

"You're not coming with me."

"I must! Now that I am alive, I need a job. That's what all Living people have. And since all the Druids have been slain and the police have taken my sword, there are no jobs left for a centurion, so I will go with you to the cemetery and be a…" Pax screws up his face. "What are you again?"

"I'm a tour guide. And you can't do my job."

"Why not?"

I am going to be so late. "Because you won't get through a single day without stabbing anyone."

"But that's why you go to work, isn't it? For the stabbing?" Pax places his hand proudly over his heart. "I promise, even without my sword, I will be a true asset to your tour guiding team. I have the most kills of the whole third Legion. I was given gold stars in my last performance review—"

"Sorry, it's a trousers-only job."

"Oh, well, you can forget it." Pax's face brightens. "Does this mean I stay here with Edward and Ambrose? And watch the Bake Off episode I missed last night?"

"You can watch whatever you want. Provided you don't make a mess and you absolutely, positively do *not* leave the house." I don't want to have to explain to anyone in the village why an enormous guy with oiled muscles wearing a Roman centurion costume is hanging out at the gardening center.

"So today will be like every other day," Pax says as he yanks open the bag of crisps and takes a handful. "Except that I can change the channel on the moving picture box by myself, so Edward and Ambrose must watch what I want to watch."

"I have no interest in the moving picture box," Edward huffs. "I have important, princely things to do."

I bite my lip as he floats through the wall.

"Don't concern yourself with Edward. He'll get over himself." Ambrose leans in to brush his lips across my cheek, making my skin tingle with heat. "Get to work and don't worry about us. I'll meet you at the cemetery gates after your meeting and walk you home."

"That would be wonderful." I glare at Pax. "To recap what we discussed, what are you going to do today?"

Pax curls his hands into fists. "I shall patrol the grounds and practice my drills—"

"*No*, Pax. You mustn't go outside or do anything to attract attention to yourself."

"But how do I know what is wrong to do?"

I sigh. "Think of what you normally do, and then do the opposite. And if someone comes to the door you should..."

"...run them through for daring to approach your property!" Pax yells, reaching for a kitchen knife.

"...ignore them and stay inside so they don't see you," I finish for him. "It's vital that everyone believes you're my friend from the twenty-first century, which means you have to act the part."

"If I am the perfect twenty-first-century boyfriend, do I get a reward?" Pax's whole face lights up. I start to correct him because he's not my boyfriend, but he's too preoccupied with his potential treat. "Will you take me to a gladiatorial performance so we can watch some criminals being eaten by lions?"

I groan. This is going to be impossible.

II

BREE

My morning tour group is a school group, and most of them spend the entire time staring at their phones instead of listening to my fascinating historical accounts of malaria and murderers. There are a couple of goth kids in the back who seem mildly interested, but they're also too cool or too shy to say anything, so the audience participation bits of my speech were rather awkward.

After the school kids leave, I have a group from the Argleton Rest Home, who shuffle through the gates looking like the last place they want to be is a cemetery. I don't blame them.

"They should visit every weekend," Edward calls to me from over the fence. "That way, when one of them expires, you can just roll them over into an open grave. Job done."

"I thought you refused to go anywhere near the cemetery," I hiss whisper through the fence, grateful that most of the tour group didn't have their hearing aids in to listen to me talking to the flower bed. "I thought you said that the ghost of Voltaire shall strike you down if you even so much as glanced in the direction of your tomb."

"I'm not glancing," he says stroppily. "I'm merely taking a stroll in the garden, hoping that the many-hued flowers will give inspiration for my poetry. I actually have a few lines I'm quite proud of. I shall recite them for you—"

"Perhaps later. I really have to get back before someone in my group has a heart attack."

The tour finishes at 1PM, and I share a Chinese takeaway with Mr. Pitts for lunch. We eat sitting at the base of the witch's monument. This sculpture by local artist Sidney Smith was installed on the anniversary of Grimdale's last witch trial to commemorate the innocent women who were hanged as witches. I remember Agnes, Lottie, and Mary watching the installation ten years ago with a mixture of fascination.

Mary admired how 'phallic' that statue appeared, and said it reminded her of her late husband (another mental image I didn't need), Lottie said it reminded her of a hot dog, and she went off to sniff the offerings at the food truck, and Agnes had sniffed her disdain and thrown Walpurgis at the mayor, causing him to cut his speech short because of a sharp pain in his chest.

"Are you enjoying the job?" Mr. Pitts asks me as he hands over a tiny wooden recyclable fork.

"Very much." I stab a piece of sweet 'n' sour chicken. "It's so peaceful here."

"I'm glad that you think so. We don't get many young people who respect this place the way you do. And that's just the problem. Our visitor numbers are dwindling, and the council is concerned that if we can't attract more young people, you and I will both be out of jobs."

I swallow my egg foo yung. "But surely they can't close this place? It's a cemetery. People need to visit their relatives."

"You're right. They won't close Grimdale, but they might get rid of the tours." Mr. Pitts pats my knee. "Don't look so worried, Bree. We'll find a way. We always do. Perhaps this tour idea isn't meant to be. Maybe the dead and their stories should stay in the ground."

I don't agree. The dead deserve the chance to live again through their stories...like Ambrose.

Mr. Pitts and I head back to the ticket office where the members of the Friends of Grimdale Cemetery have already gathered. The Friends are a group of village volunteers who oversee the management of the cemetery for the council. Maggie, of course, is the president, and she's already passing around a plate of scones with jam and clotted cream.

After Mr. Pitts' revelation, I'm not surprised that the meeting opens with the treasurer, one Mr. Jules Dodd, lamenting the state of the cemetery's coffers.

"Our outgoings are more than we're bringing in with ticket sales and plot sales. We thought the cemetery postcard collection would bring in some extra revenue, but at this stage, it's a wash. We're out of ideas and at this rate, we're going to be broke by the end of the month."

Jules' dire warning loses some of its punch as he tries to stuff an entire date scone into his mouth.

"Tourist numbers so far this season have been dismal," agree Carla, a history teacher from Grimdale Comprehensive. "I've been trying to drum up more school visits, but with the new curriculum changes, the teachers want to use their limited budgets on more historically-significant sites."

"We *are* historically significant!" I jab my finger out the window at Edward's towering mausoleum. It's so large that it shades the ticket office. How's that for historically significant? "We have one of the most infamous royal princes buried right in the heart of the cemetery, not to mention all the famous writers on Poet's Way, and the painters and sculptures on the Avenue of Artists, and the witch's monument, and—"

"But we'll never be as *exciting* as Black Crag Castle," Carla sighs, referring to a large medieval fortress 15 minutes drive from Grimdale. "We don't have VR installations or a National Trust visitor's centre or 3D printed swords to reenact famous battles—"

"There must be something we can do," Maggie brightens. "I know – we hold a bake sale and—"

"I'm afraid that all the scones and teacakes in the world can't keep up with the growing costs." Mr. Pitts shakes his head as he reaches for another scone. "The gardener has just increased his hourly rate, and we have to replace the rat traps, and OSH wants us to pay to install a sign about the rickety step—"

Jules consults his papers. "The truth is that with so many haunted tours and 'dark' attractions on the market, People aren't willing to travel to Grimdale to see a cemetery when there are equally fancy ones in central London."

"So, we need a reason for them to make the trip," I say.

All eyes swirl to me.

"Yes, Bree, that's exactly what we need," says Jules. "But on our budget, what could we possibly do? We have no choice but to—"

"Hang on a second, Jules. Bree's a *young person*," Maggie says in a reverent voice, as if she's observed me sprout an extra head.

"*And* she's been travelling the world," Mr. Pitts adds. "I bet you've visited lots of places like this, eh, Bree? You've seen how they run things?"

Mr. Pitts knows my travelling interests well. "Well, a few, but—"

"Tell us, Bree, what would convince the youth of today to visit our cemetery? Do we need more facilities? Install a cafe? A bigger parking lot? Is the lack of a tearoom holding us back?"

"No," I shake my head. "Don't do any of that. You'll spoil the magic of this place. People like me want to feel as though we've discovered something no one else has heard of yet. People love the cemetery tours – we have consistently high reviews and many people mention it's the highlight of their trip. The problem is that you're not reaching travellers where they're hanging out. The cemetery is the main reason to visit Grimdale, yet all we've got to promote it is a poorly-made website – sorry, Jules – and a notice in the Grimdale tourist center, which isn't really a tourist center at all. It's a table in the corner of the Goat. None of these is helping to put Grimdale in front of people planning their holidays. We want them to plan their entire itinerary around the cemetery, not tack it on because they happen to be in the area and there's nothing on telly that day."

"So how do we do that?" Maggie leans forward in her seat. Four pairs of eyes watch me eagerly.

"We need a story, a reason for people to travel to this particular cemetery. We need to stop promoting ourselves as a burial place and start thinking of Grimdale as a library of stories. People flock to Père Lachaise in Paris from all over the world to see Jim Morrison's grave because they've heard his *story* and they see themselves as part of it. We need to tell the stories of the people buried here—"

"No one named Jim Morrison is buried here," Mr. Pitts says. "There's Old Jim McNaughty up on the hill, but some kids graffitied a crude drawing over his epitaph, so I don't think—"

"I didn't mean *literally* Jim," I say. "We have lots of interesting and famous people buried here. We need to get on social media and start showing travellers exactly what they'll see when they come to Grimdale. We have so many amazing stories about this place. It's high time that we shared them with a wider audience. Starting with the graves on the tour – Prince Edward, and the Van Wimple family, and the catacombs..."

Carla frowns. "But if we give away our stories for free, why would anyone pay to go on the tour?"

"Because they want to see these places for real. If you want them to come to the cemetery then we first have to get them to emotionally connect to someone buried here, and then they will happily pay double the ticket price just to be a part of that story."

"Bree could be onto something," Maggie says. "We need to get on the Bookface and the Twatpad and the Bibble-box and tell them all about our dead!"

"We do have a lot of historical research," Mr. Pitts waves his hand at the dusty archival boxes stacked in the corner of the office like a giant's game of Jenga. "We could include some of the stories that don't make it onto the main tour."

Maggie rubs her hands together. "I'm sure my Albert would love to have his story told; after all, he's the only person who walked into Grimdale and never came out!"

"Excellent." Carla claps her hands. "Bree, you'll set all this up, won't you? You can get us on the Twatpad and make our videos?"

"Um...I don't know..." I think about Vera's murder and the guests arriving shortly at the B&B. *And* the fact that a living, breathing, extremely hot and bloodthirsty Roman centurion is currently asleep on my couch and he thinks he's my boyfriend. I've never even had a boyfriend. Just the word makes me queasy... "I'm quite busy at the moment. Maybe someone else—"

"No, it must be you. No one is as passionate about Grimdale as you are, and you know how to use those infernal smart-phones." Maggie slaps her knee. "It's settled. Bree is our social media coordinator."

"But I didn't—"

"Hooray! Thank you, Bree." Carla squeezes my hand. "We're so happy you've come back to Grimdale. You're going to save the cemetery."

12

BREE

Ambrose meets me at the entrance to the cemetery after my shift finishes. "How was your day?"

"Fine, except that the cemetery is in financial trouble, so the Friends want me to start a social media account."

"How will that save the cemetery?" Ambrose slides his hand beneath mine, setting the bees in my veins a-buzzing. I study his face, feeling a little perverse for the way I can admire him so openly without him seeing, but enjoying his beauty too much to stop.

If Ambrose were born in the twenty-first century instead of the nineteenth, he'd be an underwear model or something. All three of them are too beautiful to be real. Pax should probably own a gym or teach self-defense classes to swooning women, Edward could be an Instagram-famous poet with his own perfume line, and Ambrose would be a writer who travels the world making panties fall at his feet simply by smiling that beguiling smile of his...

Stop.

Stop imagining a future with them.

This isn't healthy. It's going to end in heartache – my heartache, since I'm technically the only one who has a heart that can be shattered. Well, Pax, maybe. But we don't even really know what he is yet.

Dani's right – I can't live in a daydream where my three ghosts come to life in the modern world and everything works out okay. The reality is that Pax will be thrown in jail after stabbing someone in a bar fight, Ambrose would get run over by a scooter the moment he turned Living, and Edward...well, Edward probably *would* end up being a famous Instagram poet, but he'd become so insufferable that I'd have to kill him myself.

I slide my hand out from beneath Ambrose's. I need to put some distance between us. I need to not feel the way his body makes my heart soar because then I start to hope that maybe I can find a way to turn him Living, too...

"I don't know for sure that this social media idea will work," I say quickly, wanting to focus on the cemetery and not on the way my skin tingles with the memory of his touch. "But it might reach more people who would be interested. Remember how you and I used to sit around listening to travellers at the B&B talking about their adventures? Hearing their stories made us add those places to our must-see list. This will be like that, except that with social media, I can reach travellers anywhere in the world. I'll tell all the stories of the people who are buried here at Grimdale, and do some beautiful panoramic videos about the cemetery. Maybe I'll even send out some free tickets to travel bloggers—"

"That sounds fun." His face perks up. "May I assist you with this task? I would very much like to learn more about this social media. When I was alive, I had my portrait taken by a photographer. I'd love to see how far the contraptions have come."

"Well..." I didn't know how much help a blind ghost would be, but Ambrose always surprises me. "Of course. It could be fun, and I could use your research skills to help me with some of the historical details. I'm going to do a bit of extra research on some of the more interesting graves, and then we'll have to set aside some time for filming..."

"It sounds delightful," Ambrose says, but his mouth twitches, and I notice the tension in his shoulders. He's gripping his walking stick so hard that his knuckles are even whiter than normal.

"Ambrose, what's wrong?"

"It's nothing, really. It's..." he trails off, looking helpless.

"It's Pax, isn't it?"

"Yes. He is perfectly well. He simply, um..." Ambrose is trying to keep his smile plastered to his lips, but it falters.

This can't be good.

"Ambrose. Just tell me."

"Well, he slept most of the morning. But then he woke up invigorated, or, as he puts it, 'As randy as Jupiter after seeing a particularly fetching swan,' and he decided he needed some exercise."

I groan. "And?"

"And, he remembered that you didn't want him waving his sword around where people might see, so he decided..." Ambrose screws up his pretty face.

He really doesn't want to tell me. This is not *good.*

"Spit it out, Ambrose."

Ambrose bows his head. "He decided to go for a swim."

I close my eyes. "And where is he swimming?"

"In the village duck pond."

Oh, no.

"I'm sorry. I tried to stop him, but Edward wasn't around and you know how Pax gets when he sets his mind to something."

"It's okay. It's fine. We'll just have to go and rescue him."

Ambrose slips his hand into mine, and this time, I don't pull away. We slip quickly along the woodland path into the village. The whole way there, my heart races, my imagination running wild with how bad this could be.

I reach the village green and discover, to my horror, the scene is even worse than my wildest imaginings. Volunteers are everywhere – they're supposed to be packing away the marquee and decorations after the Bake Off. Instead, they crowd around the duck pond, their mouths agape in horror, while Pax back-strokes happily and very, very *nakedly* across the water.

"Pax?" I push my way through the crowd. The skin on the back of my neck prickles with unease. What if the monster who killed Vera is hiding in this crowd? What if they can tell that Pax used to be a ghost? I scan faces as I rush toward the edge of the pond, searching for someone who doesn't belong, someone who wishes harm to me and my friends, and I see—

No.

Please, no.

At some point in my life, I have angered the gods. Because that's the only possible explanation for the fact that Kelly Kingston, Leanne Povey, and Alice Agincourt have chosen this *exact afternoon* to have a Champagne picnic on the village green, and are now on their feet on the edge of the pond, staring at Pax.

"Is that your new boyfriend, Cheddar?" Kelly scoffs. "He's just as loony as you are."

"He does have a rather nice arse, though," Leanne tilts her head to the side, watching Pax as he flips in the water and starts breast-stroking his way back toward us. "And those arms..."

She's not wrong. As I reach the edge of the water, I'm momentarily caught off guard by the beauty of all seven feet of Roman glory streaking through the water toward me. Pax sees me on the edge of the water and comes to a stop, bobbing in the water. Droplets roll off the bridge of his nose and the hard line of his strong chin and his...his...very large and stiffening *verpa*. I suddenly don't know where to look.

"Hi, Pax."

"Bree! I'm happy to see you."

"I can see."

"I have been very good. I had a sleep and ate my breakfast. I feel much invigorated. And I am not swinging a weapon around."

"We might beg to differ on that," I can't help but quip back. "Yes, you are very good. I'm sorry, this is my fault. I didn't think to tell you that you can't be naked in public."

I assumed, since you've been observing the world transform around you for over two thousand years, you'd have picked up on that.

But I might be giving too much credit to Pax's power of observation. A Roman soldier isn't taught the art of subterfuge, of blending in.

"You can't be naked in public?" Pax looks down at his body in confusion. "But that's ridiculous. How else do you greet your friends if not for a giant naked cuddle? Next thing you'll be telling me that there's no public bathroom where I can go to discuss politics and current events while I do a mighty—"

"That's not a thing anymore, either." I cringe at the memory of Pax explaining to me once that the ancient Roman version of toilet paper was a sponge on the end of a stick that you dipped into a channel of water running beside your feet while you merrily sat next to your friend in a public latrine. I'm grateful for how far civilisation has come since then! "Can you please get out of the duck pond?"

"Okay, I'll come out." Pax starts to walk toward me. Water sloshes over his muscled thighs as he emerges. "I am very pleased to see you."

Yes, yes you are.

Behind me, I hear old Widow Clarkson gasp.

"Be still my heart," whispers Carla.

"No, stop!" I don't want any more sudden geriatric deaths on my conscience. "Stay there. Where are your clothes?"

"They're over there, beside Ambrose." Pax points to a pile on the other side of the lake, near where Ambrose is hovering, and right in front of where Kelly, Leanne, and Alice are standing, because of course.

"I can bring you his clothing," Ambrose says.

"No, that's okay…" But he's already dropped to his knees, his frock coat flying behind him as he feels around for Pax's things.

Alice steps forward and picks up the bundle. She winces as her hand passes through Ambrose, who shudders and leaps away. Kelly leans down and whispers something to Alice.

"She suggested Alice push you in, dear," Agnes calls out from the other side of the pond. Lottie and Mary help Ambrose to his feet. "She wants to get you back for the fountain."

I square my jaw.

"Did she just?" I mutter under my breath.

"I've got his clothing, Bree. Stay with him. I'll bring these to you." As Alice walks toward me, she tilts the roll of clothing and a long, metal object slides out and clatters on the ground.

"It's a knife!" someone yells.

"That's not a knife, it's a sword," someone whispers.

Oh no.

I figured that at least with Pax's sword in the possession of the police, I wouldn't have to worry about him being arrested for at least a few days, but I'd completely forgotten about the replica Roman sword I had my parents buy me for my twelfth birthday after I became obsessed with Roman culture for a bit and Pax tried to teach me his drills. Pax must've found it in my old room, and now…

"But who'd carry a sword around?"

"I heard that poor old Vera was stabbed with a sword. Maybe this strange, naked man is the murderer."

Oh, this is not *going well.*

Alice reaches for the sword. "Is this a...gladius?"

"It's none of your business," I hiss, and before she can touch the weapon, I stick out my foot and send her tumbling headfirst into the lake.

13

BREE

A lice screams as she hits the water with a splash, sending a wave over the shoes of everyone gathered around the pond.

I can't believe I just did that.

But I can't let Alice get a close look at Pax's clothing. If she can tell that much about the sword just from glancing at it, she will quickly figure out that Pax's things are far too authentic to be replicas, and then where will I be?

She'd tell the authorities. They will take Pax away and study him, poke him and prod him, cut him open, and jiggle his insides. They'll drag *me* away and study me – the girl who raised a Roman centurion from the dead. They'll send me to some top-secret government facility and I'll never come out again.

And what if the monster who killed Vera finds us...

I did the right thing. Alice is in the water for her own good.

Although it *is* satisfying to see one of my high school bullies thrashing around in the duck pond, especially since she was planning to do the same thing to me. Wasn't she?

Just like when Leanne and Kelly fell in the fountain after they ruined Dad's mosaic.

Dani is going to kill me.

"Hahaha. It serves you right!" Pax clutches his sides as he steps out onto the shore beside me. "You were going to push Brianna in and she pushed you in instead."

"How did you know that?" Kelly frowns at Leanne. "How did he hear us from all the way across the pond?"

"I wasn't going to push you in!" Alice glares at me as she swims to the side. She swipes her matted hair from her eyes. "I swear. Kelly suggested that I push you, but I wouldn't have done that. I just wanted to help you."

"You were about to say something about Pax's stuff," I say. "I may be used to the three of you being awful to me, but you're not going to be rude to my...um, friend."

"I was *admiring* his sword." Alice wrings out her dress. Before I can stop her, she picks up the sword from the pile of clothing and turns it over in her hands. "This is beautifully made, not like the usual ones you see re-enactors wear. If this wasn't so new, I'd almost say it could be a genuine article from the Roman period."

That's because it was copied from a genuine article from the Roman period, with exacting instructions from a genuine centurion who'd stab anyone who got it wrong.

Pax marches over and snatches the sword from her hands. "You never touch a man's sword without permission."

"That's not what men usually say." Leanne shoves her way in front of Alice and bats her eyelids. "Hello, handsome. My name's Leanne and I'll stroke your sword any time."

"Leanne, jeez." Alice glares at her friend. "That's Bree's boyfriend."

"I don't know if boyfriend is the right word—" I start, but Leanne presses herself against Pax's naked chest, twisting her

126

fingers in his damp hair as she strokes her other hand down his muscular shoulders. A hard lump of rage forms in my chest.

She can't touch him like that! He's mine.

"By Mars' musty meatstick, I belong to Bree. Remove your hands from me, woman, before I am forced to remove them," Pax growls low in his throat, and a dark, twisted part of me loves how dangerous he sounds.

"I'd listen to him if I were you," Ambrose calls happily from the other side of the pond.

"Finally, a little violence." Agnes rubs her hands together. "Things are getting exciting around here."

I don't like guys who run around threatening women. But Leanne is my childhood bully, and all through high school, not a single person stood up to her for me or Dani, not the way Pax is doing now.

As I watch him wrap his hand around her wrist, I can't help the tears that start to well in my eyes. I never thought I'd have someone stick up for me and remove that leaden weight from my shoulders. And here he is, my Pax, proving that all those words he spoke to me as a ghost to cheer me up, he would happily make real.

"Why would you want to go out with sad little Camembert?" Leanne simpers, obviously not understanding the hundred and fifty kilos of pure Roman malice that's bearing down on her. "She was such a loser in high school, and look at her, she's still a loser now. You should come and hang out with me and my friends sometime. We'll show you how to have some real fun around Grimdale."

"Bree and I have fun already. Today we are swimming," Pax declares as he scoops her into his arms. Leanne's squeal of delight turns to a shriek as he tosses her into the pond.

"Argh!" Leanne cries as she splashes wildly. "Help me! It's deep and the bottom is *squishy*!"

"Quack!" An angry duck flaps out of the water and shits on her head. Leanne screams as the poop rolls down her cheek.

"Enjoy the blessings of Neptune," Pax calls happily. "That's what you get for touching someone who doesn't belong to you."

"I can't believe he did that!" Leanne splutters as she swims back toward Kelly. "This sweater is *cashmere*."

"This is assault," Kelly calls out, but I notice she doesn't move closer to help Leanne. "I'm going to report this! That naked thug will be in so much trouble, especially when the police find his sword—"

But Pax no longer has any fucks to spare for the bullies. His arm falls around my waist, yanking me against his muscled form. "Did they hurt you?" His hands roam all over my body in a way that makes several women whimper with jealousy. "If she hurt you, that watery tart will have to answer to my Roman blade—"

"No, I'm fine." I cup his cheek in my hand and brush my lips across his lips. I may not be ready to call him my boyfriend, but I definitely feel the need to make sure everyone knows that he's *mine*.

Behind me, a bunch of the village women cheer. Even Alice smiles.

"Disgusting," Agnes huffs.

"I think it's romantic," Mary coos.

"Hmmph," Agnes says. "I was hoping for more blood."

Leanne manages to haul herself out of the water. Kelly steps back as her friend collapses in a bedraggled heap on the grass. Kelly glares at me as she deigns to put her arm around her friend, and they start off back across the park. Only I can see the cheeky smile on Ambrose's face as he pushes his walking stick into their path, but everyone gets a fresh laugh as the pair of them trip over nothing but air and collapse into a heap...right on top of a fresh pile of duck poop.

"Oops, I'm *ever* so sorry," Ambrose calls out. "I'm so clumsy."

"That's more like it!" Agnes claps.

"As much as I don't want this morning to end," I smile as I pick up Pax's pile of clothing, "Kelly will make a fuss about this, and I need you to get dressed and come with me before the police arrest you for indecent exposure."

"There is nothing indecent about that majestic male form," Mary calls out, smacking her lips together.

"Fine, I shall obey your order to wear clothing," Pax grumbles. He starts to pull on his tunic. Several women murmur their disappointment as they begin to drift away.

My eyes briefly meet Alice's as she peels her squelchy socks from her damp boots. I don't want to say a word to her, but I know this is going to get back to Dani, so I suck in a breath and approach her.

Maybe if I try to stay on Alice's good side, it will help me if she ever discovers Pax's secret.

I probably should have thought of that before I pushed her into the pond.

"Sorry about pushing you in the pond," I say to Alice. I shove my hands in my pockets and force myself to meet her penetrating gaze. "I am a little stressed and I thought you—"

"It's okay." Alice wrings out her hair. "After all the shit I've pulled on you over the years, I understand you feel a little paranoid. Besides, it was worth it to see Leanne's face when your boyfriend tossed her in. The duck poop was the icing on the cake."

"He's not my boyfriend."

"But you said I was," Pax booms, his arms circling my waist and squeezing tight. He rests his chin on my shoulder, and with his breath tickling my ear and his very toned body and still very stiff *verpa* pressing against me, it's hard to focus on anything else. "In the shop, when you were talking to the police, you told them I was your boyfriend. I am the greatest boyfriend, much better than Ambrose and Edward. I have slain your enemies and guarded you while you slept, and last night when I did that thing with my tongue that made you curse the gods as you writhed in ecstasy—"

"Not *now*, Pax." My whole face flares with heat.

Alice's lip curls. "He's doing an awful lot of boyfriend-like activities for someone who's not your boyfriend. But sure, Bree, whatever you say. Anyway, thanks for the laugh. I'll see you and your not-boyfriend around. Oh, and since you both seem interested in Roman history, you might like to know that the archaeologists have finished excavating the skeleton this morning. He's been shipped to a lab in Oxford for analysis. They'll be a few more days at the site mapping the rest of the grave and then they'll be out of your hair."

I don't like the idea of Pax's earthly remains being poked and prodded in a lab. "What's going to happen to the Roman after the lab is finished with him?"

"He'll be on display in the Grimdale Roman Museum with all his grave goods, as part of a new permanent exhibit about the Romans and the Celts in the area." Alice's face bursts into a real, genuine smile. "I'll be setting up the display myself to make sure it helps people to learn about the lives of ordinary Romans, as opposed to the emperors and gods they're used to seeing. That's what I'm starting work on today, although I guess I'll have to stop off at home and change first. I'd better go, but I hope to see you and your not-boyfriend again soon."

Before I can say another word, Alice walks off in the direction of her flat, chuckling to herself. I stare after her, unsure of everything I've ever believed about her. I don't like this feeling. She's my school bully. I'm not supposed to like her.

Dani likes her, so I should give her a chance. And she might not have been trying to push me into the water.

But if anyone could figure out who Pax really is, it's Alice. And what happens if she does? Do they ship me and Pax off to the secret government facility? Do they send a psychic to exorcise Ambrose and Edward from the house?

If the monster doesn't tear us to pieces first.

I turn back to Pax, who is assiduously fixing his leather armour in place. Ambrose has made his way through the pond (one benefit of being a ghost – he can take a shortcut without getting wet) and is trying to explain to Pax why people don't go naked in public.

"So no swimming in the pond?" Pax pouts.

"You may swim in the pond. Just wear a bathing suit," explains Ambrose.

"*No swimming in the pond,*" I fix them both with my *don't-mess-with-Bree* face. "From now on, we have to be more careful. We can't risk Vera's killer or someone like Alice finding out who Pax really is."

Pax's face falls in confusion. "There are many things I'm not allowed to do. Can you make me a list?"

"Yes, I'll make you a list. But not right now. We're already running late to meet our new houseguests."

14

BREE

Mum: They arrive today! Remember to give them the spare keys. And to show them how to use the washing machine. And don't let Father Bryne see your old bedroom – that Twilight poster is probably sacrilegious, and I don't want to come home to find the house doused in holy water.

I drag Pax and Ambrose home and head straight to my room, where I strip off my skull-covered leggings and black tunic that I wore to conduct tours. Both are damp from getting splashed with pond water.

I take a quick shower (all ghosts banished from the bathroom) and put on a pair of cuffed jeans, then I sort through my collection of band tees until I found one that doesn't have a snarling demon or inverted crucifix on it. I brush my hair and check that the guest rooms are in perfect order. I smooth out the divot Pax's body made in the sofa.

Ding-dong!

"Here we go," I mutter. I am so not ready for this with every-

133

thing else going on, but I promised my parents I'd help run the B&B so they can have their holiday.

There's nowhere to run now.

At the sound of the doorbell, Moon scampers into the coal scuttle. Entwhistle twines around my legs as I rush to the door, eager to meet our new guests.

"Welcome to Grimwood Manor," I exclaim as I pull open the door.

Two blonde twin girls about nineteen years old and a man in his forties with salt-and-pepper hair stand on the porch with all their luggage. I catch my shock. I didn't expect all three of our guests to arrive together.

"Hallå, I'm Ida. This is my sister, Astrid," one of the girls says in a thick Swedish accent. "We have been getting to know Father Bryne. It turns out that we were all on the same train together."

"Yes, we are most interested in stories of saints and sinners..." Her twin's words fade away as she stares at something behind my shoulder. She licks her lip hungrily. "Who is this? Does he own the B&B?"

A flicker of possessiveness flares in my chest, coupled with annoyance that she assumes the B&B must be owned by a man. I throw my arm over Pax's broad shoulders and beam at her. "This is Pax. He's...er, a friend of the family."

You may feel territorial, but you still can't call him your boyfriend, a mean voice taunts inside my head.

"You need not worry while you rest your heads upon our soft pillows," Pax pronounces as he beats his fist against his leather armour. "I will slay whatever enemy dares to step within these walls."

"Er...good?" Ida raises her eyebrow at her sister, but Astrid is too busy salivating over Pax's muscled arms to offer much of a reply.

IF YOU'VE GOT IT, HAUNT IT

Back off, Pippi Longstocking. He's mine. All mine.

Pax throws all four of their suitcases over his shoulder and storms off in the direction of their rooms.

"You'll have to forgive Pax," I say as I pull the door all the way open and invite them inside. "He's Italian. They're a little eccentric."

"Now that I can attest," says Father Bryne in a lovely Irish brogue. "Last time I was in Italy, I became acquainted with a cardinal who believed he was a butterfly."

"So you know exactly what I'm dealing with," I smile at the priest as he takes off his shoes. "Welcome to Grimwood Manor. Instead of winged cardinals, we have a sword-wielding Italian and a few resident ghosts. Make yourselves at home."

The guests hover in the entrance foyer, oohing and aahing over the space. I have to admit, I love this room – there's an enormous stone fireplace on one wall with a couple of cozy chairs in front of it, a table holding brochures for tourist attractions in the area, and a bunch of portraits and art on the walls.

Father Bryne is particularly taken by an old wooden rifle hanging on the wall opposite the fireplace. "This is a beautiful piece. I'm not much for weapons, but the craftsmanship on this is superb. Is it Victorian?"

"That gun belonged to my dear friend Cuthbert Van Wimple," Ambrose says from the top of the stairs. "He brought it on all his archaeological excavations in case he ran into trouble. He once shot a snake with it!"

I repeat this information for the priest, who nods with interest.

"According to his friends, in his later years, Cuthbert placed the rifle in this display, but always told his guests he kept it loaded," I speak the familiar story along with Ambrose, who leans on the balustrade with interest. "Just in case someone needed to commit a murder toward the end of a dinner party."

"Was he making a joke about the Chekhov's gun principle?" Father Bryne asks with a laugh. "'If a writer says in the first act that there is a rifle hanging on the wall, then by the third act it absolutely must go off.'"

"He knows the joke!" Ambrose hops up and down with excitement. "Oh, we're going to get on famously."

"That's that one," I say. "Although the rifle has been decommissioned now. My parents would get in trouble with the council if they kept a loaded rifle in the foyer, and no one wants a murder after supper. Far too messy. Come on, I'll show you to your rooms."

I show the twins to the room they booked – it's near the back of the house, with wraparound windows offering views into the forest and the rear of the graveyard. They have a side door that opens out onto a little balcony. "This is a lovely spot to drink your tea in the morning," I say.

Once they're settled in, I show Father Bryne to the master suite. I glance around nervously, expecting Edward to leap out of the walls and admonish the priest for touching his stuff. But Edward is nowhere to be seen.

Which is good, but also disconcerting. Edward doesn't normally miss an opportunity to lord over our guests. *What is going on with him?*

Father Bryne walks around the space, clutching his hand to the tiny cross dangling from his neck. I half expect him to break out the holy water, but he pronounces the room, "lovely."

Now comes the strange part of the day. The guests have arrived and can do what they like. Mum prefers that at least one person is at home while guests are in the house in case they want more towels or accidentally burn the place down. Since I'm here alone (apart from Pax and the ghosts, who don't count), I'm going to stay in for the night. I'm hoping to find a subtle way of asking Father Bryne about Lazarus.

I fix myself a gin and tonic and take it into the guest lounge, in case the guests feel like being social. Ambrose follows and sits in the window seat, his hands folded neatly in his lap. Pax decides to chop some firewood in case the guests would like a fire. It's the middle of summer but the house does get very cold, and if Pax is chopping firewood then he's not stabbing anyone, so I send him off to the woodshed.

I'd just settled in with my book when I hear a rustle behind me. Father Bryne steps into the room. *Finally, something is going my way.*

"Oh, I'm sorry for disturbing you." He starts to leave.

"No, please." I nod to the sofa. "This is the guest lounge. It's your space to use. It's also one of my favorite spots in the house to have a drink and watch the sun go down. Look."

I gesture to the window. Streaks of purple arc across the sky, punctuated by the spires and crosses atop the tallest monuments.

"The Lord's creation is certainly beautiful tonight. I see why you enjoy this room. I would love to join you." Father Bryne sits down, unfolding a book on his knee.

"Would you like a drink? I'm having a G&T."

"That would be delightful, thank you."

As I hand him his glass, I notice the cover of his book – it's an airport thriller about a monk who helps the FBI solve clues to catch a serial killer who is obsessed with the predictions of Revelations. Father Bryne sees me looking and laughs.

"I know, it's not the sort of fare you expect a priest to enjoy. But I'm addicted to them. Something about the intricate puzzles appeals to me."

"And the fact that the hero is a man of god?" I ask with a raised eyebrow.

He smiles. "I admit that it's nice to see a story about a priest fighting on the side of the good guys for once. Too often we're on the side of evil, although evil priests get the best wardrobe choices."

I smile at his plain black shirt and black slacks. "So what brings you to Grimwood? Don't priests usually have a little priest house they live in?"

"Yes, I do have a lovely cottage back with my congregation," he says. "However, I am here for a youth summit hosted by Father O'Sullivan in Argleton. Different religions are coming together – Islamic leaders, Hindu teachers, various Christian denominations, even Wiccan priestesses, to create programmes that encourage our youth to practice love and charity and self-acceptance."

He seems like the sort of guy who'd be good at that. "That sounds interesting. I like the idea of all these different religions putting aside their differences to work together."

"Yes, it's rather exciting. I'm hoping we can come up with some good initiatives that actually make a difference, instead of spending the whole weekend arguing over interpretations of scripture. That remains to be seen, but I'm quietly confident."

"Good, that's good." I set down my drink. "Father, I wondered if I might ask you about something. It's about a saint."

"Any saint in particular? The Catholic church is lousy with saints." Father Bryne closes the book and looks at me, fixing me with his kind eyes. "Is this a question of faith or scholarship?"

"A bit of both, I think."

Outside, Pax grunts as he waddles up the path, a mountain of wood in his hands. Ambrose moves across the room to sit on the end of the sofa, and Entwhistle leaps onto the back of the couch to nudge the Father for pats. He obliges Entwhistle with a scratch behind the ears, and he falls over onto his back, waving his paws with ecstasy.

My chest twists up in nerves. I thrust my hand into my

pocket to feel for the saint card. I need answers to keep me and my friends and family safe, but every clue I get leads me closer to a truth I don't want to face.

"I wondered if you could tell me about Saint Lazarus," I say in a rush.

"What do you want to know?"

"Everything. About him. His life. Why was he important?"

"I appreciate you indulging a priest with his favorite topic," Father Bryne says with that kind smile of his. "In his gospel, John tells the story of Lazarus of Bethany, who is a follower of Christ and the beloved brother of Mary and Martha."

"This is a different Mary from Jesus' mother? Is it Mary Magdalene?"

"It's a different Mary. Confusingly, lots of women in the Bible are named Mary. Anyway, the sisters tell Jesus that their brother is gravely ill, and they ask him to come to their home in Bethany and see him. Jesus tells his followers that Lazarus' sickness will not end in death, but 'it is for God's glory so that God's Son may be glorified through it.' Jesus waits two days before travelling to Bethany to see Lazarus. When he arrives with his disciples, he finds that Lazarus has died."

"Maybe Jesus missed the train," Ambrose says helpfully. "That happened to me in Barcelona, when I was waylaid by—"

"Shhhh," I whisper.

"Pardon?" Father Bryne frowns.

"Sssssshould we have a refill while you continue the story?" I grab the gin and tonic bottles from the table, to distract him from wondering why I'm whispering to myself. Father Bryne holds out his glass gratefully. Ambrose mimes zipping his mouth shut.

"Thank you, this is an excellent tipple." The priest takes a sip before continuing. "Jesus meets Mary and Martha at Lazarus' tomb, which is a cave with a rock rolled over the entrance. The tomb is surrounded by Jewish mourners lamenting the passing of Lazarus. Martha admonishes Jesus. 'If you had been here,' she scolds the son of God, 'my brother would not have died.' Jesus replies with one of his most well-known statements. Do you know it?"

"I'm a little rusty on my Jesus quotes," I admit.

"Jesus says, 'I am the resurrection and the life: he that believeth in me, though he were dead, yet shall he live. And whosoever liveth and believeth in me shall never die.'"

A chill runs from the base of my neck right down to my toes.

Father Bryne's eyes glaze with fervour. He touches the metal cross dangling around his neck. It's quite an ornate thing, with extra spiky bits and thorns around the middle. I've never seen a cross like it before, but then, I don't follow clergy fashion that closely.

"Jesus asks for the stone blocking the tomb's entrance to be rolled away." The priest's voice has grown deeper, more gravelly, as if it's rising up from some underground fissure. "The mourners roll away the stone, and Jesus says a prayer. He then calls for Lazarus to come forth, and Lazarus walks from the tomb, alive and still wrapped in his white death shroud. This miracle turns many of the gathered mourners into followers of Christ. This is normally the scene you see depicted in art. See?"

He flips open his phone and shows me his home screen. It's a picture taken from the back row of an ornate chapel in some impressive Gothic cathedral. Father Bryne points to the stained glass window to the left of the altar. I can see the story now – Jesus praying with Mary and Martha and the mourners as a white-clad Lazarus walks out of his tomb.

I swallow. The scene is nearly identical to the bloody saint card in my pocket.

Father Bryne puts his phone away. "Why the interest in Lazarus?"

"Oh, it's for..." I hunt around desperately for a reason. Just then, Edward enters the room, humming to himself as he makes a beeline for the liquor cabinet and dunks his head inside. "...an art project. I'm taking a class in art history and religious iconography appears in most of the paintings, but I'm not as familiar with the stories as the other students."

"I am always happy to help. Do you have any other questions?"

I swallow. "Just one. What happened to Lazarus after he was resurrected? Like, what did he do?"

"Ah." Father Bryne folds his hands over on his lap. "Now that is an interesting question. Very few people are concerned with the fate of Lazarus outside of Jesus' miracle. The Bible does not include him again. However, some scholars have attempted to follow his life. Orthodox scholars believe Lazarus went to Cyprus, where he became a bishop and died a second time thirty years later. We Catholics believe he came to Marseille, became a bishop, and converted many to Christianity before he was imprisoned and beheaded during the persecution of Domitian. According to legend, Lazarus never once smiled during his second life, as he was haunted by the sight of the unredeemed spirits he encountered during his four-day death."

Maybe he was just sour. After all, Pax came back from the dead and he's happier than ever.

Possibly too happy, I think as I watch Pax skipping back along the path for more wood. His Roman sandal flies off and he runs after it, laughing that deep booming laugh of his. Edward glares out the window at him before thrusting his head back into the liquor cabinet.

"—of course, there are other stories."

I spin back to Father Bryne. "There are?"

"Numerous people throughout the ages have reported meeting Lazarus – a mysterious, white-clad figure who never ages and who can bring the dead back to life. Some say that Lazarus is actually a woman. Others, that he is a small child. He's appeared at funerals, on the battlefield, and in the crowd at a rock concert. He was last seen in 2006 at the opening premiere of Dan Brown's *Da Vinci Code* film. As you can tell, it's all a bit silly." He smiles. "It shows how powerful Jesus' miracle was, but also how dangerous. It is part of the human condition to wish to live forever, but our life on earth is so precious precisely because it is finite. Our only true path to immortality is to embrace the Lord."

I sense an ecclesiastical shift in the conversation. Thankfully, at that moment, Pax crashes into the room with an armload of wood, followed by Astrid, who is talking a mile a minute in her thick Swedish accent and flicking her golden blonde hair over her shoulder as she desperately tries to get his attention.

"Thank you, Father." I stand. "That was very illuminating."

"A pleasure, Bree." He raises his glass. "Any time you need help with anything concerning your immortal soul, you know where to find me."

At the rate my immortal soul is being corrupted by ghost sex and mysterious magical powers, I might have to take you up on that.

15

BREE

"So?" Mina asks as she slides into the seat opposite me and settles her guide dog, Oscar, at her feet. "Is he here?"

"If you mean Pax, my best friend slash lover slash newly resurrected Roman centurion, he's at the bar getting us drinks."

Mina fluffs her wavy auburn hair. "I'm so excited to meet him. A real-life centurion ex-ghost. Is he wearing his sword?"

"He was waving it around the shop after we found Vera's body, and the police confiscated it." I lower my voice as I notice Pax at the bar, thumping someone affectionately on the back so hard that the person falls off their stool. "So he found a replica one I had made a few years ago, but I confiscated that too because he was waving it around the village. I've hidden it in Ambrose's secret room, because Pax can't fit his goliath shoulders through the door. So I wouldn't mention swords to him. It's a bit of a sensitive subject. Did you bring the clothes?"

"I sure did." Mina pushes a stuffed shopping bag from an expensive-looking men's store. "Morrie and I went down to London to his favorite Savile Row tailor and had them made to the measurements you gave me. If I do say so myself, I have excellent taste. Trust me, instead of breaking bones on the battlefield, Pax will be breaking hearts in these trousers."

"I believe it." I finger the buttery soft fabric. "What do I owe you?"

"Oh, don't worry about it. Consider it an IOU from one magically-inclined sister to another." Mina leans across the table and whispers, "So what's it like having him alive?"

"It's..." *Wild. Terrifying. Better than I ever could have imagined.* "It's a lot."

"Bree, I have brought these strange, foreign drinks." Pax slams two G&Ts down on the table and goes to slide into the booth beside me, but then spots Oscar on the floor. "Oh, hello, doggie!"

"Pax, you can't pat that dog. He's working."

"It's okay." Mina bends down and unclips Oscar's coat. "Why don't you take him outside and throw a stick for him? He'd love that."

"Can I?" Pax and Oscar both peer at me with the biggest puppy dog eyes, one a deep brown, the other a cool, expressive ocean blue, so much more vibrant now that they're no longer see-through.

"Of course. Just remember—"

"—don't stab anyone or push them in the pond." Pax skips off with Oscar's lead clutched in his enormous hand.

"Thank you for trusting him with Oscar." I watch out the window as Pax throws an enormous stick for Oscar. The three witches dance around the golden retriever, shouting with delight. The only one who looks unhappy is Walpurgis, who glares at the pup from his hiding place beneath Agnes' hair.

"Pax may be a little scary to behold, but he has a beautiful heart. In some ways, he reminds me of my Heathcliff." Mina grabs a chip from the basket on the table. "Is Dani joining us?"

"I assume so." I glance at my phone, which still shows no

messages. "She never says no to a drink, but I texted her to ask if she wanted to come and she hasn't replied."

My stomach churns with nerves. Dani hasn't replied to any of my texts. After I threw her girlfriend into the duck pond yesterday, Dani might not want to talk to me. I thought Alice seemed okay when she walked off, but maybe she was pretending? I tap out another quick message to Dani, then set down my phone.

I guess she's not coming.

Mina clears her throat. "Do you want to wait for Dani, or do you want to tell me what you've found out about Vera's death and your strange new power?"

"I don't think Dani's coming." I place the card and the moldavite crystal on the table in front of me. I stare at the two objects as if I can somehow divine the truth from their form.

"I haven't got very far. I've been too busy pulling Pax out of the duck pond, getting volunteered to run the Grimdale Cemetery social media, and smoothing the ruffled feathers of royal rakes—"

"—and having ghost sex—" Mina reminds me with a twinkle in her eye.

"And having ghost sex," I finish, my cheeks flaring with heat. "But I did speak to Father Bryne. He's a priest who's staying at Grimwood for the next couple weeks. He's here for a big meeting of different religious leaders about how they can work together on youth programmes. It's at the Catholic church in Argleton."

"I know that church well. Quoth and I robbed it once."

"You robbed a church?"

"Oh yeah. We needed some holy water and communion wafers to defeat Dracula. I distracted Father O'Sullivan while Quoth shoved the stuff in my bag." She pats her bat-shaped handbag. "There are still communion wafer crumbs at the bottom of my purse."

I'm still getting used to the casualness with which I now discuss the supernatural with my friends. Mina says 'defeat Dracula' in the same way she might say, 'went to the movies this weekend.'

Although, the less said about my last disastrous movie date, the better.

Something else strikes me as I tell Mina what I learned about Lazarus – how wonderful it is to be sitting at the pub in Grimdale with a new friend, having a pint and laughing like two totally normal twenty-something girls. I've been all around the world and met all kinds of people, but I feel a pang in my chest when I realize that I've been searching for this exact moment.

I'm so busy having fun that I only feel a little sick about the idea that I somehow possess Lazarus' resurrection magic. Mina has some wild theory that maybe one of the saint's relics is hidden in our house, so when I'm near it I obtain his resurrection power. I point out all the reasons this is impossible and she breaks into a loud rendition of a Nick Cave song called "Dig Lazarus Dig" that is as bizarre as it is relevant. We finish our drinks and are debating getting another round when we hear a tap on the window. I look outside to see Quoth in his raven form perched on the windowsill outside, tapping the glass with his beak.

Mina, you'd better get home, he says inside both our heads. *Heathcliff has just had a disagreement with the wedding florist and now the shop is covered in peonies...*

"I'd better go." Mina grabs her purse. "I asked Heathcliff to organize the wedding because I want to concentrate on editing my book, but so far it's been nothing but trouble. He keeps firing all the vendors, adding people to the guest list, and insisting the cake is whisky-flavoured. Who would have thought my grumpy gothic villain would turn into a groomzilla? Walk me out?"

Mina hooks her hand in the crook of my arm, the way Ambrose does, and I lead her outside to where Pax, Oscar, and the witches are still playing. Quoth flutters down and rests on her shoulder.

I know you're afraid of the monster who killed Vera, he says to me inside my head. *But you aren't alone, Bree. You're surrounded by a whole horde of Livings and ghosts who will do anything to keep you safe. We will figure this out together.*

"I appreciate that, birdie," I say. My gaze falls on Basic Witch across the street. The windows are dark and police tape stretches across the door. I'm still no closer to figuring out who – or what – killed Vera, or why she was clutching that saint card. But at least Mina's going to see what she can find out from her friend Jo.

I wish Dani had come out tonight. I could really use her gallows humor and no-nonsense attitude about ghosts. I have really messed things up, haven't I? I wish—

Quoth's voice pushes out my other thoughts. *Oh, and Bree?*

I raise an eyebrow at the raven.

Take it from someone who knows. You only get so much time on this earth. Don't waste it being too afraid of what you really feel—

"Nice seeing you again!" I give Mina's shoulder a little shove. "Thanks for the clothing. You don't want to miss your bus."

Fine, fine, run away from your feelings. See if I care, Quoth croaks as he and Mina and Oscar run for the bus stop.

Pax waves goodbye to the three witches and we start walking home. His huge hand spreads over the small of my back, his fingers sizzling where they brush my skin. My heart skips as I watch his eyes dart around in shadows, and his other hand rests on the kitchen knife he has hidden in his tunic.

"You can relax. No monsters will attack you while I'm at your side," he declares as we turn toward the corner where the Squashed Navvy hangs out.

"I know. You're always watching out for me."

"I am." Pax wrinkles his brow. "So why won't you call me your boyfriend?"

Oh, fuck.

"Huh?" I feign innocence. My heart hammers against my chest. *Why is he asking that? How does he even know what a boyfriend is?*

"You won't let anyone call me your boyfriend, and you won't utter the word." Pax frowns. "I am not simple like Edward thinks. I know what a boyfriend is. I listened to you and Dani talk about boyfriends when you were teenagers. You wanted that lout Trevor to be your boyfriend, the one who dared to touch you. So why him and not me?"

"Trevor was never my boyfriend, Pax." *You and Edward and Ambrose saw to that.*

"What do I have to do to be worthy? Do I need to pass a challenge? Do I need to fight your last boyfriend to the death, because I'm ready—"

I snuggle into his shoulder. "Pax, I've never had a boyfriend before. And if I call you my boyfriend, then how do you think that will make Ambrose and Edward feel? Edward is already upset—"

"They can be your boyfriends, too."

He says it like it's so simple.

"I can't have three boyfriends."

"Why not? Mina does."

"Yes, but Mina is...is different." We turn onto Grimwood Crescent. "And I can't have two boyfriends who are ghosts. And yes, I know you're not a ghost, but putting aside the issue of the three of you, and this thing between us, I'm not ready to make anyone my boyfriend. That's a big step, a commitment. I don't know what's going to happen when my parents get back from their trip, or how much longer I'll even stay in Grimdale, so I can't—"

"But I love you."

His words steal my breath.

I stop in my tracks. My limbs don't work.

I can't breathe.

Why can't I breathe?

Pax stops too. He turns to face me, tilting his head to the side as he watches me gasp for air.

"You are frightened," he says.

"No," I manage to choke out.

His voice pitches with hurt. "You are frightened of me."

"Not of you. Never of you. I'm frightened of those words."

"Which words?" Pax's face wobbles. "I love you?"

"Don't keep saying them."

"But they're true. I love you, Bree. I have lived as the ghost of a man for a thousand lives and never felt this certain of anything. I love you. I love you like a Roman loves his war songs and his wine cup. I love you as the fish loves the ocean or the pineapple loves the pizza or a Bake Off contestant loves a KitchenAid Artisan Stand Mixer. You are the reason I rise every morning to fight another day. You are why I am going to wear trousers." He makes a face. "Why is it wrong to love you?"

Tears prick the corners of my eyes. "Because...because I don't know what's going to happen to you. Pax, you're not supposed to be here. What if...what if you become a ghost again? Or worse?"

Pax steps forward, right up in my space, his chest pressing against mine. There's nowhere I can go that isn't guarded by the hard planes of his body. Those cool blue eyes gaze down at me, as beautiful as they are lethal. The wind pushes invisible fingers through his hair, and my breath catches and my stomach draws tight. It is completely unfair that he can stand here, being so impossibly perfect, and disarm me like this when all I want to do is run.

His gaze locks on mine, and my pulse races. "So you do not feel anything for me at all?"

His voice is a low, dangerous growl.

"Pax, you know that I do. What I feel for all three of you... you are my best friends. But do you know what it's like to go most of your life knowing what happens to people after they die? Knowing that there's no happily ever after, no love that endures after death. Just centuries of loneliness as the world moves on around you. Hell, I just had to see Albert and Maggie say their goodbye. All love ends in soul-destroying grief. I've lived through that grief a hundred times over – grief that was never supposed to be mine to bear. I can't...I can't go through that with the three of you. If I let myself fall for you, and this monster takes you away from me—"

"That's not going to happen," he growls. One hand snakes around my waist, dragging me against him. His fingers splay over the small of my back, and the sensation is so *possessive* that it should have me running for my Clementine Ford books, but all it does is make my toes curl and a dark, wanton ache settle in my belly. "The monster has to get through me first."

I can't bear to look Pax in the eye, to see the sadness there as he realizes that I won't say those three words back to him. Instead, I look over his huge shoulder at Grimwood Manor rising from the gloom on top of the hill, the outlines of the graves and monuments etched in moonlight. Lights are on in the guest wing – the twins must be back from their hike.

"You can't protect me every moment of every day, especially

now that you're human. Look at the rings around your eyes. You need to *sleep*, Pax. You haven't been human in a long time, but you're human *now*. You're fragile. This...what we have...is fragile, too. At any moment, Ambrose or Edward could cross over. You could go back to being a ghost or...or worse. The monster could come for you. Or you could make a mistake and the authorities could realize you're not supposed to be here and take you away. You could catch some modern sickness that your Roman immune system isn't able to handle, and you could *die*. I love my dad and it's tearing me apart knowing what the disease is doing to him, and with you...it would be a thousand times worse. Don't you see, all these reasons are why I can't..."

Pax's whole face breaks into one of his beautiful smiles. I stop struggling, arrested by this sudden change in him.

"Bree, we are not at war over your heart. You don't have to defend yourself to me," he says. "I will wait."

"What?"

"I will wait," he repeats, his smile deepening until I'm a puddle in his arms. "I will wait for you until the gods eat the earth. When the oceans boil and the sky turns to ash, when the poets run out of words and they stop making new seasons of Bake Off, I will still be here, loving you. I will love you until the very last star flickers out, and all is in darkness. You will be my light."

"Pax, I—"

"You may be my general, but you cannot order my heart not to beat for you."

Pax places his hand over his chest for a beat, then takes it and presses it to my breast. My heart thunders against his touch. He lowers his head, those pale blue pools of his no longer hurting, but wide and open and impossibly deep. His gaze drops to my lips, and his eyes heat to blue flames.

The inches between us are kindling, ready to catch fire.

My feet itch to run, to turn around right now and sprint all the way to India before I fall for this beautiful, impossible man.

"I am yours," he whispers. "I have been waiting for you my entire afterlife. I will wait as long as you need."

Pax cradles the back of my neck, tilting my head back as his lips meet mine.

My lips part eagerly, accepting him in even though my brain is screaming that this is a bad idea. That I'm becoming attached. That as much as I try to tell myself that I can have fun with the three of them with no strings attached, I'm doing exactly what I never wanted to do and letting my heart get involved.

But it's so very hard to listen to my brain when Pax's tongue strokes mine with a wild desire that has me clutching his tunic, fisting the material to pull him closer, as if I can somehow climb inside him the way Ambrose did to me the other night. I'm trapped within the press of Pax's body, pinned by his lips and his strong arms around me. He pushes his fingers through my hair, cradling the back of my head as he deepens the kiss. He tastes like the sweet grapes of the wine he drank before his last battle, like earth and blood and war. He tastes like danger, like my beautiful ruin, and I can't get enough—

A piercing scream shatters the gloom.

16

BREE

"That's one of the twins!" I spring away from Pax. His eyes meet mine, and I know that the exact same thought has occurred to us both.

The monster who killed Vera has come for me. He's inside the house right now and—

Ambrose and Edward are in there!

I don't know if this monster can hurt ghosts, but I'm not ready to find out. I wipe my mouth as I hurry up the path and grab the key from under the squirrel. I can still taste grapes and blood and danger. Pax draws his knife.

I kick the door open and Pax moves ahead of me into the foyer. He gazes around, searching for the source of the scream. I point in the direction of the guest lounge. "I think it came from—"

I don't have to finish because another horrible shriek echoes through the house, piercing through my heart. Pax takes off in a run, his sandals slapping against the wooden floor. I'm hot on his heels.

Pax throws open the guest lounge door. "Put her down, monster, or feel the sting of my Roman steel—"

"What is this?" The twins spring apart, looking guilty and very much *not* ripped to pieces by a bloodthirsty monster. "Why are you waving a knife at us?"

It's then that I notice the only light in the room comes from a circle of flickering candles on the card table. My old spirit board sits in the center, the planchette poised on the letter D.

Behind the board, Edward and Ambrose snicker.

The fear immediately flees my veins as I grasp what's going on. I should be angry at them for terrorizing our guests, but I flash back to warm memories of eight-year-old Bree laying out the spirit board for other travellers, who would ooh and aah as the spirits of Grimwood jerkily moved the planchette to spell crude messages and knock-knock jokes. It was one of our favorite games. Sometimes, when Ambrose tapped the planchette too hard with the tip of his walking stick, it would go flying across the room. Once, Pax sliced down the center of the board with his sword.

Now, thanks to my strange powers, they're able to have more control. And I can't help it, I kind of want to see what happens. Plus, it's a distraction from what Pax and I had been doing out on the street...and what he'd said to me...

"Move it again," Edward urges Ambrose. I was close enough that he could interact with the board himself, but Edward does like to boss people around.

"But Pax is here," Ambrose says. "I heard him grunt. He'll tell Bree and she'll be angry with us for teasing the guests."

Edward winks at me. "She's not mad. I'm looking at her right now and she's trying to hide her beautiful smile."

Ambrose turns his head toward us, and the smile that lights up his face makes my knees go all gooey. I nod to Edward. He nudges Ambrose, who bends down and pushes the planchette. It slides easily across the faded spirit board.

"Argh!" Astrid shrieks. "It's moving again."

"We're not touching it, and it moves!" Ida glares at her sister. "I told you that it wasn't me moving it."

"Well, I asked if it could see us, and it said, 'thy posterior, so perfectly formed and round, Doth capture hearts with nary a sound.'" Astrid waves a pad where she'd been writing down what the spirit board spelled out. "What kind of a ghost would write that?"

"A horny one?" Ida wrings her hands.

"You wrote that to tease me, because you know how sensitive I am about putting on weight after all that pasta we ate in Italy."

"I swear, it wasn't me!"

I raise an eyebrow at Edward, but he pretends to be profoundly enraptured in a portrait of himself on the wall.

So he's moved on from knock-knock jokes to filthy poetry. That seems on-brand.

"*Edward*," I growl.

"My name is pronounced *Astrid*," Astrid says huffily. "And you don't have to sound so annoyed. We're having fun."

"And I'm critiquing your interior decor choices." Edward's lip tugs back into a smirk as he indicates the oil portrait of himself staring into the distance, looking morose while wearing a gold-lined doublet and a rather large ruffle around his neck. "I wish you'd take this down. I wouldn't be caught dead in this outfit today. That ruffle is *so* 1663."

"I wanted to tell them about the history of Grimwood Manor," Ambrose says. "But Edward won the coin toss."

I look at their feet and notice a pound coin sitting on the rug. Things have got rather more dangerous around here since they're able to manipulate the Living world.

If you can't stop your ghosts from frightening your guests with a spirit board, join 'em.

I pull out a chair on the card table and sit down. "There are a lot of ghosts in this house," I say to the twins, clasping my hands on the table. "Let's see what else they have to say."

"So there's no monster?" Pax uses his knife to hold the curtain out while he checks behind it. "No murderer waving a deadly weapon?"

"The only deadly weapon in this room is your biceps," Astrid says, licking her lips. "Why don't you sit down with us and help us channel the spirits of the dead? You have such a vibrant energy, I bet they're attracted to you."

"No thanks," Pax says with a glare at Edward. "The dead are boring. I'm going to go and watch the moving picture box."

"Go on then," Edward nudges Ambrose as Pax leaves the room and the twins settle down in their chairs opposite me. "I'll help you write the second stanza. 'Like two plump peaches, ripe and fair, Thou movest with elegance, beyond compare...'"

"My fingers are cramping," Ambrose protests, removing his hand from the planchette and flexing his fingers. "Bree's here now, you can move the planchette yourself. And then you won't get so mad when I make spelling mistakes because I can't see what I'm doing—"

"Very well. Out of my way." Edward moves around me so he can get a better grip on the planchette. As he does, he folds his body through my chair, his hips pinning me against the edge of the table. His ghost cock rubs against my ass through my jeans, already hard as stone.

My cheeks burn with heat. I'm already in a state after Pax's kiss, and the things he said to me run around and around in my head. I press my thighs together, but there's nothing I can do to stop the burning heat his touch stokes inside me.

This is insane. Edward isn't even corporeal. I should be able to resist him.

Apparently not. Apparently, I am a ghostslut. And I love it.

"I adore you like this, Little Brianna." Edward's lips graze my earlobe, sending a ghostly tingle straight through me as he nudges the planchette across the board. "You are mine. You cannot run away, which we both know is exactly what you think about doing almost every day."

I gasp. How does he know that?

"And yes, that is a deliberate rhyme. A true poet is always composing. But take it from me," Edward continues, his hand stroking over the curve of my breast. "It is far better to give in to temptation. Just think what I could do to you right here, right now, when you cannot protest."

"Bree, are you okay?" Ida waves her hand in front of my face. "You made a strange noise."

"I'm...fine," I manage to croak out. I stretch out my hand and place my finger on the planchette. "Shall we...er, channel some spirits?"

"They can't see a thing." Edward's lips trail fire down my neck. He finds a sensitive spot on my collarbone and works it until I'm all twisted up in him. "They can't see all the filthy things I'm going to do to you. I could make you come right now while the twins argue over which one of them moved the planchette."

"Please..." I whisper. I'm supposed to say, 'Please don't' but I don't quite make it to the second word.

"Oh, if you insist." Astrid answers me, obviously assuming I'm talking to her. She casts one final look over her shoulder at where Pax used to be, then places her finger on the planchette.

"As my lady wishes." Edward dives under the table.

"Bree, what's he doing to you?" Ambrose asks, his voice stuttering with excitement.

I open my mouth, but I can't answer him without saying something rather inappropriate in front of the twins.

"Oooh, did you feel that?" Ida asks. "Something warm brushed against my legs. A cat?"

"There's nothing there." Astrid flicks up the tablecloth and peers underneath. "The cats are curled up together on the sofa."

"Meow," Edward purrs as he slides his hands up my skirt, dancing his fingers along my inner thighs. I bite my lip to stop myself from making a sound.

Ambrose may be blind, but he's not stupid. He's figured out exactly what's going on. He leans down and blows out a couple of the candles, plunging the room into deeper gloom. The twins gasp.

Heat floods my body in a heady rush as Edward shoves my knees apart. I bite my lip to stop myself from begging him. The ache inside me is a throbbing, needy thing.

I don't understand what's going on in that ghost's head. Edward's been acting so strangely since Pax came to life. He's hardly been around, except when he's making breakfast or putting flowers on the table or doing uncharacteristically nice things.

But this, right now, this is pure Edward. There is nothing nice about the way he hooks the edge of my underwear and pushes them aside, and plunges his tongue inside me.

"You taste amazing," he murmurs from between my legs.

"I heard something," Astrid gasps. "I think one of the ghosts is hungry."

"I've been starving, but no longer." Every inch of my skin is aflame as Edward flicks his tongue over me in a sensual assault. He replaces his tongue with his fingers, spearing them inside me, as he moves his mouth to my clit.

He moves his fingers in a relentless rhythm, his tongue dancing over me until I am completely devoured and explored. This is complete and utter madness, but no way in hell do I want him to stop—

"Ow," Astrid frowns, kicking the tablecloth. "I think it was a cat. It feels like someone just kicked me."

Ambrose starts to move the planchette erratically around the board to distract the twins. The hot coil of pleasure unfurls inside me as Edward's reckless, princely tongue does what he does best.

And then, just as he plunges a third finger inside me and I topple over the edge of a brain-melting, body-liquidising orgasm, the moldavite tumbles out of my pocket and rolls across the rug. And Edward's hands slide inside me. Like, *inside* my skin. And suddenly, I'm no longer in my body anymore.

I'm inside of *him*. But I'm not under the table. I'm standing in the corner of the room, looking over at myself – at Bree, age about fourteen, and Dani. We're sitting at the same card table covered with a purple cloth, and we have candles flickering and the spirit board spread out between us.

"So I can ask them anything?" Dani's voice trembles as she sprinkles salt water over the table to 'cleanse the space.' I – as Edward – think this is silly, but I won't object to a little pageantry. Dani looks around the room, even though she won't see what Bree sees – us three ghosts hovering next to the table. Pax is passing his fingers through the candle flames, making them flicker and dance. Ambrose cracks his ghost knuckles, preparing himself for his task. And I am doing my best to appear bored and insouciant while mischief pools in my belly.

Bree wants us to talk to Dani. This could be an exciting night.

"You can ask anything," Bree tells Dani. "They're going to try and answer, but it can sometimes take Ambrose a while to move the pointer."

"It's called a planchette," Dani corrects her. "And how can Ambrose move it to spell things if he can't see it?"

"Edward has his hand on top of Ambrose. He helps to guide him. And he gets grumpy when Ambrose spells things wrong. Edward is a stickler for correct grammar. You should hear his rant about how wrong it is that the spirit board doesn't have punctuation."

"My kingdom for an en-dash," I – as Edward – sigh.

Bree laughs, and my heart squeezes tight. I love it when I can make her laugh like that. Dani's mouth quirks up at the side. "It would be nice to finally be able to talk to them," she says, reading some instructions from her magical rectangle. "Okay, so we place our fingers on the planchette to channel our will to reach out to the spirits."

"We don't have to do that. They're right here."

"I'd like to follow the instructions, thank you very much." Dani places her index and middle fingers on the edge of the planchette, as the magical rectangle instructs. Ambrose winces as her finger goes right through his palm. I can tell by Bree's face that she's feeling a little silly, but she places her fingers on the opposite edge of the planchette.

"Now we channel our energy into the planchette. We reach out into the space between worlds, and we..." Dani clears her throat as she consults the instructions. "We call upon any kind and good-hearted spirits present in this room to make themselves known to us. Is there a good spirit with us?"

I lean forward and whisper my reply in Ambrose's ear. Ambrose shakes his head, but he forgets that I'm running this party. I move his hand. The planchette jerks from beneath Bree's and Dani's fingers and skids across the board.

It lands on the word 'NO.'

"Holy shit," Dani breathes. "It's really happening."

"That's Edward." Bree's eyes meet mine with a warmth that makes my ghostly body tingle. "You can tell because he's being a smart ass."

"Hi, Edward," Dani brightens. "It's so great to finally talk to you. Is there anything you'd like to tell me?"

My brow furrows as I consider what I want to say. I get an idea, one that makes the corner of my mouth tug into a smirk. I move Ambrose's hand as he grips the planchette. Dani jerks her hand away, watching in awe as the pointer moves without either of them touching it.

It spells BOO.

"Edward!" Bree moans.

Beside me, Pax is cracking up laughing. I can't help but smile. I am quite hilarious. I'm still the life of any party.

Or rather, the afterlife *of the party.*

"What's going on?" Ambrose cries. "What did you do? Edward, you better not be making me spell out filthy words."

Dani's voice wavers. "Bree, are...are your ghosts taking the piss?"

"I told you." Bree rolls her eyes. "They're kind of silly."

"I can get behind that." Dani leans forward eagerly. "Okay, Edward, from your centuries spent as a ghost, can you give us some words of wisdom to live by?"

"I certainly can." I grab Ambrose's wrist.

"Edward, please..."

"I. F. Y. O. U—" Dani reads out the letters as she writes them down. "If you've got it, Haunt it. Oh, Edward."

"Oh, Edward." Bree smiles her beautiful smile at me, and a warm, happy feeling spreads outward from my heart, through my whole chest—

I blink and I'm back in the present, in my own body while it flushes with the afterburn of my orgasm. Edward has floated out from beneath the table. He rubs his thumb along my cheek, his obsidian eyes narrowed in concern.

"Come back to us, Brianna," he says in that haughty tone of his. "Your prince commands it."

I peer up at him, and his eyes soften. "There you are," he whispers. "For a moment, you were somewhere I could not follow."

"That was...odd," I whisper. I didn't just see his memory. I experienced it as if I were him. I felt what he felt when he looked at me, and it...

...it's *overwhelming*. His emotions rush over me, and they are so intense that tears pool in my eyes. *Is that what it's like to be Edward?*

No wonder he did so much opium.

"I'll say it was odd," Astrid shivers. "I heard a ghostly voice. It said the most filthy things. And the planchette went absolutely wild. It spelled a load of gibberish. Then you let out this huge moan and slumped over, like you were under a spell, and I thought the Devil himself had taken you—"

"Is everything okay?"

I whirl around. Father Bryne stands in the doorway, wearing a pair of hideous flannel pajamas. He stifles a yawn with his hand. "I heard a scream."

"Everything's okay. You can go back to bed, Father," I say, willing my heart rate to return to normal. "Ida and Astrid were just having too much fun with a spirit board."

Father Bryne glances down at the table just as Edward nudges the planchette toward the letter P. "Those boards are dangerous. You never know who might be listening to the other side."

"You certainly don't." Edward nudges the planchette until it spells out, "poos," then starts giggling as the priest whirls around and stalks away.

17

EDWARD

After the seance, Brianna begs me to go to bed with her. I
have never once had the self-control to refuse a
woman who looks at me with lust-filled eyes, her
voice husky with desire...

...and this is Brianna. Her cheeks are flushed and her voice
husky from what I did to her. I want nothing more than to kiss
every inch of her soft skin and feel her come apart around my
fingers again, and again, and again...

It takes all of the self-control I never possessed when I was
alive to back away from her. I step through the sofa over and
over, until the pain tempers my rising scepter. Only when my
ghostly body aches with agony can I tell her that I will leave her
in the capable hands of Pax and Ambrose, for I have things to do
that night.

I do have important things to do. I have almost perfected
my latest work of poetry. I've been trying to write a poem for
Brianna, and it has been quite difficult. Usually, I have no
trouble describing the beauty of a woman, or the wild, wanton
sensations that consume my body when I am in love. But when

I try to write about Brianna and how she makes me feel, the words do not come.

She may have Ambrose and Pax to fulfill all her worldly needs, but I'm determined to at least give her this poem. When Ambrose becomes a Living man once more and he can pleasure her mind and soul in all the ways I cannot, she will forget me. But at least my words will haunt her long after she leaves this infernal house.

That's why this poem must be *perfect*.

I cannot work in my boudoir, for it is occupied by that meddling priest. An Irish priest, no less. How has he survived so long without his head being placed on a pike, I'll never understand. The monarchy is rather lax these days. They are too preoccupied with opening shopping malls to deal with proper issues of state. I shall have to have my things disinfected after the priest leaves.

Because of the papal presence, I have decamped to Brianna's old bedroom. I wander amongst her old dollhouses and discarded crop tops from her teen days, sniffing that soothing pear and almond scent that wafts from her once-beloved objects, and hoping it inspires me.

Instead, I lie down on her bed, enfolded within her stack of plushie toys, and stare at the words she carved into the plaster until my eyes glaze over.

$$B + P + E + A = 4EVA.$$

A naive promise made by a little girl. Forever is a terribly long time to be without her. But at least she'll have Pax and Ambrose to care for her. At least she will be loved the way she deserves.

THE NEXT MORNING, I rise early to make breakfast. Brianna's room and the moldavite stone are close enough to the kitchen that I can touch most objects without expending much effort, although doing small, fiddly tasks such as picking out the tiny bits of eggshell from the mixture still elude me.

I never would have believed I would find a use for manual labour, but I actually enjoy making breakfast for Brianna. She can have something cooked for her before she has to set about making breakfast for the guests.

Now that I know about the water and eggs, I'm actually getting quite good. I pick up Mike's apron; it has a dragon and a golden ring and the words Lord of the Grill written on it. I approve. I can be Lord of the Grill. It takes me three goes to tie it around my waist, and it doesn't fold very well around my codpiece, but it makes Brianna smile whenever she sees it, so I shall always wear it for her.

Brianna and Pax and Ambrose enter the kitchen just as I'm fishing the blackened bacon from the pan. Her lips are raw from being kissed by an uncouth Roman. The seething jealousy pools inside me, stealing my breath for a moment. Not that I have breath to steal, unlike Pax.

"Oh, Edward, this is..." Bree tastes a tentative bite of her scrambled eggs. "Actually, quite good."

"I am rather brilliant," I say.

Brianna finishes all her eggs, although she doesn't touch the bacon. Pax shoves his big, stupid head into the plate, while Brianna helps me clear the table and sets out boxes of cereal, yogurt, and cut fruit for the guests. "Thank you for my breakfast." She nuzzles my shoulder. "I really appreciate it. And I think you like doing something nice for other people."

"That seems unlikely," I say in my best bored voice. I don't want her to think I'm becoming Ambrose. Even a ghost prince has a reputation to maintain. "I have simply discovered yet another of my extraordinary gifts – and it would be a shame to deprive the world of Edward's most eggsellent culinary delights. Downright criminal, even."

Brianna touches her hand to my chest. "You know, when you're nice, your silver cord glows a little brighter."

Ah, yes, the silver cord she sees.

"Tell me about this cord."

She chews on her bottom lip. She does not like talking about it, because it is part of the magic she does not understand. "You have one, and so does Ambrose, and so does every ghost I see now, although yours and his are stronger. They stretch out of your chest, right where your heart is, and wind all around you. They kind of follow you everywhere, like Entwhistle unwinding a ball of yarn all over the house. Then they enter my chest. They tug at my heart sometimes, and sometimes I can reach down and touch them. That's how I brought Pax back, I think. I tugged on his cord and it spun around us, pulling tighter and tighter until...until it pulled life from me into him. I think that's what happened."

She reaches into her pocket and makes a face as she tugs out that bloody saint card.

I know she's afraid, but hope surges inside me, hot and insistent, and I have to push her. "So if you tug on the cord, then I could be alive?"

Brianna shakes her head sadly. "If the cord snaps, that's game over. The ghost of Lady Macbeth snapped her cord, and so did Albert. And they're gone. We don't get a second chance to try it. I won't risk it, not for either of you. All I know is that Pax had his unfinished business, and I think that has something to do with it, too. So we can't try anything unless I can help either of you with your unfinished business, which I promise we will do, but not until I—"

"—gain control of your powers, yes, yes." That annoying, wretched hope gnaws at my belly. "But you know what our unfinished business is? You knew that Pax needed to know if his men gave him a Roman burial."

"That was only a guess. An educated guess, based on how well I know him, but still a guess. As for the two of you, I haven't spoken to Ambrose about his yet, but I'm certain I know that his unfinished business is about his lost manuscript. But knowing that isn't going to help when I don't have a way to get it back," she says. "But as for you, Edward – you're the mystery. Can you think of anything that you left unfinished?"

A memory of my funeral flashes in front of my eyes, but I stamp it *down, down, down.* "Not a thing. Every countess in my father's court would attest that I left them all sated—"

"Edward," Brianna warns with that brilliant smile of hers. "It's okay. We'll figure it out. I bet the answer is in one of the seven million history books written about you." Brianna reaches up and brushes her lips over my cheek, and my resolve nearly crumbles. "I shall see you tonight. Be a good prince today, okay?"

"I make no such promises."

From the window in the snug, I have a clear view over the fence into the cemetery. I watch Brianna as she leads her tour, and then she sits down on a bench near my grave with a stack of history books to start working on her videos. Ambrose hovers nearby. He's the only one of us who can stand to be in the cemetery, and he loves history and research and all that boring stuff.

All this talk about the stories of ghosts...

Ambrose's manuscript burns in my mind.

I should tell Brianna about it. I should tell Ambrose. I should tell him that his freedom is within his grasp.

But every time I think about it, I think about how hurt they'll be that I kept it.

Ambrose will look right through me with those azure eyes of his.

Brianna will never speak to me again.

And then Ambrose will become Living.

I'll become a shadow, a memory, a ghost without a story of my own.

They will all forget about me.

It's what I deserve.

I'll do it. I swear it on my love for Brianna. I will give her the diary.

But not today.

Not until I have finished this poem.

Not until I've figured out how to say goodbye.

18

BREE

"Good morning, Father. Did you sleep okay? No evil spirits or ghosts of seventeenth-century royal rakes haunting your room?"

"Huh?" Father Bryne closes his book – another gory religious thriller by the looks of it – and peers up at me with confusion from his seat in the snug.

"Never mind," I smile. "More tea?"

"Yes please." He holds out his empty mug for me.

It's been a week since the night of the spirit board. I've been so busy with work and researching stories for the Grimdale Cemetery videos and keeping the house tidy for the guests that I haven't got any further on solving Vera's case or figuring out how my magic works. The Swedish twins have moved on now, and a German couple are staying in their room. Father Bryne is still around – apparently, the youth summit went so well that he's sticking around for the rest of the month to help Father O'Sullivan start on one of their projects; a drop-in center for LGBTQA+ youth, which even I have to admit is very progressive for a couple of Catholic priests.

Twice I've picked up my phone to call Dani and tell her

about it, before remembering that Dani hasn't returned any of my texts. The thought of my best friend being upset with me makes my stomach twist, and I have to rush back into the kitchen and pretend to be busy so Father Bryne doesn't notice my discomfort.

"What are you doing today?" Father Bryne sips his tea while I stack the guests' dishes into the dishwasher. "Another shift at the cemetery?"

"I have a day off from tours today, but I'm heading over to the cemetery to do some filming." I've told the priest all about my videos. He even helped by gifting me a book on Victorian funerary architecture.

"That's a great idea. The weather looks lovely for it." He pauses. "Bree, I've been praying for you lately."

"Oh?"

"You don't need to be frightened. I know you're not a believer – I'm not trying to force anything on you, but rather to give you an extra layer of spiritual protection."

"You think I need spiritual protection?"

"I worry for your immortal soul that you concern yourself so much with the dead. You think nothing of channeling ghosts through a spirit board, and I would hate for you to unwittingly call forth a malevolent spirit—"

CRASH.

I stare down at the broken pieces of crockery at my feet, my heart hammering.

What if he's right? What if when I brought Pax back, I also brought back the monster that killed Vera? What if I'm the cause *of that horror? After all, they both happened around the same time and—*

"Oh, no. Are you okay?" Father Bryne rushes to my side, snapping me out of my disturbing thoughts as he grabs a broom from the corner.

"Of course. I'm just clumsy." I kneel to pick up the larger broken pieces, grateful that Father Bryne can't see the horror playing over my face. "And don't worry about me, Father. My immortal soul is safe. The spirit board was a bit of harmless fun, and as for my project, I believe that the dead have their stories, and they should be shared with the world. I can't give them the kind of immortality that Lazarus enjoyed, but this is the next best thing."

We sweep up the mess in silence. I toss out the broken pieces and pick up my phone and ring light, and escape the house and the kindly priest. I am in no mood for discussions of my immortal soul, which I'm pretty sure at this stage is corrupted beyond repair.

"Bree, wait for me!"

I whirl around. Ambrose hovers over the steps, his frock coat flapping around his legs. Even in the strange mood I'm in, his beauty leaves me breathless. Those high, noble cheekbones, that strong jaw. The tailoring of his coat perfectly accentuates his lean figure, muscled shoulders, and trim waist. One curl of hair has come loose to flop over his forehead. His azure eyes sparkle with joy – as they do every time he's near me.

It's painful how attractive I find him. There is something addictive to his enthusiasm – the way his whole face lights up as if I'm the first ray of sunshine after a terrifying storm, or the extra-hot mustard on a hot dog, or a new country's visa stamp on a passport.

"May I assist you with your videos?" Ambrose asks in a breathless whisper.

I don't know if I'm up for company after my revelation from Father Bryne, but saying no to Ambrose is like kicking a puppy. "Sure."

My hands are full of equipment, so Ambrose walks behind me as we make our way down the secret path and through the

STEFFANIE HOLMES

broken fence. He chatters nonstop about the Van Wimples, who were his close friends and the first on my list of video subjects for today. The metal ball on the end of his stick raps on the concrete, and I'm glad no one else is around to hear the strange tapping sound as it follows me.

The cemetery is blessedly empty. We don't run tours on a Monday, so the only people I see are Mr. Pitts scrubbing down the ticket booth sign and an elderly couple laying flowers on a new grave. I hurry the long way around them to the Van Wimple mausoleum.

I set up the ring light on its tripod and make sure that the moldavite stone is in my pocket. I take Ambrose's hand and press the remote control into it, still marvelling that it doesn't fall through his fingers.

"Do you think you have the strength to push this button when I tell you to?" I ask.

He nods eagerly.

"Okay, then that's your job. And you can hold this in front of your chest with your other hand." I pass him the notebook where I've been scribbling notes for the video script. "I'll tell you when to turn the page."

"Of course," he beams. "I am happy to be of assistance."

I know that I'm taking a risk. If anyone walks around the corner, they'll see a remote and notebook floating in midair in front of me. But if Ambrose can't be alive like Pax, then the least I can do is give him a proper job to help. The Van Wimple mausoleum is around a bend in the path and slightly elevated, so I'm confident that I'll be able to see any approaching visitors before they see me. It makes Ambrose so happy to help, and it's so much easier with two of us...

This is just the kind of project Dani would love.

I squash that thought down, *hard.*

"Ready?" Ambrose waves the remote at me.

I smooth down my hair and tug on the bell-sleeved black dress and bat necklace I'd chosen for a suitable 'girl who works in an old cemetery' vibe. "Ready."

"And *action*." Ambrose clicks the button.

"Hi, I'm Bree, and I'm one of the tour guides here at the historic Grimdale Cemetery, in the beautiful village of Grimdale. Today we're going to visit one of the most elaborate monuments in the cemetery – the mausoleum of the Van Wimple family. The Van Wimples owned Grimwood Manor from the mid-eighteenth century until my great-grandmother won it from them in a game of cards, or so the story goes—"

I'm about to launch into the history of the Van Wimple shipping fortune when Ambrose clicks off the camera. "Technically, it was a game of backgammon," Ambrose says.

"Mum always told me it was cards."

"I was there, Bree, sitting in the corner. And it was *definitely* backgammon."

"It doesn't matter," I wave my hand.

"Backgammon is more accurate."

"Fine. Press record again."

Ambrose does, and I repeat my intro, this time using backgammon. Ambrose nods along happily, and I continue with my story. "The Van Wimples earned their fortune through shipping, starting with a trade route with the Americas and quickly rising to become one of the foremost British shipping companies. They owned several properties all over England, but Grimwood Manor was their favorite – the family would stay for the hunting season, opening up the house to all manner of guests and throwing some of the most impressive and elaborate parties of the age.

"The most famous member of the Van Wimple family was Cuthbert Van Wimple, the third son to inherit the company. From an early age, Cuthbert had an interest in the burgeoning area of Egyptian archaeology, and when he wasn't working in the London office, he would head across the seas to Egypt to take part in excavations in the Valley of the Kings. Cuthbert's interests are reflected in these obelisk-shaped columns and these winged goddesses above the door to the tomb. It was in Egypt where he met his future wife, Penelope—Ambrose, what?"

"I'm sorry." Ambrose makes a face as he clicks off the camera again. "It's just that you've skipped over Cuthbert's archaeological work. He was instrumental in the discovery of the tomb of Imhotep the royal scribe. Cuthbert tripped over his sandal and his foot went through the roof of the tomb!" His eyes sparkle as he recalls the story. "It was quite a tale – his foot was dangling through this hole in the desert, and the workers had to dig all around him, throwing sand in his face as they hunted for the tomb entrance—"

I sigh. "Ambrose, I know that you lived this, and you know these people, but if I make this video a two-hour lecture, no one is going to watch it."

"I would." Ambrose's lower lip wobbles. "I'd love to listen to you talk about history for two hours. I'd love to listen to you talk about dirt for two hours."

"Yes, well..." A blush creeps across my cheeks. "Not everyone feels the same. We have to make it short and snappy to keep people's interest on the internet. And that means glossing over some details. Okay?" I fluff my hair and step back a little. "From the top. Cuthbert was invited on a cruise along the Nile hosted by the prominent Wilmont family. He is showing off a lapis lazuli necklace he found in the tomb when in walks a beauty who —"

"I hate to interrupt again, but Penelope was actually on the upper deck when Cuthbert brought out the necklace—"

"Ambrose!"

"Sorry, sorry," he throws up his hands. "It's just that it wasn't exactly how it happened."

"If you interrupt me *one more time*, you don't get to help."

Ambrose makes a face, but he mimes zipping his lips shut.

I manage to film three videos about the Van Wimple mausoleum without Ambrose interrupting, although he keeps making pained faces and waving his finger around like he was dying to add more.

It makes me think how much better at this job he'd be than me. Ambrose is a born storyteller. He always enthralls me with tales of his adventures, and he used to love helping me with my homework. He could make subjects like history and biology come alive with his enthusiasm. I'd give anything to be able to read his manuscript...

His manuscript...

Yet another thing I haven't had a chance to think about yet – Ambrose's unfinished business. His enthusiasm for my cemetery history project makes me more certain than ever that his unfinished business is the book that would have immortalized him as one of the greatest adventurers and travel writers of his age. But I'm no closer to figuring out if my magic can even bring him back, or where I might be able to get a copy of his book.

I haven't even told him what I suspect. I can't do that to him – he's already excited enough about Pax coming back to life. I can't tell him that I think I know what his unfinished business is until I know I can help him. I won't build him up and then destroy his hope like that.

Kicking a puppy, remember?

My stomach rumbles. It's lunchtime, but I don't feel like walking back to the house and seeing what disaster Edward will create under the guise of helping me. A flock of sparrows descends from the ancient oak tree behind the ticket booth, murmuring over the war graves.

It's peaceful here.

I know Vera's killer is out there (that's why Pax has been attempting to hide in the bushes behind the fence all morning to guard us, as if no one can see his enormous shoulders sticking out. Romans weren't exactly known for their stealth). I know that I'm no closer to figuring out what the Lazarus card means for me and my power, but behind the high iron fence of Grimdale, surrounded by the sleeping dead and my own personal Victorian gentleman escort, I feel safe.

Mr. Pitts keeps a selection of snacks for staff and volunteers in the ticket office. I grab a packet of crisps and a Mars bar and sit on the steps leading to Edward's mausoleum with my food. Ambrose sits beside me, hovering slightly above the step, his carved stick leaning against his thigh.

His knee presses against mine, sending a surge of heat through my skin. My heart stutters, and I look down to see the silver cord stretching between us. Two other cords – one for Edward and one that pulses with blue light for Pax – twirl through the air before meandering off in the direction of the bushes outside the cemetery wall.

I turn my attention back to Ambrose, who has one hand behind his head and is leaning back, his face serene with joy as he breathes in the sweet fragrance of the hyacinth and lavender in the garden that borders the mausoleum.

Gods, he is beautiful.

Imagine if he were real, like Pax. Imagine if I could touch him, really *touch him. And hold him. And kiss him. Imagine if we could go on adventures together, or do all the things in bed that he's been learning from Pax and Edward—*

But then I imagine getting the resurrection magic wrong because I don't know what the fuck I'm doing. I imagine the horrible feeling of the cord snapping, and the light in Ambrose's azure eyes going out as he crosses over into the light.

I imagine never seeing him again.

My throat tightens.

I stuff a few chips into my mouth and hold out the bag for Ambrose to sniff. He leans over and breathes in. "Oh, but I have missed the taste of salt. One of my earliest memories is of my mother taking me to get fish and chips in Blackpool, and the smell of the hot, salty, vinegary food and the crisp ocean air was something truly magical." He turns to me, his mouth quirking up into a hopeful smile. "Maybe one day soon I will get to taste these salty treats for real."

Damn. I was hoping he'd give me more time before he asked about it. "I'm sorry, Ambrose. I know you're excited to find out if I can resurrect you the way I brought back Pax, but I've been so busy with everything going on that I haven't had a chance to figure out my magic."

He tilts his head to the side, and those blue pools of his seem to look right through me. "Have you been too busy, or are you putting off looking into it because you don't want to face the fact that you have this magic inside you?"

I look away. I can't bear to look into those beautiful blue eyes and lie.

"I know you're frightened." Ambrose places his hand on my knee. An electric pulse shoots along my leg. My breath catches. "I'd be frightened, too."

"No, you wouldn't." I laugh despite myself. "You'd love having magic. You'd spend all your time trying to bring back famous adventurers, and all your friends, so you could have a big party. And you'd probably solve world peace."

"Yes, perhaps that is true." Ambrose's fingers squeeze my thigh, and I find myself unable to get enough air into my lungs. "But I'm not the one with the magic – you are. There is a reason you possess this gift, Bree. You're special."

"That's just a nice way of saying that I'm a freak. An even bigger freak than previously thought."

"I've never thought you were a freak. Neither has Pax or Edward. To us, you're a wonder. I think that you are trying to ignore what happened with Pax and the silver cords you see because you are afraid. But isn't it better to face the truth, so you can understand your magic? So you can learn to wield it? Look at your friend Mina. She has magic in her veins and she is, to quote one of my favorite twenty-first-century sayings, 'living her best life.' That could be you."

"Yes, or I could be thrown in an asylum or taken to a secret government facility to be chopped up and studied—"

"Are you really afraid of that, or are you afraid that you'll find out you *are* special and different?"

Ooof.

Ambrose always had this uncanny ability to cut through to my deepest, most secret feelings.

You're right." I screw up the crisp packet in my fist. "I hate admitting it, but I *am* afraid. I left Grimdale because all I ever wanted was to have a normal life. And then Dad got sick and I wanted to be with him but he's in Europe and I...I feel as if I'm holding on to my life by a thread. At any moment it could all unravel completely. Everyone will find out what I can do, and they'll shun me, and it will be like school all over again. I'll have no one—"

"You have me," he says softly. "You'll always have me."

He's breaking me wide open. I have no defense against his words or the raw, haunting adoration in his eyes.

"Yes, but what good is it when the only people in your life are ghosts. I'm sorry, Ambrose, I don't know what I'm saying. I'm scared and I wish my dad was here and—"

My words are cut off by Ambrose's lips on mine.

His kiss is soft at first, and I can taste his sweet agony on his lips. He threads his fingers in my hair. Sometimes they fall through the strands but sometimes they catch, and he pulls me closer to him, tilting my head as he meets me stroke for stroke.

But before long, the kiss becomes something more. Something deep and profound. Whatever gentlemanly restraint Ambrose possesses crumbles, and his lips on mine are strong and sure and eager. A warm longing pools inside me. I want something that I can't articulate, and it makes my head spin. *He* makes my head spin.

This is...

A twig snaps.

My eyes fly open. Through the back of Ambrose's head, I see the couple who were visiting the grave earlier. They're on the other end of the path, near the Witches Monument, and they're staring at me like I'm some freak with her mouth hanging open and her face flushed as she kisses the air.

Because that's exactly what I'm doing.

I jerk back from Ambrose and snap my jaw shut.

"Sorry. I'm sorry." I mutter, my skin flaring with heat for a completely different reason. The couple slinks away, whispering to each other.

Ambrose reaches for me, but I shy away.

"What if you weren't sorry?" Ambrose says, his ocean eyes rippled with sunlight. "What if you decided not to care what others thought of you? What if you were Bree Mortimer, living your best life with a resurrected centurion and two ghosts who love you?"

Love. There's that word again.

My chest constricts. I can't breathe.

Ambrose takes a shaky step toward me, his ghostly arm outstretched. "I know you're not ready to say the word, and I'll not force it upon you." His full lips curl back into a sad smile. "But I need you to know that even if you can't bring me back to life, I am content to remain here with you. I am happier than you could ever imagine because you are back at Grimdale."

I glance over my shoulder. The couple has hurried away. There's no one else around. My fingers tremble as I grasp Ambrose's outstretched hand. He nestles his head on my shoulder.

We stay like that for a long time, in the company of the resting dead. I watch the sparrows in their murmurings. We listen to the wind whisper in the trees.

We stay long enough that I can almost believe this is what I want.

Damn him, Ambrose is right.

Maybe I am the cause of all of this. But if that's true, I need to take responsibility. I can't run away from the magic inside me.

If I want to keep everyone safe from whatever monster is out there, my magic might be our best shot.

Which means it's time for me to become a basic witch.

19

BREE

Mum: Bree, I just heard that the old woman at the witchy shop was murdered! Why would you not tell us a thing like that? There must be something in the air in Grimdale. We're off to Oslo, Norway today – your father is going to see some loud rock band you'd probably love. I'm spending the evening in the hotel bar, hoping for a burly Viking to whisk me away for a night of passion.

A couple of nights later, while I'm waiting for a stack of books on magic to arrive from Mina's store, Pax and Ambrose and I head out to the pub for another important lesson in 'how to behave like a normal, twenty-first-century guy and not a bloodthirsty Roman soldier.' Father Bryne left ahead of me on a night out with members of his youth delegation, and the other guest room is empty for a night before two New Zealand backpackers join us tomorrow.

It's quiz night, and I'd hoped to rope Dani into being on our team. She's always a font of strange and weird facts, and she's insanely competitive. No matter what's going on in her life, it's practically impossible for her to turn down a quiz night, especially if I've got Ambrose whispering answers to all the history questions in my ear.

But when I text her, all I get is a short reply:

I can't. I'm busy. Sorry. Another time.

What other time? I want to yell into the phone. I can't ignore the feeling that she's ghosting me.

Get it? Ghosting me. Urgh, I'm ridiculous.

Is Dani afraid of Pax? She was pretty freaked out when she found out he was real. Is this about Alice? She said she understood why I threw her in the pond, and she seemed okay when we left things, but maybe she told Dani a completely different story.

That has to be it. Because Dani was freaked out about Vera's murder. She wouldn't stay away unless she was really hurt.

Am I asking too much of her?

"Have I been a bad friend?"

I don't realize I said that aloud until Ambrose squeezes my hand. "You've always been the most wonderful friend to me."

Pax stiffens, reaching for the knife he keeps concealed in his trousers. "Did someone say you were a bad friend? I will slice off their fingers and serve them as spaghetti—"

"Here's your next lesson in being a normal dude – don't fly off into a rage every time you think I've been slighted. If you see me about to walk off a cliff, then run in and stop me. But you don't have to stab everyone who hurts me. When you're a ghost, it's kind of adorable in a possessive morally grey romance hero kind of way, but in real life, it will get you thrown in jail."

"But..." Pax's face falters. "It's my duty to protect you."

"You *are* protecting me. You're at my side twenty-four hours a day, so no monsters can get me." I rest my head on his shoulder. "And right now you can protect me from becoming dehydrated by getting me a drink."

Pax marches off to the bar, crunching the crisp pound notes I got for him from the ATM earlier. I'm not yet ready to teach a Roman about credit cards. He'd probably run up a massive bill shopping online for busts of Caligula and Druidic protection amulets.

While Pax gets our drinks, I scan around for a place to sit. Father Bryne is over at the bar with a bunch of guys who have the earnest arrogance and beige dress sense of fellow religious leaders. He beckons me over with his kind smile. I wave back politely but decide that with Pax's general belief that Christians are lion food, the good father's quiz team will be a last resort.

Maggie is at a booth in the corner with a bunch of her friends. That's a possibility, but they're pretty serious about quiz night, and their table is quite crowded, which could be awkward for Ambrose. I check the tables for anyone who might be closer to my age with space for another two players (and a ghost with decent general knowledge) when I spy someone sitting by themselves at my favorite booth.

I suck in a breath through my teeth and stride over.

"Dani! Hey!"

"Oh, Bree." Dani's smile wobbles as her head jerks up. "I didn't think you'd come tonight."

"I didn't think *you'd* come." *Since that's what you told me in your text.* "But I'm so happy you did. Pax and Ambrose and I are looking for a team and we don't want to cramp Maggie's style, so can we join you?"

"Oh, well, I—"

Before she can protest, I pull out my seat and sit across from her. *If we're going to have it out, we might as well get it over with.*

Ambrose hovers behind my seat, near the open window. I

can see the three witches crowding around outside. Walpurgis pads across the table to sniff Dani's pint of cider.

Dani won't meet my gaze. My stomach churns with distress. I don't want to be fighting with my best friend. I don't even know *if* we're fighting. Or why.

"Dani, are you okay?" I whisper. "I've sent you at least a dozen texts and you don't reply. I haven't seen or heard from you in ages."

"I know. I'm sorry." She doesn't sound sorry. "I keep meaning to call you back, but I've been so busy at work. There seems to be a run on death lately."

Dani says the word death sharply, and I get the feeling that she's referring to Vera.

"Don't I know it?" I lower my voice. "Is Vera one of your...er...?"

"One of my clients?" Dani says the word unironically. "Yes. The police took their time with the autopsy, so it's been slower than normal. Her funeral is Wednesday."

I can't help myself. I shouldn't press her, but Ambrose's words from the cemetery echo in my head. I need to protect everyone, including Dani. I need answers. "Did you notice anything unusual about her body? Anything that I might be able to use to find the killer?"

That darkness flashes in Dani's eyes again, and I lean back as if I've been slapped.

"I don't know..." Dani shrugs. "I can't put my finger on it, but something about her injuries is familiar to me, but I can't think why."

"That's what I said!" Ambrose bobs up and down with excitement.

"Ambrose says he thought the same thing, but it's not exactly helpful. Anything else?"

Darkness clouds Dani's eyes. "Nothing supernatural, but

the wounds were brutal. The person who killed her is a psychopath. No ordinary human would do such a thing. Bree, I really think you should leave this one up to the police."

"But you know they're not going to look in the right place." I dig the saint card out of my pocket and show it to her. "Vera had this in her hand when I found her. That's Saint Lazarus. Jesus brought him back from the dead, and according to this kooky priest who is staying at Grimwood, some people believe he still wanders the earth with the power to bring people back to life. That can't be a coincidence."

Dani's mouth falls open in horror. "You removed that from a crime scene? What's *wrong* with you? That could be a vital clue about the killer."

"That's just what I'm trying to tell you."

"Bree, you can't investigate this case."

"Why not?" I can't help the edge in my voice. "I could be the one who raised this monster. Vera was killed around the same time I raised Pax. What if—"

"Even more reason for you to stay away." Dani's lip trembles. "I don't want my best friend to end up on my embalming table, cut to ribbons with her intestines flung around her ears."

"That will never happen. You know that I don't want to be embalmed. I plan to have a Viking funeral. Burn me in a boat on the duck pond with all my possessions." That way I can never come back as a ghost.

"Bree, I'm serious. Whoever this killer is, he's dangerous. And unhinged. He killed Vera in broad daylight in front of everyone, and didn't seem to care if he got caught."

"I have Pax to protect me." I point over at the bar, where Pax has his head down, drawn into a deep conversation with Father Bryne and his friends. There is lots of gesticulating, but it seems friendly enough. No one's been stabbed or crucified. Yet.

"But who knows how long he'll be around?" Dani says.

"What do you mean by that?"

"We don't know what's going to happen to Pax." Dani pulls out her phone and clicks on an image. She slides the phone across the table to me.

I gasp as I look at the woodcut drawing of a demon. He has blazing, evil eyes, bulging muscles, and horrible curved horns. He's dancing atop a pyramid of skulls. It looks like the kind of image Dani and I used to doodle in our notebooks in high school.

"Ooh, hold that up, dearie," Mary leans through the window. "We want to see."

"What are we looking at?" Ambrose asks.

"A picture of a rather horny fellow," Lottie says, peering close.

"Oh, so a portrait of Edward," Ambrose says with a smile.

I glance at Dani with interest. "Why am I looking at a drawing of a demon?"

"That could be what Pax becomes, for all we know. Or he could become this," Dani scrolls through her phone, showing me a horrific jackal-like creature with rows of serrated teeth. "Or this." She flips to an image of a zombie-like being, its body laid waste with rot. "The only way to kill one of these is to cut out its heart."

"But you've seen Pax." I gesture to the bar, where Pax is buying a round for Father Bryne and his friends. "He may be able to spend all my money, but he's no monster. He's just...Pax."

"For now. I've been doing some research on revenants – the dead brought back to life. In every case in folklore, raising a revenant always ends badly. Pax may seem ordinary now, but he's not, is he? He isn't supposed to be here, and at some point, that's going to catch up to him." Dani taps the image of the jackal creature with her finger. "Maybe that's what this other monster is – a revenant Vera brought back who turned on her."

"Look at those claws," Lottie clucks, crowding in beside Mary. "I bet he doesn't have any problem scratching his back. Do you have any idea how annoying it is to die with an itch? I have a spot between my shoulder blades that's been bothering me since 1701."

Dani flicks her finger across the screen, showing me another terrifying image – a vampire biting the neck of a white-shrouded woman, his fangs sinking deep into her virgin flesh.

"These creatures show up in different forms across all mythologies. Revenants. Edimmu. Upyr. Dybbuk. Gjenganger. Nachzehrer. Sometimes they are part of vampiric myths. They're almost always malevolent and murderous. The dead don't just come back unchanged, Bree. That kind of trauma destroys their soul."

I shake my head violently. "That's not Pax."

"Are you certain? I heard from Jo that Sergeant Wilson is convinced that Pax is Vera's killer, and you're covering for him. They're rushing the blood analysis of his sword through, hoping that will seal his fate."

"Pax would never do anything like this. You won't find Vera's blood on his sword."

I don't know whose blood you will find, though.

"You can't know anything about Pax, because bringing the dead back to life is not exactly an area of scholarly research. So I'd defer to the demonology experts on this." Dani raps her phone with her nails. "I don't know *what* Pax is or what he'll do, so I don't want—"

"Bree, be careful!" Mary cries. "That girl you threw in the duck pond approaches."

"Perhaps she means to finish you off," Lottie covers her eyes with her hands, peeking through her fingers. "I can't watch."

"You should have held her head under while you had the chance," Agnes grumbles. "The youth of today lack all sense of *commitment*."

"There you are." Alice sinks down into the seat next to Dani, planting a kiss on her cheek. Dani's cheeks darken with joy. Alice steals Dani's cider and takes a sip. "Hey, Bree."

"Alice." I nod, instantly feeling uncomfortable.

"I didn't know you'd be joining us." Alice shoots a glance at Dani. "Do I need to run home and put on my swimmers? Or are you packing a cream pie in that cool purse of yours?"

"You're safe." I clutch the bat-shaped purse I got after seeing the one Mina had. A blush creeps across my cheeks. Dani looks positively *murderous. So she is mad at me for the duck pond.* "I'm so sorry about—"

"I told you, it's totally fine." Alice laughs, and I might be wistful thinking, but it actually sounds genuine. "I told Dani about our little misunderstanding the other day. She thinks it's hilarious, too. Perfect revenge for that time I stole your clothes in year 11, right?"

"Sure," Dani mutters. She does not look like she thinks it's hilarious. At all.

"I remember that day," Ambrose frowns. "You got out of the shower to discover your things gone. You made yourself a bikini out of toilet paper and ran outside to find a teacher. All the kids called you The Mummy for a month. You cried on my shoulder every night."

The memory slams into me – the way my skin burned in humiliation as I ran into the gym with bits of toilet paper trailing behind me. I glance over at the bar, where Pax is collecting our drinks. I'm glad he isn't here to hear that, or Alice would find herself pinned to the dart board...

Before I can stop him, Ambrose reaches forward and slaps

the drink in Alice's hand. She cries out as cider splashes all down the front of her dress.

Dani frowns at me as she grabs napkins from the dispenser to soak up the mess. I glare at Ambrose, but he settles back into the shadows, completely oblivious. The witches hoot with delight.

"Serves her right!" Agnes cries.

"Meeeeorw!" Walpurgis agrees as he bats a chip with his paw.

"I don't know how I did that." Alice dabs at her collar. "I'm such a butterfingers."

"It could have been the pub ghost," Dani says with a meaningful look in my direction.

"I really didn't mean to push you in the pond," I say, desperate to save this situation. "I just—"

"It's cool. I get it. Self-preservation. I would have done the same thing in your shoes." Alice shoves the basket of chips toward me. "You sure you and that hot guy of yours want to hang out with us? You're in for a pretty boring night. Dani and I weren't going to sign up for the quiz. We're busy planning my birthday party."

"Bree can't join us. She was just going to join Maggie's team," Dani says.

"Your birthday's coming up?" I keep my tone casual.

Inside, I'm crushed.

One of the reasons Alice was so popular at school was that she threw the most epic parties. In intermediate, every kid used to wish that they'd get invited to her sleepovers. Alice and her parents would deck out their enormous rec room in various themes. Once, they built an entire fairy grotto inside her house – with giant light-up toadstools and smoking fairy drinks for everyone. Another year, her father dressed up as a dragon and led the party guests in a dragon egg hunt around the whole village. Another year, they hired a famous children's performer from the telly and had a candy buffet.

And when we got to high school, her parties got even crazier. Her mother hired London clubs out for the night and bussed teens down for an insane, hedonistic adventure. Then there was the year that they hired Lachlan Hall in Argleton for a Middle Ages banquet, with everyone decked out in full medieval garb. There was a jousting tournament and a bard who serenaded Alice all night.

Alice's parties were epic.

Not that I know firsthand. Dani and I never got to go to one of Alice's parties.

We were never invited.

And now she and Dani are planning one *together*.

"Yeah, it's in a few weeks," Alice smiles. "I'm going to have a toga party. My boss has let me rent out the Roman Museum for the evening, on the promise that we don't wreck anything. I've got this crazy band coming up from London – they're called Caligula's Cads and they dress up as Roman soldiers and do punk songs about building an empire and slaying Gauls. We're serving ancient food and my own signature cocktail. What's it called again, Dani?"

"The Mint Julius Caesar." Dani won't look at me.

"That's the one."

"It sounds fun," I manage to choke out.

"It's gonna be epic. You *must* come," Alice says.

"I think Bree has something else on that night," Dani says quickly.

"Oh, well, that's a shame." Alice dabs the last of the cider from the table. "Hey, I see your friend has been roped into an arm wrestling match with Pastor Tim. Do you want me to extract him? The pastor is a notorious cheat."

"If you don't mind." I'm more concerned about Pastor Tim

being thrown through the window by the force of Pax's substantial forearms.

"I'm on the case. I'll bring back your drinks while I'm at it."

Alice weaves off in the direction of the bar, and I lean across the table and tap my finger against Dani's pinkie.

"What's going on?" I ask. "Why don't you want me to go to Alice's party?"

"Why? Because of exactly this." Dani waves her hand in the vague direction of Pax. "I know you're so happy he's here, Bree. But Pax doesn't belong here. And as much as he doesn't mean to, he's pulling you into his world."

"That's not true—"

"You threw my girlfriend into the duck pond!"

"And I apologised!"

Dani covers her face. "I knew you wouldn't get it. Pax is going to mess up this party for Alice. You're not the only one who's trying to find a place for herself in this village. I have a job I love and the girl of my dreams and I finally feel like I belong. If a Roman centurion starts stabbing people at my girlfriend's party, that all goes out the window."

Hurt stutters in my chest. "You're saying that you wish I never came back? That your old friend Bree always ruins everything for you?"

"That's not what I'm saying at all. I just—"

Dani reaches for me, but I grab my purse and Ambrose's arm.

"Ow, Bree?" Ambrose cries. "Why are you dragging me away? You and Dani were finally talking—"

"Pax?" I call out. "Put down that rabbi. We're leaving."

20

BREE

"**N**ow, Pax, you oversized sack of potatoes, what is this?" Edward gestures to the crystal water glass set up on the table beside a dazzling array of different-sized knives and forks.

Pax's face brightens. "It is a secret weapon. You smash delicate glass, then use shards to stab your enemy—"

"Wrong!" Edward boxes Pax around the ears. "Try again, and this time, try not to be so bloody *Roman*."

It's a couple of days after my fight with Dani, and I'm watching Edward school Pax on table manners. Edward has spent most of the morning painstakingly arranging the dining room into a table fit for a prince, and he's now making Pax remember what every single tiny fork is used for.

"It is not polite to scratch one's scrotum at the dinner table," Edward whacks Pax around the ears again. Truthfully, I'm sure he only agreed to teach Pax because it would allow him the opportunity to get away with slapping the Roman around. "Nor is it appropriate to dip one's giant Roman schnoz into the gravy—"

"But we do that all the time!" Pax complains. "Ambrose is doing it right now."

"Ahem..." Ambrose straightens up from where he has had his head stuck in the gravy float. He looks sheepish. "We ghosts must take our simple pleasures where we may—"

"Shhhhh," I whisper as I hear Father Bryne's door creak open. "He's coming downstairs."

I leap out of the dining room, pulling the door shut behind me so Father Bryne doesn't notice the table setting or the forks moving through the air of their own accord. I dart into the kitchen and pull the French toast I made earlier from the warming drawer.

"Good morning Father. Did you sleep well?" I set down his breakfast and hand him a bowl of blueberries, which he distributes liberally on top of his French toast.

"Yes, thank you. The beds here are so comfortable. This house has such a lovely feeling about it – a real weight of history." He peers around the kitchen with a smile as the ghosts leap through the wall behind him. *If only he could see the royal rake with ridiculous codpiece and the glass shard in his backside, or the Victorian gentleman with his head stuck in the cream bowl.* Father Bryne takes a bite of his breakfast. "Delicious, as always. You're up early this morning, Bree. Do you have something interesting to do today? More filming for the cemetery social media?"

"I'm going to a funeral." I indicate my black dress and my good pair of New Rock boots. "This old woman, Vera, was murdered in the village a couple of days before you arrived. I found her body."

"Oh, that's horrible. I shall accompany you. A lovely woman such as yourself shouldn't have to attend a funeral alone."

"I won't be alone," I say quickly. "Pax is going with me."

For my sins.

"Even more reason for me to join you." Father Bryne wipes

his mouth on the napkin. "Your friend possesses many great qualities, but gravitas is not one of them. Besides, it is a priest's sacred duty to bear witness to a spirit's journey to return to the Lord. This Vera may not be one of my parishioners, but I'm sure she'll appreciate my—"

"Vera owned the village witchcraft shop, so it's not going to be your crowd—"

"Nonsense. The church has amended our views on witchcraft." Father Bryne chuckles. "I certainly won't be burning anyone because they enjoy dancing around in the woods in their underwear."

"Don't believe him," Agnes growls from the window. "He's got the look of a witchfinder about him."

"Well, okay, if you wish." I glance at my phone. "I'm leaving in fifteen minutes. Is that enough time for you to have breakfast and change?"

Father Bryne scoffs down his toast and retires to his room. I check in on Pax's table manners lesson and inform him that if he wants to attend the funeral with me, he needs to put his trousers on. I find him throwing forks at Edward's portrait. One is sticking out of the center of Edward's forehead. Edward sees this and grows even paler.

"I can see that you have your work cut out for you," I smile at Edward.

"You don't cut things with forks," Pax says with a grin as he tosses another utensil. "Forks are for *stabbing*. I'm doing great, aren't I, Edward?"

"Oh yes," Edward says miserably. "We'll have you curtseying for the King in no time."

I leave them to it. Ambrose, of course, offers to escort me to the funeral. Father Bryne emerges from his room and meets me (us) in the hall. He wears a black shirt and slacks, his collar visible at his neck. "Lead the way," he says.

205

We step outside. Father Bryne puts his arm through Ambrose as he offers to escort me. "Why don't you show me the secret way into the cemetery? I haven't had the chance to go on one of your tours, so I'd love a little behind-the-scenes tour before the funeral begins."

I lead Father Bryne down the secret path, wincing as I notice his slacks catching on the brambles. If he notices, he doesn't care. Ambrose tap-tap-taps behind me.

"What's that noise?" Father Bryne asks.

"Oh, it's a grim-bird," I say, thinking quickly. "It's a type of bird unique to this area. It sounds strange, doesn't it?"

I help the priest stoop to get through the hole in the fence. Ambrose gives a little shudder as he passes after us. He's the only one of the ghosts who will step foot inside Grimdale Cemetery, but even so, being close to so much death doesn't feel nice to him.

We're a little early, but I can see a few cars already parked in the street. People in black mill around the gravesite. We wander down Avenue of Artists toward Edward's mausoleum. I tell Father Brynne a few stories about some of the most fascinating graves, and he nods along with interest.

Vera's plot is in a quiet corner of the cemetery, on the very edge that abuts the Witch's Monument. Very appropriate. A small crowd has already gathered there. I spy Dani – who is acting as the celebrant – in a dark gray, immaculately tailored suit, her head inclined toward one of the mourners. When she looks up, I give her a tentative wave, but she looks away.

An ugly lump forms in my throat.

Maggie sees me and runs over to embrace me. "Vera would be so happy you came, dear."

"Oh Maggie, dear! You shouldn't lie in a cemetery. The ghosts will hear you. Of course Vera wouldn't want this young lady here," an elderly woman admonishes her. She waves a carpet bag that could be classed as a deadly weapon. "Vera hated the youth of today, always coming into her shop and touching things and asking questions—"

"One did wonder why Vera chose to continue in the retail business," another old woman remarks. "She hated it so much."

"But our dear Vera hated everything," the carpet bag lady coos. "Why, you should have heard her rants about doddery old men blocking the checkout line at the supermarket, and chalky-tasting apples, and not being able to get the last bit of HP sauce from the bottle—"

"Bree!" a familiar voice calls out. "Is that you?"

"Mina?" I turn around to see my new friend, wearing a black maxi dress with fashionable drapey details. Oscar wears a matching black bandana. In the tree behind her head, I could see Quoth nestled in one of the branches.

"Croak," he nods at me.

Hello, Bree.

"Did you get those magic books I sent you?"

"Yes, thank you. I've started reading the one on practical magic for the modern witch. So far, I haven't turned myself into a toad, so that's a promising start." I give her a quick hug. "You never said that you knew Vera."

"Oh no." Mina smiles uncomfortably. She gestures to the woman with the carpet bag. "I'm here with Mrs. Ellis. This Vera seemed like a woman after my Heathcliff's heart."

"Your friend seems popular." I watch as Ms. Ellis makes a beeline for Father Bryne. She grabs his arm and begins talking a mile a minute, batting her eyelashes aggressively. He shoots me a pained expression, but I shrug. *You wanted to come to the funeral, Father.*

"Ms. Ellis was my high school English teacher," Mina says. "She's trouble. You stay away from her unless you want to hear about the particularly ambitious sex positions she and her husband were attempting when he had his heart attack."

I make a face. "Noted."

Mina and I stand toward the back while Dani officiates the short ceremony. Vera's casket is closed, which seems sensible. Mina's friend Mrs. Ellis gives a short eulogy about Vera and her life. I can't look at Dani without tearing up but at least there are lots of handy tissue boxes around.

After the service, I shift from foot to foot, trying to build up the courage to go and talk to Dani, when a woman in a sharp black suit appears in front of me.

"Bree Mortimer?"

"That's what it will say on my gravestone," I say, then cover my mouth. "I'm sorry, I didn't mean—"

"My name is Caitlin." She hands me a card. *Okay, I guess Caitlin has no time for my terrible cemetery humor.* "I'm Vera's solicitor. I've been trying to track you down for a couple of days. I gave a card to your boyfriend, but he ate it."

"He *ate* it?"

"He had his pinkie out like this." Caitlin demonstrates. "He pronounced it delicious."

Oh, Pax.

At least Edward will be proud that his etiquette lessons are sinking in.

"Why did you want to talk to me?" My stomach churns with nerves. I think about what Dani said, that Sergeant Wilson believes Pax is the murderer and I'm covering it up. Did the police say something to Caitlin? Is she offering her services because they're going to arrest me and Pax?

But what Caitlin says next is even more of a shock. "Could you come by my office tomorrow at 10 AM? Vera has left you something in her will."

21

BREE

At 10:03AM the following day, with Pax, Edward, and Ambrose in tow, I knock on the door of Caitlin's law office, which is an adorable lime-wash cottage just off High Street. A harried-looking man answers the door. "You're late," he barks as he whirls around and stomps inside.

"How am I late…" I trail off as I become aware that he's no longer listening and has, in fact, disappeared.

I duck through the narrow front door. Pax has to back up and re-enter three times to fit his shoulders through the tiny doorway.

"At least he has shoulders," Edward mutters as he floats inside. Ambrose taps his way in after him.

We make our way through to a small office at the rear of the cottage. Caitlin sits behind her desk, and an assortment of people are gathered around her. They all glare at us as we enter.

"Hi," I wave. "I'm Bree, and this is my friend Pax. I'm sorry, I thought I was supposed to get here at ten—"

"Have a seat, Bree. Dominic, could you fetch Bree some tea?" Caitlin is all business. She shuffles papers across her desk. She introduces the other beneficiaries in the room – Vera's daughter, who looks to be about thirty and like she's ready to unsheath her claws. I see that Vera passed on her cordial good nature to her offspring. There's a brother named Paul, a niece around my age, an uncle named Rupert, and a couple of others, all staring daggers at me and Pax. I am the only non-family member who will receive something from Vera.

"There is a lot of tension in this room," Pax whispers to me as I take a seat. "I could cut it with my sword if only you'd allow me to carry it."

"Shhh," I hiss back. "No swords for you. Now be a good centurion and loom menacingly over me so Vera's relatives don't get any bright ideas. And stop pulling at your trousers. You look hot AF."

"What does hot AF mean? Does it mean Hot As Flavius? Because I assure you that randy old goat could not—ow!" He whirls around and glares at Edward, clutching the back of his head. "That hurt."

"What?" Edward's lips curl back into his signature sneer. "I'm just over here as a non-corporeal being, minding my own business. You must've got smacked in the head by your own ego."

"Now that we're all here," Caitlin says sharply, pointedly glaring in my direction. I sit up straight and fold my hands on my lap. *That lady is scary.* "We can finally begin."

Vera's daughter sniggers. Pax grips the back of my chair and glares at her until she looks away.

Relax, they're probably afraid the old lady cut them out of the will and left the entire estate to me in a twist worthy of an Agatha Christie novel.

Truthfully, I *am* a little worried about that myself. I have enough on my plate without suddenly becoming the owner of a cat-infested cottage on the edge of the village and a shop filled with possibly dangerous magical items.

Caitlin explains the legal process around the will and the items in Vera's estate. She begins to read the will aloud. The whole scene plays out exactly as it would in an Agatha Christie mystery, with each member of the family being bequeathed items from the estate.

I breathe a sigh of relief when the house and shop go to the daughter, with a small sum of money in a retirement account going to Vera's brother. A selection of antique sewing machines passes on to her niece, who beams with happiness. It looks as if Vera made someone happy, at least.

"Last of all, for Bree Mortimer, Vera leaves this." Caitlin picks up a box from beside the desk and shoves it across to me.

"What is it? Please don't tell me it's the skull of her first husband."

No one laughs. I take the box uneasily. All eyes are on me. Something prickles on the back of my neck, warning me not to open the box in this company.

"Why did she want me to have this?" I ask.

Caitlin shrugs. "Don't ask me. If it's in the will and it's not illegal, I see it done."

Ooookay then. I scuttle back to my seat, the box burning a hole in my hands, as I wait for the legal proceedings to finish. *What on earth or the celestial heavens could be inside?*

AT HOME, I check that Father Bryne has left for the day. The ghosts crowd around as I dump the box's contents out on the dining room table.

"Huh."

"What?" Ambrose leans forward, trembling with excitement. "What is it?"

"It's a load of nonsense," Edward says with a sneer.

He's not wrong. Inside the box is a strange assortment of, well, *junk*.

There are a bunch of pages that look to be torn from a ledger of some kind. Judging by the scrawled handwriting in the 'item column' listing cauldrons and ritual knives and votive candles, I suspect it's some sort of inventory from the stop. There are a bunch of drawings of what look like magical symbols and creepy demons sitting on people's chests, similar to the websites that Dani showed me at the pub, a velvet bag with some dried herbs inside, one of Maggie's candles – cardamom, 'for relaxation' – and a small, lurid booklet titled *History's Deadliest Killers – 20 of the worst serial killers and bloody monarchs in history*.

"Why did she want me to have this?" I ask.

"Perhaps she didn't like you very much," Edward says.

"Ha, ha, very funny." I roll my eyes.

Vera gave me these things for a reason, the same as she gave me the moldavite stone. And the saint card.

I can't explain why I know this, but I feel it in my bones. There's a message here for me, but I don't understand it.

I pick up one of the images of the demons. What did Dani call them? Revenants and vampires and something that sounded like cheese. My hand reaches for my phone and I'm scrolling for Dani's name before I remember.

I can't call Dani.

She's mad at me.

She doesn't want me at Alice's party.

I slump in my chair.

"Bree, it's going to be okay," Ambrose drops beside me, his hand rubbing warm, tingly circles on my back.

IF YOU'VE GOT IT, HAUNT IT

"We don't know that." I lay my head in my hands. "That... beast or monster or whatever is out there, and we know nothing about it. And our only clues are my strange magic and this box of junk, and my best friend hates me and I don't know what to doooooo..."

"You could try sticking your head in the liquor cabinet," Edward suggests. "That always works for me."

"Remember when Dani had us experiment with the moldavite stone?" Ambrose asks. "Because of those experiments, we learned that the stone enhances a power you already possess. I think we need another experiment. We need to learn more about your power. And I offer myself up at your lab rat."

Panic claws at my chest. Ambrose squeezes my thigh. I look up at him and see the steadiness in his eyes, the complete and utter faith that I won't hurt him. I wish I had such faith in myself, but I keep remembering the horrible feeling when the woman's cord snapped in Mina's shop.

"I don't know how to use my powers. What if I hurt you or make you cross over—"

"I think you do know," Ambrose murmurs. "You've been reading those books about witchcraft. I think you have some idea, but you're just afraid to try."

Damn you, Ambrose.

"I won't allow anything bad to happen," Pax growls. "If you'd allow me my sword—"

"No," Edward and I say at the same time.

"I really think you should give this a go," Ambrose prods me. "Perhaps the more you practice, the less scary it will become. You should assume the best."

"Okay." I get shakily to my feet. "I'll do it."

"You will," Edward shoves himself in front of Ambrose. "But you will do it on me."

"Edward, no," Ambrose says. "I'm the one who—"

"*I* am the royal prince, and this home is rightfully mine." Edward thrusts his noble nose into the air. "If Brianna is bringing anyone back, it's me."

I study Edward's haughty expression. He looks the same as ever, utterly convinced of his own superiority. And yet...there's something else in his eyes, something I've rarely seen before as his gaze darts from Ambrose to me – a grim determination masking the faintest hint of fear.

Is Edward actually offering himself...as a sacrifice?

Is he trying to protect Ambrose?

No. That can't be true.

Can it?

Ambrose's shoulders sag briefly, but then he brightens. Ambrose's good humour can never be defeated for long. "Yes, of course. Edward is the next oldest after Pax. It makes sense that he should go next."

"Exactly. First, I shall present my last will and testament, in the unfortunate event that this doesn't work."

"Now, wait just a second—" I protest, but Edward grabs a piece of paper and a pen. It takes him a few tries to pick up the pen, and I can see that his writing is shaky. His dark hair flops over his eyes as he writes, and he keeps his hand cupped around the paper, so we cannot see what he's written. When he's finished, he folds the paper and places it facedown on the table.

Edward flops down on the sofa opposite, spreading his legs and draping his arms over the back of the sofa and flashing me the smirk of a lazy, unaffected prince. All traces of that fear have disappeared from his anthracite eyes. "You may do your worst, Brianna."

What's in that note?

The edges of Edward's silk shirt flap against his chest. I forget about the note as my eyes are drawn to that triangle of flesh cutting down from his regal neck, leading the eye down to his codpiece and...

I swallow and jerk my eyes up. Big mistake. Edward catches me looking. Those devastating dark eyes of his drink me in with a hunger that is positively sinful. His wicked, pouty lips curl into a smirk that makes me press my knees together.

How can he do this to me with a simple look?

What would it be like if Edward were a Living? What dark and depraved things would he do to my body?

Perhaps the more important question is, what would I *let* him do?

I suck in a deep breath, willing my traitorous body to behave. I need to focus on this. My hands tremble in my lap. "Okay, I'm ready if you are."

"I have been ready for this since the night I got a glass shard poked through my posterior." Edward grins, spreading his arms wide. "You may begin."

"I don't know how."

"Do you see the silver cords?" Ambrose asks. "I think you should try touching them. Can you manipulate them?"

I stare down at the three cords extending from my chest, each one weaving in meandering coils throughout the room before sinking into the chests of my three men. Pax's is tinged with a cool blue light. I assume that has something to do with him being resurrected, and that's why I see his cord when I don't see the cords of other Living people.

Ambrose's cord pierces his elegant frock coat. Edward's cord stretches across the coffee table between us before diving inside his open silk shirt. His eyes follow my gaze, drawing me in, daring me to make a move.

My skin buzzes from the heat of his gaze. Are we working magic, or fucking each other with our eyes? I guess I'm about to find out.

"Here goes nothing."

My hands tremble as I reach down. I touch my finger to Edward's cord. At first, I feel nothing, but as I run my finger along its length, I get the faintest sense of tugging in my chest. I glance up at Edward. His eyes bore into me as the corner of his mouth quirks.

"Do you feel something?" I ask.

"A slight burning in my chest. But I don't know if it's from the cord or from my mounting desire to drape you over the piano bench, push those pretty legs of yours apart, and lick you until you come undone on my face," he says in that insouciant tone of his.

I squeeze my legs together, but there's nothing I can do to tame the aching need for him.

"That sounds fun," Pax pipes up. "Let's do that instead."

"Stay out of this, Roman," Edward snaps. "Try again, Brianna. You must give me more."

"Okay. I'll try." I can't stop my hands shaking as I wrap them around the cord. The light falls through my fingers but *somehow* I grip it. The cord is real. It has substance, even though it is also not there at all.

I remember something from one of Mina's witchcraft books. It had a whole section on how a witch can tap into her powers. The spell told you to imagine yourself in a place where you feel comfortable and happy. It told you to visualize yourself with your feet on the ground, your bare toes digging into this happy place, and to picture a white light rising from the earth around you to encircle your body. The book said that the power will flow into your womb.

I close my eyes. I imagine myself standing in Grimdale Cemetery, at the head of Poet's Way, facing Edward's tomb. I wiggle my toes in my boots, imagining digging them into the soft earth and fallen leaves.

I suck in a breath.

I *feel* myself pulling magic from the earth, feel it wrapping around my body, skipping around my womb to climb toward my chest. As it climbs, the magic tries to lift me off the ground, so I dig my toes in deeper.

I open my eyes and glance down at the cord, which seems to hum as the silver light shimmers around it. I give the cord a small tug.

Edward's face contorts.

"More," he rasps.

Something in his tone makes some dark and devious part of me yearn to obey.

I look at my hands again, wiggling my toes and imagining myself grounded in the cemetery dirt. For the first time, I feel something *beneath* my skin. Energy crawls in my veins – and it isn't the humming bees that Edward and Ambrose and Pax stir inside me. This energy is more of a whirring, a winding, of something being coiled up tight. And it's all *mine*.

I yank the cord.

Edward flies off the sofa, his body crumpling as he lands half on top of, half *inside* the coffee table. The contents of Vera's box topple onto the rug. He lets out a horrifying sound I've never heard from man or ghost before.

"Do you feel something?" Ambrose asks.

"Yes," Edward wheezes, clutching his chest as he rolls on the floor. "I feel agony."

Ambrose leans forward eagerly. "Is it the exquisite agony of unrequited love that you describe in your poems?"

"Alas, no," Edward grits out. "It is a dull, ordinary agony."

I drop the cord.

"It's okay," Edward sits up. He clutches his chest, his hard curls flopping over his eyes, which in this light are flecked with gold and swimming in pain. "Try again."

"No." I sink back into the sofa. I cover my eyes with my hands. I can't bear to look at the pain on Edward's face, knowing I caused it.

"Bree, please—" Ambrose pleads.

"Yes, Brianna." Edward's tone is determined. "I was once thrown from my father's house into a pile of brambles, and my manservant spent the next week pulling thorns from my buttocks and massaging my skin with essential oils. That hurt more than this. You must try again."

Ugly, desperate tears spill down my cheeks. "I *hurt* you. When Pax came back, it didn't hurt, did it?" I glance over at the Roman, who shakes his head. He watches me with concern. "I think that without your unfinished business, I'm not supposed to touch the cords. It feels wrong."

Ambrose's lip wobbles. "But I don't know what my unfinished business is."

"We'll figure it out," Edward says with surprising tenderness. "We will make you live again, but Brianna must master her power—"

"Hello, Bree? Are you home?"

Heart pounding, I shove everything back into the box. I reach for Edward's 'last will and testament', but he swipes it off the table and tosses it into the fire.

At least with Father Bryne home, the ghosts can't ask me to try any more of these experiments. "Yes. I'm in here, Father. Please, come and tell us about your day..."

He enters the room just as I kick the box under the table, and sets a white box on the table in front of me. "Father O'Sullivan and I had a productive meeting with the local Hindu community leaders about a joint event, and I brought you doughnuts from the bakery in Grimdale. It was my way of saying thank you for putting up with a priest...Bree, are you all right?" He peers at me in concern. "You look a little flushed."

"I'm..." I watch as Edward leaps from the sofa just in time to avoid being sat on by Father Bryne. Something about the priest's kind voice makes me long to open up to him. I can't tell him about the monster or my powers, but... "I'm having a fight with a friend."

Pax peers at me in surprise as he selects a doughnut from the box. Father Bryne clasps his hands on his lap, the large cross at his neck hanging above them. He studies me with a rich intensity, as if he truly cares about what I'm going to say. "You can talk to me. It might do you good to get it off your chest."

"This friend and I...we were inseparable as kids," I say. "We went to high school together, and it will come as no shock to you that we weren't exactly popular."

"I am shocked," he says, his eyes sparkling. "A kind, funny girl like you with excellent taste in gin should have been the most popular girl in school. But I am to understand from all the teenagers I've talked to over the years that a most particular kind of cruelty is reserved for teenage girls."

Tears spark in my eyes, but I blink them back. "You got that right. We were the outcasts, the freaks, but as long as we had each other, it didn't bother us that no one else at our school liked us. We were always there for each other, no matter what the other was going through. When high school finished, I went travelling and she went to uni. We haven't seen much of each other, but we've still kept in touch. And now we're both back in Grimdale and I was so happy to see her that I guess...I expected everything to be the same. Only now she's got this new girl-friend, and I guess she wants to impress her. But she seems to think I'm going to ruin her life and her relationship with my weirdness."

"And is the anger toward her really about her rejection of you?"

"No, I..." I stop. "Yes. I feel angry because this girlfriend is one of the people who used to be horrible to us, and I think that for all we said we didn't care what people thought of us, we both dreamed of fitting in and feeling like we belong. And now Dani does fit, but that has to mean I don't belong. I'm not angry, not really. I'm afraid that I'm losing my friend, but I don't know what to do about it. I can't stop being who I am, or who I love."

"No, we certainly can't." Father Bryne glances over at Pax, who is shovelling a second doughnut into his mouth his with pinkie finger quirked out to the side. Behind his head, Edward nods his approval at Pax's improved table manners. "You know what I'm going to say, don't you?"

"That I should forgive her," I scoff. "I don't think it'll work, considering she's the one who rejected me."

"Forgiveness can be confusing," Father Bryne says, touching his finger to his cross. "It's hard to make our feelings reflect the choice we make to forgive. We may want to forgive our friend, but we still feel angry, or hurt, or forgotten. It is a powerful choice to decide not to hold another's sins against them, for we are all sinners in our hearts."

I trace my finger along the edge of the table. "I don't know where to even start."

"Instead of dwelling on the hurt that this friend caused you, think about what makes her such a valuable friend in the first place. Those we love have the power to hurt us the most, but short of shoving everyone away and being alone all our lives, we have to open ourselves up to the possibility of hurt, so we can enjoy the gifts of their love."

I glance over at the three ghosts – Edward with his proud nose thrust in the air, Pax with cream filling stuck to his chin, and Ambrose with his beautiful, eager smile as he leans in for a sniff. Their silver cords wind around them, tangling us together in this mess.

I place my hand over my heart, feeling the cords pulsing through my fingers, thinking about the horrible agony on Edward's face, and about the sickening *snap* of the theatre ghost's cord breaking as the light took her away. And about the hurt in Pax's voice when I could not return his love, or the certainty in Ambrose's voice that everything would be okay.

Father Bryne's words echo in my head.

Those we love have the power to hurt us the most.

The only way to be safe is to never, ever fall in love.

22

BREE

Days go by. I don't call Dani. I stare at the images in Vera's box a little longer. Twice more, on my own, I practice the grounding spell, imagining my toes digging into the graveyard dirt as I call up the power. Each time, the magic flows more easily in my body, brimming with nervous energy. It has nowhere to go. I don't know what to do with it.

I'm annoyed and anxious at being no closer to solving Vera's murder. Dani doesn't want me to investigate it. But Dani and I aren't talking, and I know exactly who can help me figure this out.

"Welcome to Nevermore Bookshop," Mina answers the phone on the second ring. "Where all your book boyfriends come to life."

"It's me," I say. "I've had some developments in the whole Vera murder thing. I wondered if you might be able to meet for dinner tonight?"

"Sure. The Cackling Goat at seven?"

"Actually..." I think of Dani wandering in as Mina and I

discuss the case. "How about I come to you? The Rose and Wimple have a half-price roast on Wednesdays."

"True that. And Robert always gives me extra roast potatoes. I'll see you and Pax there. And the ghosts, too, although I won't see them." She laughs.

Blind people make the best blind jokes.

"Brilliant. Oh, and maybe you ask your friend Jo if she's finished with Pax's sword? He feels naked without it."

"Can do. See you then."

I hang up and pack up Vera's things. If anyone can make sense of the old lady's bric-a-brac, it's the vampire-slaying amateur sleuth, Mina Wilde.

23

BREE

When Pax steps off the bus ahead of me in Argleton, a woman actually clutches her carpet bag to her chest and *swoons*. I can't help but notice that it's the same old lady Mina warned me about at the funeral. I grab Pax's arm and steer him toward the pub before he becomes her next victim.

"Wait for us." Edward trails behind, with Ambrose touching his arm. I feel a burst of affection at seeing Edward being so nice to Ambrose. He's been extra pleasant lately, and I'm still unsure about his true intentions for making me practice my magic on him instead...

But before I can say anything, Edward walks Ambrose through a parking meter.

"Sorry." Edward doesn't sound sorry at all. "Old habits die hard."

"Yes, quite." Ambrose dusts himself off and picks up his walking stick, and off we go.

The Rose and Wimple is an enormous Tudor building on the other side of the green. It doesn't host quite as many community events as the Cackling Goat, which means that it's bliss-

229

fully empty when we enter. Mina's waiting at a table out the back, with Oscar lying across her feet and Quoth in human form beside her. His long, dark hair sweeps her shoulder as he cuts cheese from a ploughman's platter and feeds it to her.

Pax and I purchase a couple of ciders, plus two glasses of red wine for Edward and Ambrose to sniff, and join her.

Mina drops a bundle wrapped in a beach towel on the table. "With Jo's thanks," she beams. "Apparently, there is absolutely no trace of Vera's blood on the blade, although she said there are traces of other people's blood – but it's badly degraded, as if it's hundreds of years old. I told her that Pax must've cut himself doing historical re-enactment."

"That's my sword." Pax reaches for the weapon. I grab his wrist.

"Do *not* swing that thing around in here," I warn.

"That's what she said," Quoth says with a wink. Mina shoots him a look and he shrugs. "Sorry, Morrie wasn't here, and it felt like a vacuum."

"My *sword*." Pax picks up the entire bundle and cradles it against his face, like a baby. He whispers a Latin prayer. It's adorable.

"So, now I have reunited man and pointy weapon thing, I demand to know what you inherited from Vera." Mina drums her hands on the edge of the table.

"What Mina means to say is hello, how are you?" Quoth says with a quiet smile.

"Sorry! Yes, hello, hi, how are you? Things have been so dull around here since I solved my last mystery." Mina raises her hands, showing off some rather impressive sparkly purple nails. "I'm *dying* to sink my claws into a new mystery. So go on, what've you got?"

"It's all very strange. Vera left me a box of junk. There are pages torn out of a shop ledger – just lists of names and dates and what they purchased. Vera did online sales all around the country but apparently still kept handwritten records. And there's all these other weird items, too." I lift the box onto the table and dump out the items. "I don't know what to make of it."

Mina starts to sift through the items. She frowns as she traces her fingers over the bag of herbs. Quoth picks up the ledger pages and starts to scan them.

"Looks like your friend Maggie's candles were popular." Quoth's brow furrows as he stares at the pages. "You're right – these are just records of purchases made in the shop and online."

"Maybe there's a secret message hidden inside them?" Ambrose suggests.

"You may be right, Ambrose." Quoth squints at the pages. "We might have to rope Morrie in on this. If there's a code, he'll be able to crack it."

I stare at Quoth in awe. "I'm never going to get used to him hearing the ghosts."

Mina pats his arm. "It figures that the grim, ungainly, ghastly, gaunt, and ominous bird of yore from Poe's poem would end up with the power to see ghosts."

Quoth had finally told Mina that he can see and hear ghosts. His impressions of the restless dead aren't as vivid as mine, but his ghostly powers are still new. It's strange to sit across from him and listen to him acknowledge Ambrose like a real person.

"He can hear me?" Ambrose's mouth hangs open in wonder.

"Yes. Ambrose, meet Quoth. Quoth, Ambrose. And the surly one with his head in the wine is Edward."

"My pleasure," Edward says in a voice that is anything but.

"If Quoth can hear and see us, doesn't this mean that he could be a target for the monster, too?" Ambrose asks.

Quoth's head snaps back. "I didn't think of that."

"Neither did I."

"Think of what?" Mina frowns at us both. "You know, it's very strange to only be involved in half of the conversation."

"Vera could see ghosts, too," I explain. "And she deliberately left the Lazarus card for me as a clue. And then this box of stuff...the ghosts and I think she was targeted because of her powers, which means..."

"Which means unless we catch the monster who killed Vera, you or Quoth could be its next victim?" Mina squeezes Quoth's hand so hard that his knuckles turn white. He winces but never asks her to let go.

"Yes. Dani doesn't want me to investigate. She thinks the police should handle it. And I get it, but I need to do this."

"Okay." Mina's jaw sets in a hard line. "Then we've got to figure this out."

She goes back to moving the objects around in different configurations, and Quoth and I go back to reading over the lists, looking for something that could be a clue.

"I should ask the three witches," I say, setting down my stack of papers with a sigh. "They hung out in Vera's shop. They might've seen her tearing out the pages and could tell us what it means—"

"I found something," Quoth interrupts. He points to a name on his list. "This person purchased moldavite. Isn't that the stone you use to interact with the ghosts?"

I pull the moldavite from my pocket and drop it on the table. Quoth picks it up, turning and examining it in the light. He squeezes it. Ambrose waves his hand, and it goes right through Quoth's shoulder, making him shudder.

"It doesn't work for me," he says, rubbing his shoulder. "But what happened to me...what Mina did – it's not normal. Even within the magical realm that we're dealing with here. I don't think I am the same as what you are, Bree."

"I don't think I'm anything, really," I say.

"She's being modest," Edward says. "She is the morning and evening star—"

"Edward is a poet," I say to Quoth. "Aren't you glad you can hear him?"

"Um, guys?" Mina taps the table. "Back to the realm of the Living? Quoth was asking about the moldavite?"

"Well, what if the people who brought moldavite from Vera are also...whatever you are," Quoth says.

"I bet tons of people purchase that stone. It was just in a dish beside the rose quartz," I say.

"Yes, but..." Mina frowns as she holds the page right up to her nose. "Okay, no. I can't read this at all. But Vera wanted you to have this folder for a reason. Maybe this person purchased the moldavite because they want to use it for their own ghost friends."

Holy shitballs, she's right.

I grab the list and stare at the name. Penny Hatterly, with an address in Crookshollow. That's less than three miles from Grimdale. Have I been living practically next door to someone with resurrection powers this whole time and not even known about it?

What if I'm looking at a person who is just like me?

Quoth points to Penny's entry in the book. "We should talk to Penny Hatterly. She's only twenty minutes on the train."

Mina's face lights up. "We could go on the weekend. I have to be at the shop on Saturday, but Sunday is Heathcliff's day behind the counter, so I'm free." She stops. "That is, if you want some company?"

"I'd love that." I smile at her. "The ghosts will want to come, and I need a little help wrangling Pax."

Speaking of Pax, I cast my head around, searching for him. I didn't have to look far. He leans on the bar, regaling a small crowd with one of his tales of brawn and bravery. I notice Father Bryne is among the men with him. He lifts his orange juice and flashes me a cheeky smile, and I can't help but smile back. For a priest, he seems kind of cool.

"Bree, do you want to play?" his voice booms across the pub. "It's a famous Roman drinking game. Bibamus moriendum est."

"No thanks," I call back. "You have fun getting wasted. And remember, no stabbing."

"No stabbing!" Pax picks up a fork and slams it into the bar, leaving it standing up by its tines. He tries to pull it out, but it's embedded too deep in the wood for even Pax to wriggle out. Pax glares at it with a mixture of horror and fascination.

"That does not count!" he yells at me.

"Fine. It doesn't count."

Pax goes back to his drinking game. Edward goes back to staring morosely into space. And Mina and I return to puzzling over Vera's box of random belongings. I open the lurid little book of serial killers and scan the contents: Countess Bathory. Vlad the Impaler. Jack the Ripper...

Dani would enjoy this book. She used to obsessively listen to serial killer podcasts. One year she dressed as Jeffrey Dahmer for the Halloween dance and the school called her mum in a frenzy and her mum absolutely tore the principal a new one—

I realize that Mina has been talking to me. I release myself from the memory. "Sorry, you were saying?"

"I was just wondering if you've had any luck working with your magic?" Mina asks.

"Well, I read the books, and I managed to do something, but that something hurt Edward, so I haven't tried again." I shrug, not wanting to think about it. "It's weird. Even though I saw myself do magic, I don't *feel* magical."

234

"I know, right? I feel like a completely normal person, and yet..." Mina wiggles her fingers at Quoth, who nuzzles her shoulder. "I've done some pretty freaky things, and not just in Morrie's bed. I found that when I needed it most, my magic just came to me. I'm sorry, that's not very helpful."

"Not really." I don't like talking about magic. I don't like thinking about magic. I down the rest of my cider and shove the contents of Vera's box aside. "Shall we have a look at the menu? I can't monster-hunt on an empty stomach..."

24

BREE

"Brianna, there you are." Edward floats through the wall of the bathroom. The lights flicker as his hand sweeps over the fixture. "I didn't think I'd ever get you away from the Roman Oaf. I have something I want to tell you."

"Can it wait until I have pants on?" I grumble as I hop across the floor, struggling to get my foot into my tight black jeans. Curse all ghosts and their inability to understand one's need for privacy.

"No!" Edward's voice rises with urgency. "It cannot wait!"

I stop hopping and stare up at Edward. He plasters his usual smirk on his face, but it's ill-fitting. The gold flecks in the corners of his anthracite eyes dance in the flickering light.

"Edward, are you okay?"

"Why wouldn't I be okay? I am a royal prince and artistic prodigy surrounded by imbeciles, present company excepted, of course." Edward holds out a hand. "Now, if you please, I require you. I have...er, composed a new poem. Yes, I have written a new work and I wish to share it with you. And it absolutely *cannot wait*, not while my loins burn with inspiration."

I sigh. It doesn't matter that my hair's a mess and my sock's twisted around my foot. If I don't listen to Edward's poem, he'll sulk and pout all weekend, and make all our lives miserable. Better to get it over and done with.

"Okay." I yank my jeans over my hips and manage to secure the button, making a mental note to eat less of Maggie's baking from now on. I sit down on the edge of the bathtub, fold my legs, and clasp my hands. "I'm all ears."

"That's a rather disgusting expression – it brings to mind an image of your beautiful body covered with wiggling earlobes, when I know from experience that you have but two cute ones, right here." Edward leans forward, his leg brushing mine as he lightly touches my ears.

It's a strange and intensely intimate gesture that leaves my ears tingling. From the way Edward's mouth crooks when he steps back, I know he's trying to hide something from me. Something's up with him, and it's more than his frustration at not being able to be brought back to life.

"Why won't you come to bed with us?" I blurt out before I can stop myself. "The night with the spirit board shows that you have no problem touching me, but you won't join Pax and Ambrose anymore. Why not? I miss you."

Pain flickers in Edward's eyes, but he whips his head around, glancing over his shoulder at the small bathroom window high in the wall.

"Pax is out chopping more firewood," he murmurs, ignoring my question. "And I have distracted Ambrose by telling him I'd play a game of statues with him in the garden, and it's my turn to freeze."

"Edward!"

He turns back to me, and his eyes are back to being their usual dark, fathomless orbs. His mouth curls back into his quintessential Edward smirk. "I predict he'll be looking for me for at least the next sixteen minutes, which gives me plenty of time to..." he stares down at his hands, and that oddness is back. "To tell you that I—"

My phone vibrates. I hold up my hand as I dig it out of my pocket. "Hold that thought."

Edward looks a little seasick, but all thoughts of his poetry fly out of my head when I see the caller ID. I plonk the phone down on the sink and prop it up with my shampoo bottle.

"Hi Mum, Dad!"

Edward's fingers brush my shoulder, and he shoots me a final, forlorn glance before floating back through the wall. I long to go after him, but it can wait until after I've spoken to my parents.

"Hello, darling!" Mom yells into the phone as the video call starts playing.

"Argh!" I cover my ears as her voice echoes through the bathroom. "Mum, I can hear you just fine. You don't need to yell."

"Sorry, I forget sometimes that overseas calls aren't a big deal anymore." She throws her arms out and steps back, revealing the jagged edges of a majestic fjord out their hotel window. "Your father and I are in Norway!"

"That's exciting. What have you been doing?"

"Oh, *everything*. We were in Oslo for three days, seeing all the art museums. That Edvard Munch is one disturbed individual. I suspect he was never hugged as a child. Oh, and we went to this strange park filled with statues of naked people. I've never seen so many bottoms in my life, and that includes the nudist beach we accidentally crashed in Santorini."

I remember the park. I wandered around there for hours when I visited Oslo, thinking about how much Edward would have enjoyed all the art in the city. "Well, they're naked because the artist, Gustav Vigeland, wanted to show the cycle of life and how we return to nature when we—"

But Mum is not listening to my art lesson. "The food is terrible. What I wouldn't give for a lovely Cornish pastie or a shepherd's pie. Everything here is smoked herring. I ordered pancakes for breakfast yesterday and I swear they were slathered in herring!"

Dad makes a face and I laugh. "I'm sorry to hear that. Hopefully, you find some non-herring-based fare soon."

"I hope so too, dear. Now we're exploring the fjords, and if this dreary rain lets up we're going to a Viking museum tomorrow."

Mum gushes about the scenery and complains about the food for a little longer, and then she gets a call from her German friend to meet down at the bar. "The olive in my martini might be my only chance at sustenance."

Dad shuffles over to fill the screen. He's looking more tanned than I remember. His hair's a little longer and there's a line of fine hair around his jawline, and he's wearing his Jethro Tull t-shirt. Seeing him makes my chest tighten.

"Hi, Dad. Are you as big a fan of herring as Mum?"

"Honestly, I think it's delicious, but don't tell your mother." He smiles. "We had reindeer steaks last night."

"Oh yes. And what did Rudolph taste like?"

"Absolutely divine. I had two helpings. Your mother said I'm banned from Christmas."

We both laugh.

"How are things..." I swallow, trying to find the words to ask what I want to ask. "I mean, how are you doing with all the travelling?"

"I'm enjoying myself very much. Your mother and I should have done this years ago." He shows me a troll figurine they brought at the hotel gift shop. His other hand stays clenched on his chest and I can't stop staring at it. Dad must notice because he says, "You don't have to worry about me, Bree-bug. I'm happy. This disease isn't going to change your old man."

But it already has.

I swallow. "I know, Dad."

"Tell me about yourself. How are things going at the house? Are the guests giving you any trouble?"

"Everything's fine." That's a woefully inadequate statement for my current state of affairs, but that's all I can offer. "Father Bryne is staying on for the rest of the month, and he's a lovely guest. Mum will be pleased that I haven't scared him away with my gothic fashion or my general nihilism. I'm going on a little adventure with my new friend, Mina, this weekend. And I've been working on a fun project for the cemetery, making videos about the history of some of Grimdale's most famous corpses..."

...and bringing my dead ghost friends back to life, and trying to learn how to control my magic, and going to visit some lady named Penny Hatterly who may or may not be a resurrection witch, and hunting for the monster who killed Vera and might be after me next, and fighting with my best friend...

I plaster a smile on my face that I hope is convincing.

Dad leans forward a little. "Is everything okay, Bree-bug? You seem quieter than usual. We're worried about you managing the B&B by yourself with your cemetery job on top of it, and with this murderer on the loose...it's okay if you're a little overwhelmed. If you need us to come home..."

"No, don't cut your holiday short. I'm fine." I don't want to retell the story of finding Vera's body. I don't have the stomach for it.

"I know, why don't you ask Dani to help you a couple of days a week? I'm sure we could stretch the budget for that, and then the two of you can—"

"Dani and I had a fight."

Saying the words out loud makes my stomach twist. I

remember the cold way she spoke to me at the pub, all those things she said. I pretend to flick some lint off my sleeve so Dad doesn't see me wiping the tear out of my eye.

"I'm sorry, honey. You know, I'm here if you want to talk about it. You might feel better."

I sniff. Dad knows Dani and loves her like another daughter. We used to spend every weekend at each other's houses. Dad used to help Dani with her woodshop projects because her mum is hopeless with DIY. My parents and Dani's mum Sue are good friends, too – they're usually on the same pub quiz team.

I stare at Dad's mosaic of two fish kissing that hangs over the clawfoot tub. "Dani has a new girlfriend."

"Oh, that's wonderful."

"It's Alice Agincourt."

"Alice?" Dad's voice thickens. He knows that name well.

"Dani says that Alice has changed, and maybe she has. She certainly seems nicer the couple of times I've spoken to her. She even said that she wanted to be friends with me and Dani in high school, but she was too afraid of Kelly's wrath."

"Oh, Bree-bug, I'm not surprised Alice felt left out – you and Dani always had such fun together. Didn't your old man tell you that bullies pick on other people because of their own insecurities? I know it doesn't help much when they're being horrible to you, but everything those girls did was about them, not about you."

You're right, Dad. It doesn't help to know that your bullies are insecure when they're tormenting you. Alice was a big part of why I left Grimdale as soon as I could, and now...and now she's stealing my best friend.

"Alice is having a huge birthday party," I say, wiping my eye with my sleeve. "She invited me, but Dani doesn't want me to go. I guess she thinks that I might embarrass her."

Dad's voice cracks. "Oh, Bree-bug."

"I get it. Mine and Dani's individual weirdness always complemented each other. But maybe we're different now? Maybe too many years have passed since high school. I didn't keep up with her while I travelled the way I should have. But now she's got this new girlfriend, and I guess she wants to impress her, and I'm..." I can't tell Dad about the ghosts, but it's not really even about them, anyway. "I'm sad because all Dani and I ever wanted was to fit in and feel like we belong. And now Dani does fit, but that has to mean I don't belong. I'm not angry, at all. I'm afraid that I'm losing my friend, and so I snapped at her and stormed out, and we haven't talked since."

"Dani is a very special friend," Dad says. "That kind of friendship doesn't come easily, and the older you get, the more you realize how precious it is. Do you want to know what I think?"

I wipe my tears away again. "Sure."

"I think you should forgive her."

"That's exactly what Father Bryne said."

"On this occasion, I happen to agree with the priest. I know Dani hurt you, but if you look inside, you'll understand why she did that. She's just as scared as you are. We're all a little scared, all the time. I think that's part of what makes us human."

"Thanks, Dad." This time, I don't bother to wipe the tears that streak down my cheeks. "You are wise."

"It's the kind of wisdom you only get by being a parent and spending eighteen years of your life terrified that you'll fuck up your kids beyond recognition."

"That ship sailed a long time ago." I wave at the screen as Pax calls my name from somewhere in the house. "I have to go. You should join Mum for a drink at the bar. And maybe take her to get a burger tonight."

"The only burgers here are made from reindeer."

"Just don't tell her – I bet she won't even notice."

243

I hang up with Dad just as Pax bangs his fist on the door. "Bree, are you in there? Edward says I have to curtsey in his presence, and I'd like your permission to put him through the paper shredder–you are crying?"

Pax's eyes narrow in on my wet cheeks as soon as I open the door.

"Yeah." I allow myself to fall into his arms. "I got a call from my parents, and it made me think about my fight with Dani. But Dad cheered me up and gave me some advice. I think I know what I have to do."

I burrow deeper into Pax's broad chest. His strong arms go around me and squeeze tight. My breath stutters as his musky, leathery scent washes over me. I feel so *safe* with him. Nothing can hurt me when I'm in his arms.

"I am sad that after all these years of living in the house, I have not got to meet Mike in person," he says, his lips pressing against the top of my head. "He is a wise man. If he was a Roman, he'd be a seer."

"He probably would," I smile.

"That's not a good thing. Seers usually take many hallu-cinogenic drugs and go insane," Pax says with a serious expres-sion. "As a career, it doesn't have the best advancement opportunities. Now, about Edward and the shredder—"

25

BREE

The next day, I leave the house at lunchtime, fueled by Dad and Father Bryne's sensible words. I stop by the pub for a couple of mince pies and some chips to go, and then walk down to the end of High Street to Dani's work. Wigham's Funeral Home has been part of the village since 1823. But the current two Wigham sons have no interest in the death business, and I know Dani hopes that she might one day be able to buy the funeral parlour and make it her own.

There are no funerals scheduled for today. I walk in and wave to Darren, the balding son of the current owner who doesn't look too happy to be working reception over the summer. "Oh, hello, Bree. I didn't know you were back from Ithaca."

"Hey, Darren. I just came to visit Dani." I hold up the lunch bag.

"Sure thing. I'll buzz her up."

A few minutes later Dani appears, dressed in her work attire – an austere dark grey pantsuit. I notice a little of her signature style in the wide lapels and corset tailoring detail on the back of her jacket. She nods at me, and I follow her silently into the building.

Dani leads me through the maze of hallways and reception rooms. She opens the door at the back of her office into the contemplation garden. It's a tiny walled garden filled with the sweetest-smelling flowers and herbs, and beautiful statues made by local artisans that symbolize love, mourning, and remembrance. Even though we're close to High Street, I can't hear any traffic or village noise. The only sound that breaks the silence is the twittering of birds and the steady burble of the small pond in the center.

Sometimes, when clients are having a hard time making arrangements through their grief, Dani brings them out here. Wighams even host intimate funerals in the small space.

I sit down on one end of the bench, facing the pond. I place the bag in the middle of the seat.

"I brought you some lunch."

I can't look at her. I can't bear to see anger or scorn or embarrassment on her face.

"I have a sandwich from home," she says. "Mum makes me cucumber and cream cheese, just like she always did at school."

"Oh, okay then." I reach for the bag. "More for me."

"Gimme that." Dani snatches it before I can grab it. I peek out of the corner of my eyes as she opens it up to inspect the contents. "If you eat two pies, you'll be sick. Remember that time we took the ferry over to France, and it had a free buffet so we gorged ourselves on croissants, but the sea was so choppy that you threw them all up again?"

"I do remember." My stomach churns at the thought of what all that bread looked like as I heaved it over the railing into the ocean while Dani held back my hair. "I wish you didn't."

Dani sits on the end of the bench, not as far from me as it's possible to get, but not close, either. She takes out one of the pies and lifts off the pastry lid, using it like a spoon to scoop out the mince filling. I pick up my own pie and take a huge bite.

We chew in uncomfortable silence for a few moments.

I swallow. "That France trip was the first time we ever left Grimdale together on our own."

Dani chews thoughtfully.

"The other girls used to brag about heading down to London for the weekend to go shopping, but we decided to pool all our money and go to Paris for a week over the summer break. We stayed in that horrible hostel, remember?"

"I remember," she winces. "Bunk beds with broken springs and the druggies in the elevator and gunshots at night."

"I'm sure it was just old pipes banging—"

"They were *gunshots*. And that stupid circling light on the top of the Eiffel Tower that blared through our window every twenty seconds. I kept thinking the Inquisition had come give us the thumbscrews."

"You said you would never leave Grimdale ever again," I smile. "But the food was amazing. Crepes for breakfast, lunch, and dinner."

"By the time we came home, I thought I *was* a crepe."

"And the art galleries! You nearly got us kicked out of the Louvre for touching that statue—"

"I thought it was made of chocolate," Dani says wickedly. "It's not my fault they don't label things properly."

"Remember our goth photoshoot at Père Lachaise – all those mopey pictures we took draped over Jim Morrison's grave—"

"—and those Japanese tourists thought we were famous musicians and took all those photos with us!"

We've both laughing now, remembering that wild, crazy

trip. When I catch my breath again, I look her square in the eyes and the words just burst out of me.

"Dani, I'm sorry."

I don't know why I didn't say it sooner.

"I'm the one who's sorry." Dani bites her lip. "I got so messed up. I never should have said those things—"

"But you only said them because I—"

I look into her friendly eyes, rimmed in unfallen tears, and we burst out laughing again.

"We've just a couple of freaks." Dani throws her arm around me. "We stick together, got it? No matter what."

"No matter what." My chest does a funny fluttering thing. I look down to check on the cords stretching from my heart, but they're still there, still intact.

I have my friend back.

"Are any ghosts with us right now?" Dani asks. "I want to say some sappy shit and I don't need Edward correcting my grammar."

"Nope. It's just the two of us." Ghosts don't like to hang around funeral homes – they remind them that they're dead. I told Ambrose and Edward to stay away. Pax is waiting outside on the street, staying true to his promise to guard me, no matter what. But he can't do much damage outside a *funeral home.*

I hope.

"Okay." Dani's shoulders shake. "Me first. I'm so sorry for not texting you back. I'm sorry for what I said about Alice's party, and I'm sorry because I should have known better how all of that would make you feel. It's horrible being left out of stuff, and I hate that I made you feel that way."

"I understand why you did it, though."

"Do you?" Dani swipes a strand of auburn hair behind her ear. "I don't know that you do. You left *me*, Bree. You went off to have your adventures and it seemed like you didn't need or want me anymore. As much as I understand exactly why you did it and I've always been so proud of you for getting on that plane and following your dreams, part of me feels like you didn't just leave Grimdale, but you left me. Like I wasn't good enough or exciting enough of a friend for you, and you had to go out and find a new life."

"But that's not—"

Dani holds up a hand. I snap my mouth shut and let her finish. "I know it's not fair. I know that's my shit, not yours. But it's how I *feel*. I was always the one who needed you more than you needed me. For so long I wasn't able to live the way I wanted to, be the person I know I am inside, and I wouldn't have survived that without a friend who liked me for who I truly am. But all through high school, all you ever talked about was getting away from Grimdale, and how much happier you'd be without this place. Then you did it. I guess part of me wished that I wasn't so easy to leave. I know that's not how you meant it, but what I know logically and what I feel aren't always the same thing. Even in the dark times, you made my life so much fun. When I decided to come back to Grimdale I knew that I had to do it without you. It hasn't always been easy, and people are dicks sometimes, but I've found my place here."

"You really have," I pat her knee. "I'm a little jealous. I'm still searching for my place, and sometimes it seems like I don't fit into your life anymore."

"You will always fit. I might not need you anymore to make me feel like me, but I want you in my life, Bree Mortimer. But I want Alice, too."

"Yeah." My cheeks flush. I knew we'd get around to talking about Alice eventually.

"I know you don't understand. I don't always understand it either. But even back in school, I think we had a spark. Sometimes, she and I would hang out in the music suite after school, and I got the sense that she wished she was hanging out with us, instead of with Kelly and Leanne. And when she and I started...the first time she smiled at me, at *me,* I realized that someone else sees me as *me.* And she's still got some of that Alice mystique. I feel six feet tall whenever I'm around her."

"You *are* six foot tall." I elbow her in the ribs.

"Hush, you. The point is, I finally got the girl of my dreams," Dani says. "I don't want to mess it up. Everything feels so fragile, like if I make one wrong move, Alice will go back to Kelly and Leanne and you'll go back to your adventures and your ghosts and I'll be alone again. And Pax..."

I look over the wall to where Pax doing his military drills in the village rose garden. "Pax is likely to mess it up and scare Alice off. I get it. Not all of your points are bad. Is it my turn to apologise now?"

"Sure."

"I'm sorry that I didn't understand this sooner. I'm sorry that I left you behind. I didn't want to. I hated leaving you. It was one of the hardest things I've ever done. And I think...I knew if I talked to you all the time, I'd miss you and I'd want to come home, so I removed the temptation. I guess I'm good at running away from my problems."

"It's okay."

"It's not okay. And I'm sorry that I haven't made a better effort to get to know Alice. It still frightens me a little to see you with her. I worry that she's going to tear your heart out and stomp on it, the way she did so many times to both of us in high school. Kelly and Leanne haven't changed a bit, and I guess it's hard for me to think that Alice might be different. But most of all, I'm so sorry that I made you feel like you were alone. Me getting out of Grimdale had everything to do with me running away from the ghosts and nothing to do with running away from you. I've thought of you every time I wandered through a cemetery or saw a killer post-punk band. I'm sorry we lost touch."

"Okay," Dani pulls me in close, folding her arm around me. I rest my head on her shoulder. "Let's agree to put an end to this silliness. Best friends forever, right?"

"Forever."

My heart full, I sit back. "So, about Alice's party. I think I should come. Alice invited me. She was *so* genuinely nice the other day—"

"You mean when you pushed her in the lake?"

I wince. "Yeah. So I think it would be a good chance for me to get to know her."

"But Pax..." Dani frowns. "I can see his head above the wall, you know. He's slaying a parking meter, isn't he?"

"I can neither confirm nor deny."

"He's going to want to go to this party. He won't let you out of his sight for one night."

"What if I made him promise to be on his best behavior? Edward's been giving him lessons on etiquette, and he's improving. He zipped up his own trousers the other day, and he now eats everything with his pinkie out like this." I demonstrate, and Dani cracks up laughing. "What if I get Edward to turn Pax into a proper gentleman in time for the party?"

"Let me get this straight, you propose to teach a blood-thirsty Roman centurion how to behave by giving him lessons from a seventeenth-century royal rake who thinks that cocaine gives his salad a little zest?" Dani's eyebrow raises at an angle that would impress Pythagoras.

"I'll be there to keep an eye on him. I promise he'll be on his best behavior. And besides, if it's Roman-themed, he's going to blend right in. Please, Dani." I squeeze her hand. "I want to do this for you. I want to be part of your life, and for Pax and Alice to be a part of our lives, too. Remember how we always wished we could go to one of Alice's parties? We'll have an absolute blast together – you and me and your hot girlfriend and my Roman centurion and menagerie of ghosts."

Dani's face twists. "Okay. But Bree...I really mean it. Don't ruin this for me. I have been working hard on myself over the last few years, but I'm not made of stone. I can't take that kind of setback."

"I swear it."

We link our pinkies together and say, "Per Iovem lapidem," which is an oath Pax taught me and I taught Dani. It means "By Jupiter and his stone!" The stone bit is because it's an unbreakable oath, or it might be that Pax was stoned on Roman mushrooms when he made all of his oaths. The real answer has yet to reveal itself.

"I gotta get back to work," Dani gives me a squeeze. "But I'll call you tonight. We can plan our outfits for the party."

"It's a deal."

Dani gives me a thumbs-up as she heads to the door. Halfway there, she stops and turns around. "Bree?"

"Yeah?"

"You did listen to me about the murderer, right? You're letting the police handle it? I'm not doubting your sleuthing abilities. I saw those injuries. I know a human didn't kill Vera, and I don't want you to end up like that."

"I get it." I swallow, thinking about the box of Vera's belongings under my coffee table, and our visit to Penny Hatterly this weekend. "And yeah, I'm trying to leave this one to the police."

The lie tastes like chalk in my mouth.

Dani's shoulders sag in relief. "Okay. Good. Well, you know your way out. Go get your Roman and I'll see you guys at the party."

As soon as she's gone, Edward leaps out from behind the

wall. I glare at him as I wipe away the pastry crumbs we left on the bench.

"This place smells of death," he grumbles.

"I told you I was going to a funeral home and not to follow me."

"And you thought I'd listen?" He looks offended. "Why, Brianna. How little you know me."

I think the issue is that I know you too well.

"What do you want, Edward?" I stuff a couple of chips into my mouth. "I promise I'll listen to your poem tonight."

"Oh, no, do not trouble yourself with that." Edward busies himself sniffing the fragrant flowers climbing up the wall. "I decided that the poem needs more work. I couldn't find any words to rhyme with bosoms. You did not tell Dani that you're trying to learn your magic and find the monster."

"I was a little busy ensuring I didn't toss fifteen years of friendship out the window by making a heartfelt apology," I shoot back. "A burden you haven't yet faced."

"Why apologise when I am always right?" Edward's mouth quirks up into his signature smirk. "Perhaps now you will stop moping about Dani and focus more on your magic. And now we just have to teach the Roman oaf not to stab Alice's dinner guests if they tie their togas wrong. It should be easy."

By the gods, what have I done?

26

PAX

"Pax. Can you stop for a sec? I want to talk to you."

I lower my sword arm as Bree steps out of the woodland path. She's wearing a blood-red garment with short, puffy sleeves and a bow above her breasts, and a pair of black trousers. The barbarian garments accentuate her lovely figure. My beanstalk grows engorged just gazing upon her.

She's also carrying her sword – the one she had made for her twelfth birthday that is identical to mine.

I drop to one knee, offering my sword. "I am here for whatever you require of me. If you like I can lead you into the forest and I can spread your legs over the altar of the old gods—"

A flush creeps along Bree's cheeks, right to the tips of her ears. "While that sounds fun, it might somewhat frighten the delicate sensibilities of the archaeologists still working there. I was wondering if we could talk about Alice's party."

"Yes! We can now attend the party because you and Dani have made up honorably, and you didn't even have to cut her head off." I bow a little to show how impressed I am. "I usually can't get my friends to see sense until I separate their head from their neck."

"Er, yes, that's right. Very good." Bree plops down on the garden step, balancing the sword on her knees. She dusts off a statue of an oversized badger. "I want to go to this party. And I know that you won't let me go on my own."

"This monster could be there. He could be at this Penny Hatterly's house when you visit her on Sunday. I must stay by your side at all times." Even though I am tired to my bones from barely sleeping – I sleep only when Bree is at the cemetery and Ambrose watches her – I will not forsake my duty.

"And I get that. I'm so grateful. Having you with me means I can have somewhat of a normal life – normal being a relative term." An adorable little crease appears between Bree's eyes. "But it's very important to Dani – which means it's important to me – that none of her friends realize that you're an ex-ghost I brought back to life. Which means that you can't be Pax the Roman centurion anymore. You have to be Pax, my slightly eccentric Italian boyfriend."

Boyfriend? There's that word again. "You want me to be your boyfriend?"

"No. Everything I said still stands. I'm not ready for a real boyfriend. I want you to *pretend* to be my boyfriend."

"Is this acting?" I frown. "Because Edward always says that actors are a carbuncle on the arse of society. And in that play we saw, all the actors wore ruffles that made them look like they'd swallowed Apollo's discus. I don't want to be an actor."

"No, Pax, I don't want you to become a Shakespearean actor." Bree smiles as she sets the sword on the step, but her smile is tinged with sadness. I don't like this smile. It reminds me of my mother when she sent me off to war with a kiss on the forehead and tears brimming in her eyes. "I just want you to do a bit of pretending. The truth is, if you are going to be a living, breathing human from now on, then you have to learn how to be a human in the *twenty*-first century, not the *first*. Society has changed a lot since Roman times, and so many of the traditions you're used to are, well, weird or illegal or problematic now."

"I'll do anything." I want Bree to smile again. A proper smile, not this half smile with pain at the edges. "I'll wear trousers. I'll learn to crochet. I'll give up meat."

She raises an eyebrow. "Really?"

"No. That was a joke. Hahaha." I look at her face. "Wait, I have to give up meat?"

"No, but you need to learn to eat it with a knife and fork. How are your lessons with Edward going?"

"Good."

"He says you put the fork through his eye."

"Exactly." I grin. "I am learning how to use a fork effectively. What else do you need me to do?"

She looks like she's trying hard not to smile. "Well, for starters, the party is at the Grimdale Roman Museum, and it's Ancient History themed. It's fancy dress, so we'll both wear togas—"

"I cannot wear a toga," I say. "They are for statesmen. Politicians. I would never become a politician – those weak, flappy-skinned man-boys who fight battles with words instead of swords. Bah!"

I spit on the ground.

Bree regards my spit with her lips pursed. "This is just the thing. You can't spit on the ground at the party. And you can't lecture people on the historical accuracy of their clothing. And you can't bring your sword."

I frown as I stare down at my tackle. "You want me to cut off my beanstalk? I will do this for you if you ask it. But I will miss it greatly, and I won't be able to bring you the same pleasures. Are we offering it to a fertility goddess? This is a very strange custom but if that is your way, I will honour it so that your womb swells with my seed—"

"Pax, *no.*" Bree laughs as she holds me. "Putting aside the fact that that's not how fertility works, and that we've never even *discussed* having children, I would never want you to hurt yourself like that. *And* I would miss your beanstalk too much to offer it to any god. I mean *that* sword. The stabby one." She points to my gladius, which I have laid lovingly at the foot of the Diana statue. "You can't bring it, okay?"

"But what if the monster comes after you?"

I can feel the monster nearby, feel his otherworldly gaze watching us, waiting for the moment when I am weakest to make his move. Bree will not end up like that woman, ripped apart on the floor. I will die again before I allow that beast to touch her.

"You mean to tell me that these guns aren't strong enough to protect me?" Bree squeezes my biceps. "And here I was thinking that Pax Drusus Maximus didn't need a sword to protect his woman."

"I don't!" I growl, my hands balling into fists.

She smiles. "Then it's settled. I'm serious, Pax. And these rules aren't just for the party. They're forever. If people figure out what you really are, they might take you away from me."

"That will never happen. I won't allow it."

"You might not have a choice." Bree blinks, and I see tears pool in the corners of her eyes. The dark pool of rage inside me rises. I hate this monster for making Bree sad and afraid. When I get my hands on him...he'll *wish* he was a Christian being thrown to the lions, that's all I have to say. "I don't want to lose you, okay? So will you work on being more normal?"

"I promise, I will work hard." To demonstrate, I take my sword in my hands and walk over to the small pond. I don't want to throw it in, but if it will show Bree that I am serious about being with her, then I will do it.

I pull back my hand, but something tightens around my wrist. Bree. Her eyes sparkle. "Wait just a second. I'm not just going to make you change everything about yourself without a fair exchange. You learn from Edward and me about how to be a normal twenty-first century fellow, and I will learn from you."

"I'm a humble soldier." I bow my head. "There is nothing I can teach you."

"You can show me how to swing that sword."

"I cannot." The very thought of it horrifies me. "Swords are not for women."

"Bullshit." Bree's mouth quirks up in a smile. Her tears have gone now, and instead, something devious dances in her honey-coloured eyes. Bree leans in close. She takes the sword from my hand and slides it into my belt, but then her hand explores me, finding its way beneath my tunic. She grips my already hard beanstalk and strokes it slowly. *By Jupiter's jolly joystick, she is enchanting.* Bree's voice purrs against my skin. "Haven't I shown you how very good I am with a sword? Besides, weren't there Amazons?"

"Amazons cut their breasts off," I growl as I grab her breast in my hand. I can't help myself. I run my fingers over her nipple through her garments. Bree gasps. Her eyes stare up at me, wide and pleading as her hand pumps faster. "I don't want to maim your beautiful body like that."

"Actually, I was watching a documentary the other week and it said that Amazons didn't actually cut their breasts off. It's a rumor the Romans made up to make them appear more 'un-Roman' so that everyone would feel okay about subjugating them." Bree gasps as my fingers find her nipple again. I push up the edge of her shirt, exposing her soft flesh. She feels so amazing to touch. All I want to do is fall to my knees and worship her.

"Oh." I didn't understand most of what she just said, and not just because it's hard to focus when she has her hand around my verpa. "Yes. Come to think of it, I never met an Amazon with her breasts cut off. We used to drink with them on campaign sometimes, and whenever I asked about it, they said they were on their way to the breast-chopping doctor when war broke out, so they hadn't had a chance to do it yet. They were fun ladies, they could drink me under a table. What does subjugate mean?"

"It means to bring someone under your power," Bree breathes as I shove up her top and bra and take her nipple in my mouth, rolling that little bud around my tongue. "Kind of like what you're doing to me right now..."

"Ah, then you have subjugated me, for I am utterly in your service." I fall to my knees, ripping her hand away from my beanstalk. I grab her trousers and rip open the offending buttons. "Subjugation is fun. We shall do this more often."

"Yes please," Bree murmurs.

The lawn is soft on my knees as I wrap my hands around her thighs. I nibble the soft skin between her legs. Bree bucks against me. She is so slick that wetness drips down the side of her leg. I lick it, tasting a trail back to her sweet cunt.

She wants to fight. She already has the heart of a warrior. I can give her the skills to match.

"Pax..." Bree moans. "Please..."

I cannot deny my goddess.

I bury my face between her legs and *devour* her. She tastes amazing, like the sweetest Roman honey wine. I lick and swirl around her clit, writing my prayers of supplication with my tongue.

There's nowhere in the world I'd rather be than between my goddess' thighs.

I slide my tongue between the lips of her pussy, kissing her everywhere, committing her skin to memory.

Bree's legs tremble as I drive two fingers inside her. With a battle cry, her walls contract around me and she collapses forward, her legs no longer able to hold her upright.

She is my goddess, and I will worship her until she can take no more.

"Pax, that was...argh! Hey!"

I wrap my arms around her legs and stand up, throwing her over my shoulder. She yelps in surprise, but she does nothing to stop me as I run into the forest with her. My hands slide up her naked legs to cup her glorious ass cheeks. I dive my fingers between her legs to feel her wetness.

We reach a clearing higher up the ridge. I come here often – it was the place where we made our last stand against the Celtic army, my brothers and I with shields locked, fighting side by side.

On the ground where I spilled the blood of Druids, I lay down my Bree on a bed of wildflowers, and I worship her until she begs for mercy.

Bree rolls over and picks up my sword from where I let it fall. I flush with embarrassment. A Roman should never drop his sword, not even for fornication.

Before I can stop her, she gets to her feet and starts cutting it madly through the air.

I go to take it off her. "You shouldn't swing that. You'll put your own eye out."

"Well, then, teach me, Roman."

"I cannot. Swords are not—"

I duck as Bree slashes the blade through the air and nearly gives me a close haircut. "Remember that feminism happened, Pax. Swords are for *everyone*, and I need to know how to defend myself."

"You don't need to defend yourself. You have me."

"But you might not always be around."

"Why wouldn't I be around? Do you mean if I get drunk and pass out?" I pound my chest. "Because my friend Flavius once poured an entire amphorae of wine down me. He had to roll me onto the battlefield on the back of an ox but I still slew thirty-five Celts and captured their Druid—"

"Damnit, Pax, will you just teach me some moves?" Bree smiles her heart-melty smile at me. "And then afterward you can come inside and Edward and I will teach you how to make small talk with party guests about topics other than stabbing."

"Okay. I will teach you."

She yelps as I grab my blade from her hands and march off into the trees.

"Where are you going?" Bree demands as I stop by a tree and saw off two low-hanging branches. "Why aren't you going back to the house? I brought my sword, but we left it on the steps—"

"You don't want to cut your boobs off like a real Amazon by accident? Then you don't start with a stabby sword." I find the perfect tree with nice, straight branches. I cut off two that are roughly the same size, throw them over my shoulder, and head back toward the house. Bree follows close behind.

I sit down on the edge of the garden and use my dagger to carve the sticks into two blunt wooden swords. "We use these.

When I see that you won't accidentally behead yourself, you can try with the proper sword."

"Okay, that's fair." Bree tests the sword by slashing it wildly around.

"That's not how you do it. You're *asking* for your opponent to make pretty patterns with your intestines."

I wrap my arms around her and show her the proper stance. I place my fingers over hers and show her how to grip the hilt, and how her other arm would hold her shield. I love being this close to her, with her almond and pear scent invading my nostrils. My verpa is already stiffening again, especially when I see her gripping that wooden sword.

Hmmm, maybe we Romans were wrong not to allow women to fight. They would have distracted the enemy with their deadly beauty, and we could have cut them down without losing a single soldier.

I shall have to mull over this *feminism*.

"This is your gladius," I explain to Bree as I stand behind her, moving her limbs through a military drill. "It's a one-handed sword. We use these in battle. Your comrades protect you on either side, and you stab with this, or cut throats."

I step back and demonstrate.

"Okay, well, what if I don't have comrades on either side of me?" Bree holds up her hand. "I know, I know. You will never leave me, but let's say it's a once-in-a-lifetime event where you happen not to be there, and I get in trouble. What do I do?"

I show her the basics – how to hold her sword, the most vulnerable parts of the body, and how to block blows. She is terrible at it, but I don't know if this is because she is a woman or if my beanstalk has made her drunk with pleasure.

"Okay, it's your turn now." Bree grabs my hand. "Come inside. Edward is probably waiting for us."

I follow Bree into the guest sitting room. The guests are out for the day. Edward paces at the window, his mouth fixed in that ugly scowl he's been wearing a lot lately. He plasters on a pleasant smile when Bree walks into the room, and gestures for me to have a seat opposite him.

"Welcome back to the Edward School of Decorum," Edward intones. "Today, we will work on respecting personal space and conducting proper conversations. You enter this classroom an uncouth, bloodthirsty bastard, but under my tutelage, you shall emerge a worldly gentleman."

"I am not uncouth. I am the height of Roman civilisation. I'll cut your nutsack off for saying such things." I advance on him, reaching for my sword, but Bree grabs my arm.

"Silence while your prince is speaking," Edward swats my arm as if I'm a pesky fly. "In fact, for you, Pax, silence overall may be preferable."

I glance across at Bree. She's staring at Edward with a strange look on her face. Almost as if she *agrees* with him.

She wants me to be this...this not-Roman man. At the Roman party!

Bree is my general, my goddess. She commands and I obey. I will kill for her. I will lay down my second life for her. If she doesn't want Pax to be Pax anymore, I will become whatever man she wants.

I lean forward. "Go on. Teach me how to be a foppish Briton man."

27

BREE

"So how is Pax's party training going?" Mina asks as Quoth makes sure she and Oscar are happily ensconced at the table before walking off to the counter to get our drinks.

We're sitting at Oliver's bakery in Argleton, Mina's favorite place for coffee and pastries, fuelling up before we hop on the train to visit Penny Hatterly. Ambrose is with me (he's currently got his head stuck in the sweet cabinet), but Pax and Edward decided to stay home to get in some extra etiquette lessons. When I left, Edward was instructing Pax to walk around the room with a book on his head and Pax was pummelling Edward with said book.

"It's...interesting. Edward has made some progress with the trousers, but table manners are still a work in progress. Pax stuck a fork through his eye."

Mina winces.

"It's okay. Edward is a ghost so he suffered no permanent damage. I can't say the same thing for the fork sticking out of my parents' antique hutch dresser."

Quoth returns with our coffees and a selection of fresh date scones still warm from the oven. As we tuck into our breakfast, Mina asks, "Tell me about what you can see?"

Quoth and I exchange a look. I know she's not asking for a description of the bakery.

"Well," I start. I'm not used to people believing me so readily, or being so interested in my ability to see ghosts. Even with Dani, I always had to be careful what I said, because I didn't want to freak her out. But Mina is a part of my world. *The magical world.* I'm still struggling with that. "There's Ambrose on my left."

"Hello, Mina," Ambrose says with his bright smile.

"He says hello. And there's a woman in a medieval dress wandering across the green in the direction of the stables. She has an axe sticking out of her back."

Mina winces.

"And the old priest in the belltower of the church." Quoth points. I squint, and then I see the shape moving across the window of the gloomy tower. His cassock is splattered with blood.

"What do they look like? Are they just blobs of mist and light?"

"No, they look like people, just see-through. Ghosts are dressed in the outfit they died in. Sometimes they're carrying an item of importance to them, or their murder weapon. Ambrose is wearing a spiffy frock coat and carrying his walking stick."

"That's what causes the tapping I hear sometimes?"

I smile. "Yes."

"And each of them has a silver cord?"

"Yup. Some are brighter than others." Sometimes I only see the cords if I deliberately look for them. Others, like Ambrose and Edward, I now see all the time, snaking through the air around us.

IF YOU'VE GOT IT, HAUNT IT

"That's news to me." Quoth shakes his head. "The cords are something only Bree can see."

"It's so interesting. There's this whole world going on around us that we're not even aware of," Mina smiles. "Well, you two are."

Yes, and most of the time, I wish that world would shut up.

We finish our breakfast and head to the train station. It takes a bit of coaxing to get Ambrose to walk through the electronic turnstiles, much to the chagrin of the people waiting behind me, but we do it. Thirty minutes later we're off the train in Crookshollow and we've walked to a lovely brown house on the end of a terrace with a front garden overflowing with flowers. A sign on the gate reads, 'My Broomstick Runs on Red Wine.'

I swallow.

It looks like we're in the right place.

The woman inside this house might have the same power I have. She can tell me how to use this magic, what to do about the silver cords I see everywhere, and why all this weird stuff is happening.

I could *finally* get answers.

So why are my feet itching to run far away?

"Are you ready for this?" Mina squeezes my hand.

Fuck no. "Ready as I'll ever be."

Ambrose beams at me. "You can do this, Bree. I believe in you."

I knock on the bright pink front door.

My stomach twists. I think I'm going to throw up.

No one answers.

A mixture of relief and desperation floods my body. I don't know what the fuck I'm feeling right now. I knock again, just in case, but no one comes to the door.

"That's a shame," Ambrose says sadly. "We can come back another time."

As I turn to leave, a horrible feeling washes over me. I can't explain it, but it's the same sickening sensation that hit me in Witch Please – a sense of something being utterly *wrong*.

Oh no. Oh no no no no.

I stop in my tracks. Ambrose crashes into me, his warm body sinking into mine, giving me brief flashes of his life.

"Bree?" Mina asks.

Ambrose disentangles himself from me, and his memories vanish. I swallow. I don't want to do this. I don't want to see what's inside that house. But that's exactly why we have to do it. "Something's wrong. We have to get inside. Don't ask me why I know."

"Okay," Mina says.

"Okay? Just like that, you're agreeing to break into someone's house with me. Hang on." I jiggle the front door, but it's locked. "I don't even know how to break into someone's house."

"Of course I believe you," Mina says. "That's what magically-inclined friends are for. And as for breaking in..." She bats her eyelashes at Quoth. He flashes her a look that's part resignation, all adoration, then disappears around the corner of the house.

A moment later, a huge black raven soars past us, circling up to enter an open upstairs window. I hear a fluttering inside the house, and a moment later, a very naked Quoth flings open the door, his hand doing a bad job of covering his junk.

"If you could pass me my clothes..." Quoth says. Even through the curtain of black hair over his face, I can see his cheeks are beet red.

I duck around the side of the house and pick up the pile of clothing in the flower bed, and hand them to him. I look away while he changes quickly in the foyer. Ambrose lurks in the corner, half inside the umbrella stand, sniffing the air, which smells heavily of incense and something tangy and metallic.

"Did you see anything in the house?" I ask Quoth nervously. Inside the foyer – which is decorated with more witchy signs and dreamcatchers – the creepy, tight feeling inside me that something isn't right intensifies.

"No, but I wasn't looking," Quoth says, his eyes focused on the closed door at the end of the narrow hallway as he pulls his trousers on.

Mina pinches his bum.

"You should wait out here," I told Mina, but I should've known better than to tell Argleton's foremost amateur detective not to investigate. She grips Oscar's harness tighter and shoves past me. Quoth walks behind her. I take Ambrose's hand and follow them.

We pass the front reception room, which is crammed full of crystals and mandala blankets. It looks as if this woman was single-handedly keeping Vera's shop in business. There are no signs of life, but that insidious feeling creeps up my spine.

We move toward the back of the house. The feeling grows stronger – it squeezes my chest. I don't look down because I know what I'll see.

I shove the door to the kitchen open and stop, my hand flying to my mouth.

Penny – or what's left of her – lies on the floor. A rust-colored pool spreads out from her to stain the grout in the tiles.

Her body has been ripped and slashed until she is almost unrecognisable.

28

AMBROSE

I know something awful has happened by the way Bree stiffens. A tiny, choking noise escapes her throat. I move behind her, wrapping my arms around her, trying to show her that she has nothing to be afraid of while I'm with her.

My actions would have more meaning if I actually could protect her from the monster. I curse my insubstantiality and then feel instantly guilty. It's wrong to want to push Bree into using her magic before she's ready. It's not her fault that I have no idea what my unfinished business might be.

When it's my time, I'm certain she will make me whole and human again, like Pax. But it is not yet my time and right now, Bree needs me.

She trembles in my arms – a full-body tremor that speaks of her horror. She buries her face in my shoulder and I wish that I could give her more than this. I wish that I could kiss her pain away. I stroke my ghostly fingers through her hair and after a few moments, she settles enough to talk to me.

"Oh, Ambrose," she sobs. "We're too late."

"This is sick," Quoth whispers.

"What is it?" Mina asks. Her guide dog, Oscar, whimpers. I hear his toes pawing at the tile, clearly in distress. "What's happened?"

"I—" Bree hiccups. "I can't—"

"I know it's horrible," I say. "But Mina and I can't see what's going on. Can you tell us what's happened?"

"She's dead. She's been mutilated, ripped..." That's all Bree can get out before she collapses against me again.

Something niggles at me. That same uncanny sense of deja vu I had at Vera's death. Something about these murders feels familiar.

"Describe the wounds. *Please.*"

"I...I..."

"He's...he's slit her throat and cut her open," Quoth fills in, his voice tinged with sorrow. "There are pieces of her skin scattered around from where he opened her up. Her small intestines have been pulled out and tossed over her right shoulder..."

Intestines over the right shoulder...

...throat cut...

...ripped apart...

A sinking feeling wells in my chest. "I think I know who the murderer is. But it doesn't make any sense."

"Ambrose, how can you possibly know that?" Bree asks. "We know nothing about this monster except for the types of wounds he inflicts."

"Precisely. I've heard about these wounds before. What you're describing...they sound like the murders of Jack the Ripper."

29

BREE

Penny's silver cord hangs in the air above her body, its silver thread practically invisible. I touch the end – it's been severed, as if by a magical blade. Something about the cord tells me that Penny didn't become a ghost. She is gone. She can't tell us anything.

Ambrose's words echo inside my head as I call the police, sit through another tense interview with Hayes and Wilson while I come up with a plausible explanation for why both Mina and I have once again appeared at their crime scene, and they churn around and around through a tense taxi ride back to Grimwood with Ambrose floating excitedly in the seat beside me.

As soon as I'm back within the safety of Grimwood Manor's walls, I curl up in the snug with a cup of tea and flip open the booklet in Vera's box, landing on the biography of Jack the Ripper and his horrible crimes in Victorian London in 1888.

This is what Vera was trying to tell me with this book. But it still doesn't make any sense.

The booklet only has two paragraphs of text and a bunch of gruesome old photographs and letters, so I pull over my laptop

and do a web search for the Jack the Ripper murders. There are hundreds of websites describing every facet of the unsolved case in excruciating detail. My eyes flick over the autopsy reports of the first two victims – Polly Nichols and Annie Chapman.

Polly was found lying with her throat brutally cut from left to right, severing the spinal cord, windpipe, and gullet. Her abdomen had been cut open from the center of her bottom ribs along the right side, and under her pelvis was another jagged wound, and three smaller cuts down the right side of her abdomen. My hand flies to my mouth as I recall Vera's wounds. Ambrose is right – they were almost a perfect match.

The second Ripper victim is Annie, and she was found on her back with her legs bent up and her left arm across her breast. Her small intestines had been pulled out of a jagged cut in her abdomen and laid across her shoulder. Her neck had been savagely cut, as well. Just like Penny.

But it makes no sense. What does it mean? Is there a Jack the Ripper copycat killer? But so many of the details aren't correct – Jack killed his victims outside, in the street, at night. He chose women who were sleeping rough – although not necessarily prostitutes, as the media at the time claimed.

These murders are not taking place in the Ripper's stomping ground of Whitechapel, London, but in the sleepy county of Barsetshire.

Both Vera and Penny were killed on their own property. At Penny's house, the backdoor was open and there were two cups of coffee still warm on the kitchen table. Whoever Penny's killer was, she trusted them enough to let them inside.

Of course, there's another explanation that makes sense if magic is involved, but it's so terrifying and ridiculous that I can't even—

"Bree, are you okay?"

I glance up. Ambrose hovers in the doorway, his face a picture of misery. I'm reminded of the first day I arrived home from travelling, when we sat together in the snug and had a drink. And of the moment when he fell into me and I glimpsed into his memories, and *sensed* myself through his mind. I wonder what he senses in me now.

"I don't know if I'll ever be okay again." I run my hands over my face. "I wish I could bleach my eyeballs so I didn't have to see Penny and Vera like that, with their throats cut and those horrible expressions on their faces."

"I have never felt as lucky to be blind as I do with these murders," Ambrose says. "May I sit with you? I cannot claim to offer such comfort as—"

"Please. Come sit." I pat the cushions next to me. Ambrose is exactly who I need with me right now.

Ambrose sits, or rather hovers. His fingers graze my knee, searching for mine. I slide my fingers into his, enjoying the touch that is not quite touch, the warmth zapping through my body, taking away some of the edge off today's horror.

"I know it's terrifying, Bree. But at least one good thing has come out of today. We have an identity for our monster."

"No, we don't. All we know is that some sicko is pretending to be Jack the Ripper, and I—" I stop when Ambrose's hand squeezes my leg.

"Bree," he says my name softly, desperately. "You know that's not what we're dealing with."

I swallow. *That's exactly what I'm afraid of.*

"Okay, fine, yes. Someone has used the same magic I possess to resurrect Jack the Ripper, the way I did to Pax. And they are somehow using a Victorian serial killer to bump off anyone else who uses resurrection magic."

"Was that so hard to admit?"

To admit? No. To face? Hell fucking yes.

I set my laptop down beside me. "I have a question. How do you know about the Jack the Ripper murders? Didn't they happen after you died?"

"Between my adventures, I lived in this house," Ambrose explains. "I didn't have an income of my own beyond a meagre military stipend for the injury I obtained in service. I could not afford my own rooms. As you know, Cuthbert Van Wimple was a dear friend to me, and he allowed me to live as a houseguest in Grimwood when I was in England. I wrote my memoirs and travel books in this very room, and in the bedroom that was your childhood room. This house has always been one of my favorite places in the world.

"When I appeared here after my death, it seemed strange at first. It was not congruent with the stories of ghosts I've heard. Why should I haunt a home that isn't even mine? But in many ways, Grimwood *is* my home. It's the only stable place where I've laid my head and I felt truly safe and accepted."

I believe him, and that makes me so angry that I see red. From what little I've been able to find about him in Victorian accounts, Ambrose's contemporaries saw him as a novelty, a curiosity who demanded little more than their passing interest. Despite being one of the most accomplished pedestrian travellers of all time, no one ever took his writing or his discoveries seriously.

Ambrose continues. "When I was Living, I spent my days at Grimwood writing and my evenings in the drawing room with the Van Wimples and their guests. Cuthbert and Penelope always had houseguests and dinner parties, and the conversation was wonderful. So after I died, I did the same thing. Every night I'd go down to the drawing room and listen to the Van Wimples and their guests talk about the news of the day. For a long time, it was all about the wars in France. I find war so dreadfully boring, so I lost interest. But then, one day, they started to discuss a series of murders happening in Whitechapel in London."

I raise an eyebrow. "Jack the Ripper?"

"The one and same. The papers were reporting all kinds of grisly facts about the case, and Cuthbert took great delight in reading them out. Some of the imagery is burned in up here." Ambrose taps his forehead. "When you described the injuries, something about them reminded me of the Ripper's crimes."

"That makes sense. At least one thing about this makes sense." I rest my head in my hands. "Two people who had the same powers as me have been killed by Jack the Ripper. Does it mean that someone else is out there with these powers who wants us all dead? But why bring a dead serial killer back to life? And how is this magic user controlling the Ripper? Wasn't Jack the Ripper never caught? So how would someone know who he was to raise him in the first place?"

"I think we can safely say that whatever this Ripper is doing, he's after people with your powers," Ambrose suggests. "Which means we're right to be concerned for your safety. He could be after you next."

"He doesn't know what I am. And if he has the same register from Vera's shop as me, then my name won't appear on it. Vera gave me the moldavite. I didn't purchase it."

"So you don't think this killer knows about you?"

"If he did, we'd have seen him at Grimwood by now. Anyone with knowledge of resurrection powers who saw me pulling Pax out of the pond would know exactly what I am."

"But you have to be careful, Bree," Ambrose pleads. "You can't do anything to draw attention to yourself or to Pax or the fact you can see ghosts."

"I know." I swallow hard as a tremor cascades through my

body. I try to banish the vision of my body lying in a pool of blood after being slashed by the Ripper.

It's okay. It's going to be fine.

All I have to do is blend in, act completely normal, and not reveal to Jack the Ripper that I have resurrection power. Easy, right?

30

EDWARD

Another girl murdered.

A long-dead serial killer on the loose.

And how have I spent my day? Teaching a Roman oaf how to converse about art.

Brianna's lip trembles as she slumps onto the sofa, her fingers clutched around a whisky glass as she recalls the shambles of a day. I long to go to her and pull her in my arms and make her laugh to take away the fear. But I can't.

I'm useless.

And so I run.

I cannot bear to see Brianna hurting and know that I can do nothing.

I cannot abide the raw fear in Ambrose's eyes as he holds her, knowing that I could have given him the gift of being able to hold her for real but I chickened out. Again.

I tried to do the right thing. I tried to tell Brianna about Ambrose's manuscript, but she got that call from her parents. I saw how her face lit up when her father's face appeared on the screen, and all the pretty words I practiced dried on my lips.

She has so much pain and uncertainty in her life right now.

My betrayal will break her.

I *will* tell her. I will set her free of her obligation to care about me. But not yet. Not while she is hurting.

And so, as Pax dances around the room, sword drawn, rage burning in his eyes, I do precisely what the useless, lazy, decadent prince always does.

I slip away, unnoticed.

Not missed by any of them.

I leave, so that they don't have to suffer the misery of my presence.

I dive into the walls and climb until I'm in the attic. I hear a SQUEAK of indignation from the direction of the piano, but for once I'm too upset to care about that loathsome fuzzy hell-demon. I think of Ambrose's manuscript hidden inside, and of the frantic, scribbled note I'd written when we experimented with Bree's powers.

I was ready to sacrifice myself, but I still couldn't bear to tell Brianna the horrible thing I've done. I couldn't live with Ambrose's broken smile when he finds out the truth. I would rather die.

I bite down on my twisted, bitter thoughts that are turning me inside out.

I shove my head into the main power box.

The pain is immediate and exquisite.

It is precisely what I deserve.

It has been so long since I've felt physical pain that can match the emotional agony of being half in Brianna's world, but always without.

"More!" I yell, holding my head right in the center of the box.

I hold it there until I smell smoke, until I cannot feel anything anymore.

"Edward? Edward?"

I open one eye. It's a terrible idea. My body, such as it is, is on fire. And not in a fun, going to bed with a beautiful duchess way.

It's as if every single cell in my body is simultaneously afflicted by syphilis and the bubonic plague.

All I can see are bright red dots swimming in front of my eyelids. I squeeze my eye shut again, but it doesn't stop the red dots. Or the excruciating pain touching every corner of my ghost body.

"Edward, where are you?"

The voice sounds achingly familiar. Inside the ruins of my chest, something bright and hopeful stirs.

Brianna!

"Edward, please? I need to find you."

"Brianna—" I try to speak, but my lips hurt too much to move.

I open my eyes. And get the fright of my life when I see nothing at all. Even the red dots have disappeared.

"Help!" I croak out. "I've gone blind!"

"Oh, there you are." A hand grazes my arm, sending searing pain down my side. "And you haven't gone blind. You blew the circuit breakers and cut power to the entire street."

"Ah." That's the only sound I can muster through the ruin of my lips.

Why does my face feel like it's been stretched on a rack by the Spanish Inquisition?

Why does my chest feel like an elephant is dancing upon it?

"What, no smart-arse comments?" Brianna plonks down on the floor beside me. It takes me a few moments for my eyes to adjust to the dim light cast from the moon outside the dirt-smeared window. I'm still in the attic. She must have climbed up here to check the circuit breakers and found me like this. How mortifying. "You're in a bad way. Getting electrocuted can really mess a person up. Next time you want to get your jollies, come to me."

"I didn't—"

Her hand brushes my side, but my body is so battered from the electric shock that the slightest touch hurts. I flinch away. I don't deserve her sympathy. Or her ministrations.

Brianna withdraws her hand, her face falling.

I've hurt her.

Even trying to save her, I hurt her.

"I'm worried about you," she says.

"You should not think of me, Brianna. I cannot die as you can. I am nothing to be worried about."

I am nothing.

"Don't say that. You won't change how I feel about you. I care, Edward." Brianna bites her lip with determination, and it takes everything in me to hold my battered ghost body back from sweeping her into my arms and kissing that worry away. "You're hurting. And not just from the electricity. Don't lie to me. You've been hurting for a long time now and I don't know why. I wish you'd talk to me so I could help."

Don't lie to me.

Oh, my Brianna. If only you knew.

"Edward, talk to me. What's this about?"

"We should have been with you today." I settle for a part-truth. "I should never have talked Pax into staying at home to practice his manners. If this Strangler—"

"Ripper."

"—if this Ripper had still been at the house, you would need Pax and his sword. If things had gone differently and he wasn't there—"

I turn away. I can't bear to think that we could have lost her today, and it was because of me.

Again.

Brianna's hand falls half on, half inside my shoulder. It hurts, but I don't flinch away this time. I deserve the pain. "It's okay, Edward. Really."

"It is not okay. No matter what I do, I mess it up."

"What is this?" Her fingers tighten on my shoulder. She spins me around so I'm facing her again. Her champagne eyes taunt me from behind a curtain of her honey-brown hair. "This isn't like you, this...moroseness."

I snort, blowing a lock of dark hair out of my eye. "This *is* me. Ambrose will tell you. Pax will tell you. They have lived with me for many more years than you've been alive."

"How come I've never seen you like this?" she demands.

"Because...because I sense the same darkness inside you, and I know how it can consume a person utterly. I never want to be the reason for you to feel hopeless or helpless." I pause. "And because when I'm around you, the world feels bright and full of hope."

"Oh, *Edward.*" Brianna grips both shoulders with her hands. She shoves me until my knees give out and I sink to the floor once more. She drops down beside me. "That's how I feel when I'm around you. Bright and full of hope. So why are you hiding in the attic and hurting yourself? I thought you hated it up here?"

"When you told us to go away, it was I who had the brilliant idea to live in the attic." Suddenly, I *need* her to know this. "We could be close to you without disturbing you. Ambrose and Pax found me up here one day and saw that I was right, and so we stayed. At first, it was fine—"

"You're lying," Brianna says with a heart-melting smile.

I nod. "It was a nightmare, living among the dusty remnants of the house's history, breathing in Roman stench, and being subjected to Ambrose's constant good cheer. But it was a nightmare I could tolerate for you. But then..." I shudder at the thought of the horrors we endured under Ozzy's reign of terror. I glance over my shoulder to make sure he's not lying in wait to ambush an unsuspecting Brianna. But the little fuzzy hellspawn has made himself scarce.

Brianna leans forward suddenly, throwing her arms around me. The expression is so sudden and unexpected that she nearly knocks me over. She squeezes me so tight that one of her arms falls into me and I glimpse her memories – a snippet of the day after she told us to leave. Her feelings rush over me – lonely, afraid, guilty – as she searches the house all over, frantically calling our names, but we did not come out.

My fault. Always my fault.

"I'm so sorry," Brianna whispers, her words brushing my ghost-skin, hurting and healing in equal measure.

"You have nothing to be sorry for. I was a bother to you."

"I have so much to apologise for. I was being selfish when I told you to leave. I thought about myself and what I needed, and I didn't even consider what it must've been like for you to be tossed aside. I didn't know the lengths the three of you would go to to give me what I wanted, because you care about me so much..." She swallows once, twice. Saying these words is hard for her, but I don't understand why. After all, they are simply the truth. "You may be dead, and very, *very* annoying, but you still had feelings. And I...I forgot that. It was so wrong of me."

Now I'm making her feel awful about herself. This wasn't how this was supposed to go. What kind of a monster am I?

Brianna nuzzles into me. "Look at us, a couple of moody bitches. We need to put on some late 90s emo music and side-part our hair."

"None of those words make any sense to me." I run my hand through my dark curls. "It's taken me centuries to perfect the 'just rolled out of bed and fallen out a window' look. Don't you try to change me now, woman."

"I wouldn't dare."

"Did I ever tell you about my death?" I ask, suddenly desperate for her to know. I can't give her Ambrose's book, not now, not yet. But I can give her one gift, one piece of me that no one else has.

I have never told Brianna about my death, or my funeral.

I have never spoken of it to a single soul.

Pax was there, but he mistook the black-clad mourners for Gallic warriors and was too busy trying to stab them to pay much attention, a fact that I have been eternally grateful for. The three witches were also present, although for all their faults they do adhere to a certain measure of ghostly privacy, and have never brought it up.

"I thought you couldn't remember?" Brianna says. "That's what you always told me, that ghosts can't remember their own death."

"I think that we choose not to," I say. "I believe that in death we learn so many painful, terrible truths about the futility of life that we cannot bear to hold those truths to our bosom. But I am an old ghost now. I have remembered pieces over the years. More, since you came into our lives."

"Do you want to tell me?" Brianna leans her back against a stack of old boxes Mike moved up here a few years ago. I rest my head on her shoulder, lending strength from the fizzing spark of our bodies touching.

I take a shuddering breath.

"I do not remember how I came to fall out the window. That will remain an eternal mystery. But I do remember the fall. I remember the horrible *crunch* when my body landed in the garden. But I did not die straight away."

"Oh, Edward." Brianna's voice cracks.

I stroke my fingers along her leg, wishing by all the gods I never believed in that I could cross the final barrier that separates us. "I lay on the bare, cold earth for hours staring at the stars streaking across the sky. I cried out, but I don't know if my words were only inside my head."

"Didn't anyone notice you missing?"

"I could see the lamps flickering in the windows," I say bitterly. "I could hear their laughter and singing. Inside, my friends drank my wine and smoked my opium and never even thought to come and look for me."

"Oh, *Edward*."

I gaze up at her as a fat tear rolls down her cheek. I reach up a finger to blot it away, but I'm not powerful enough. It drops from the tip of her chin and falls right through me.

I continue. "I faded as the sun rose, until the pain in my body became a ghost itself, until I somehow freed my spirit from the confines of my broken sack of bones and skin and sinew. My body lay outside for three days. I wandered through the house, yelling at my friends to go outside and find me, mourn me, miss me. *Anything*. But they could not hear me. The only person who *could* hear me was an extremely annoying beast wearing Roman garb, who informed me that I was dead."

"I can imagine that was very frustrating," Brianna says, a hint of a smile on her face.

"Can you now? Can you imagine standing in the shadows,

watching your body rot in the garden, while your so-called friends swill your absinthe, bathe in the fine French wine you collected in your secret cellar, eat your game hens, and carry on as if it mattered not whether you were present at all? And what was worse was how they talked about me. They spoke of the great con they had laid upon the prince of the realm, putting up with his company so they could partake of his riches. They said my poetry was terrible."

"That's a horrible feeling when your friends betray you." Brianna places her hand over mine. I know she's thinking about Dani and Alice. They may have made up, but Brianna won't so easily forget all the horrendous things Alice did to her in school. I know that I won't.

"The most wretched, horrible truth is that they were right about me," I say. "I saw it all from the outside, just how shallow and vapid my life had become. I left court because I wanted to be more than the life my father had laid out for me, and yet I had squandered my gifts on sin and debauchery. I enjoyed it all immensely, of course, but my friends were not the wild thinkers and brilliant artists I had talked up in my mind. They were not creating, but destroying. They had destroyed a piece of me, and I would never have the chance to get it back."

"Why have you never told me this before?" Brianna asks, her fingers dancing over mine in a most distracting way.

"Because I know what you've read about me in the history books. Edward the rake. Edward the wastrel. Edward the disgraced prince who squandered his fortune and made a mockery of everything his father stood for. And I am proudly these things, but I wanted to be so much more. I wanted to be an artist because I craved something that I could not get within the stuffy rules and expectations of court life. All the backstabbing politics and pointless posturing wore down my spirit. I craved a deeper meaning to life. I wanted color, and freedom, and *passion*. And yes, sex and opium and loud, satanic music."

"Of course," Brianna smiles.

"And so, I became drawn to the bohemian world of poetry and painting, and I loved it. I thought I had found my place in the world. But on the eve of my death, I saw...my father was right all along. I became exactly who he said I was – a useless profligate who contributed nothing of substance to the world."

"That's not true," Brianna says. "You can't say that you've given the world nothing. You have a pamphlet of poetry published, which is more than Ambrose can say about his book—"

Please, please don't mention Ambrose's book.

I clear my throat to continue my story. "On the third day after my impression of the flight of a preening ostrich, Lady Pendlehurst began to complain about an odour. Yet still, they did not look for me. It was only when a wild dog wandered into the grounds and tried to chew my leg off that they came outside to shoo it away and found my body."

Brianna's fingers tighten over mine, her whole body stiffening.

I cannot bear to look at her, to see the pity in her eyes. Brianna is never supposed to pity me.

"And so, a prince was dead, but the country didn't mourn him. I had made my good friend Hugh Bancroft the executor of my estate so that he might make arrangements for my funeral."

"Hugh Bancroft, the poet and essayist?"

"The very same. It is he who commissioned that ghastly monstrosity out there." I point to the dusty dorma window that looks out over the cemetery and my mausoleum.

"I wouldn't have had quite so many cherubs," Brianna says. "But I think the mausoleum is very *you*."

"Hmmmph."

"Go on with your story. You were telling me about your funeral. Your friend made the arrangements and commissioned the mausoleum."

I nod. "A fair crowd did show up, I'll grant that. All of the famous painters and sculptures and poets flocked to Grimdale for the spectacle. Curious people from all over the country showed up, mainly in the hopes of a glimpse at the king. But neither my father nor my brother bothered to turn up."

"Oh, Edward."

I wave a hand. It was to be expected – the final humiliation from a man who never loved me for who I am, but only saw me as a vessel for his own immortality. "I did not miss them. Pax and I watched from the windows in your old bedroom as the mourners crowded into the cemetery. The air that day was beautifully scented with hyacinth and calla lily. The house brimmed with activity as my so-called friends made toasts and composed sonnets and painted portraits in my honor. And at the center of it all was Hugh, who doled out my gold for a bountiful feast and a three-day party at the estate. That was where I presume my so-called friends emptied the rest of my cellar. That's why I can't remember where it is – the trauma of the funeral has robbed me of the memory."

"I think it's nice that all your friends were there," Brianna says. "I think that when I die, I'd like my funeral to be a fun party, not a sad, sombre occasion."

I squeeze her hand so hard that she yelps. "We're not talking about your death. We're not going to even think about that. And you don't want a funeral like mine, filled with people who only pretended to like me, but who really liked my money and my influence and my opium."

"But Hugh—"

"Hugh was the worst of them. He gave a moving speech at my funeral. Perhaps you've read it? It's printed in all the biographies of my life. He concludes with his most famous poem, written to honor my life – 'Thou comest a thief.'"

"I know it well," Brianna closes her eyes as she recites that fateful opening line. "'In somber shades, where twilight's tendrils creep, Where whispers hush and shadows softly weep…'"

I slap my hand over her mouth. "I cannot bear to hear those words spoken. For they are *mine*. Hugh stole that poem from me. It was my greatest achievement, my finest work. And he claimed it as his own."

"Edward, I'm so sorry. I didn't know." Brianna squeezes my hand again. Her fingers fall ever so slightly through me. How I wish I could feel what Pax feels, her flesh on mine, her heat and breath and *life*. "I didn't know. It's a beautiful poem."

"Hmmmph." All the more fitting that my final work should be my own funeral dirge, and should make another man's fortune.

Even now, the hurt of Hugh's betrayal burns bright and hot in my ghostly veins. And yet, I know that I am no better man. I have betrayed my best and closest friend.

I will make this right. I will give Brianna Ambrose's book.

But not yet.

I'm a coward. A rotten, profligate *coward*. But as I gaze upon Brianna's perfect face, I cannot bear to be her monster. She believes I am redeemable. When she knows the truth, she will see me only as my father saw me, and she will be right.

I'll give the book to her soon, Ambrose. I promise. I am sorry that I'm robbing you of these precious days you could be with her as a Living. But in your kindness, I will have these final days with her, these last precious memories where she believes I am capable of goodness.

Before I break her heart.

31
BREE

"You look handsome." I stand back and admire Pax.

"I *do* have excellent taste," Mina says from her position on the bed, lost amidst a pile of clothing. She insisted on being the one to dress me and Pax for the party. Before Mina became a bookshop-owning, vampire-slaying, amateur sleuth, she studied fashion and even worked for a famous designer in New York City. Mina may be blind, but her fashion sense is off-the-charts cool. She scoured the charity shops to find our outfits and altered them herself until they were perfectly tailored.

I decided not to wear togas, as it would be too distracting for Pax to wear something that his society dictated wasn't for him. He kept pointing out that women aren't supposed to wear togas, and none of my protests about feminism and costumes could convince him that I wouldn't be struck down by the gods.

Instead, we're pretending to have misheard the theme, and dressing as if we're attending a 'yoga' party. I even called Dani and cleared the costume idea with her and she said that Alice would find it hilarious, so we're rolling with it. Mina found Pax a black tank top with mandala designs all over it, and a pair of tight yoga pants that leave nothing to the imagination. I've got a matching yoga set in an emerald-green marbled design. Mina stencilled, "We're ready for Alice's Yoga Party. Let's start stretching!" onto the back of both our tops. She even took a pair of plain white canvas sneakers and painted the same emerald marble design onto them for me. I suspect Quoth the artist might've had a hand in that.

"I look like a Gaul with these ridiculous trousers," Pax tugs at the yoga pants.

"You look hot as fuck," I grin, drooling a little in my mouth as he turns, revealing the curve of his muscled thighs and arse through the skintight yoga pants.

"There is no belt to hang my sword."

I grab the hilt before Pax can shove the tip of his sword through the Lycra. "That's by design. People in the twenty-first century don't tend to carry swords with them to parties."

"But what happens when someone insults your intelligence or implies you have sexual relations with your mother?"

I grin. "Then you destroy them with your wit. That's how Dani and I survived high school. Barely."

"I will be by your side the whole night," Edward says to Pax in what I'm guessing is an Edward idea of a reassuring tone. "I will whisper witty repartee into your ear so that you will not resort to your uncouth Roman insults."

"You will *not*." I put my hands on my hips. "We already agreed that you and Ambrose are staying home."

"Is Edward being difficult?" Mina asks.

"Very."

"I don't see why I can't go to the party," Edward sticks his lips out. "I am the king of parties. The last party I attended was your seventeenth birthday sleepover, and you didn't mind my presence then."

"That was because Dani was the only person who came, and she knew you existed."

"It might be good if Edward came," Ambrose suggests. "He could stick close to Pax and help smooth over any etiquette misunderstandings. It might give you a chance to relax."

I squeeze his hand. "And I suppose you want to come, too?"

"Well, it would be awfully lonely here at the house by myself while the three of you are off having fun..."

"And with Jack the Ripper on the loose, I don't believe the Roman should be the only one charged with protecting you." Edward raises his fist. "I was quite the pugilist. I used to fight in underground London boxing clubs as 'The Dark Prince.' I wore a mask, of course, because my handsome features would certainly give away my identity and bring a mountain of trouble down upon my head. But I am not afraid to get these hands dirty in Brianna's defense. I am certain I could take out a cretinous monster if the mood so struck me."

I smile. I like this version of Edward – the prince who is tawdry, spoiled, and utterly certain of his own superiority. I haven't seen much of morose, pouty Edward since our talk in the attic, and I hope that means he's feeling better about himself. "*Fine.* You both can come. But you have to promise that you're not going to do anything spooky or annoying or reckless. I don't want you to talk to me or expect me to talk to you. I want everything to be perfect for Alice."

I want everything to be perfect for Dani.

"Don't you worry." Ambrose's grin lights up his whole face. "We will be the picture of discretion. Won't we, Edward?"

"If I managed to keep my affair with the Queen of France secret for four centuries, I think I can be trusted not to open my mouth at this party." Edward's familiar smirk warms my heart. "Oops."

I check my hair while Edward gives Pax one last pep talk

about proper party behavior. ("Remember, always pass the opium pipe to the left. I once passed it to the right by accident and it was the most terrible faux pas.") Then I said goodbye to Father Bryne, who was heading out to the pub shortly. I checked he had his spare key for the back door, and locked up behind me.

The three of us walk the long way into Grimdale – it's well-lit with streetlamps, so it's less likely the Ripper would attack us. Pax walks ahead, his eyes darting everywhere. Ambrose walks beside me, his arm looped in mine and his stick tapping out a faint rhythm, and Edward slouches along in the rear. Although I can't help but notice that he has a long rapier hanging from his belt.

"Pax isn't the only one who knows how to use a sword." Edward winks at me as he grabs his codpiece lasciviously.

"Careful. You could put someone's eye out with that," I shoot back.

I've seen the sword on Edward a few times before. He occasionally draws it out to have sword fights with Pax, although Edward's fancy footwork and insistence on 'gentlemanly rules of combat' tend to lose to Pax's 'stab everything' technique. I don't know how Edward can make the ghost sword appear and disappear at will when he didn't die with it, but that's ghost mojo for you. It doesn't always make sense.

All I know is that I'm happy at least one person has a weapon on them tonight.

My stomach twists with nerves. Jack the Ripper could be around any corner. Since Pax was at home during Penny's murder (and both Mr. Pitts and Maggie saw him performing his military drills around the garden), the police seem to have dropped him as a potential suspect for now. But they don't seem to be any closer to an answer. We're not doing any better. We called two of the other women on the list, but neither answered their phones. Mina and I have been scouring the internet for information on the Ripper case, but nothing tells us how to catch him or figure out where he's going to strike next.

We may know the identity of our monstrous killer, but we're no closer to stopping him.

I tense as we pass the corner with the blocked-up railway tunnel, but the ghost of the Squashed Navvy is nowhere to be seen. My eyes keep darting over the shadows, expecting a killer to jump out at us at any moment.

We should have asked Maggie to drop us off at the party. Or Dani could have picked me up.

We make it to High Street without incident. When we skirt around the village green, the three witches chase us from the pub.

"You look like a troupe of travelling minstrels," Agnes glowers at my skintight yoga pants.

"Why, thank you." I beam, squeezing Pax's arm before he can get stabby.

"That wasn't a compliment. Do you know what they did to women who travelled with minstrels in my time, girlie?"

"Showered them in riches and minted their faces on coins?" Now that we're so close to the museum that I can hear the party, I'm feeling less afraid and more sassy. *We're going to have a fun night. We deserve it after everything that's going on.*

"I think they look very nice," Mary says affectionately. "Especially Pax. He looks as if he's going to give Alice a very *large* birthday package."

"Oh, yes, she'll enjoy unwrapping him." Lottie licks her lips as her gaze travels over Pax's yoga pants. "I think we'll accompany you to this party. Just to make sure you get on okay—"

Agnes grabs Lottie by the collar. "You will not go anywhere near a place where people dress like *that*. You don't know what kind of shenanigans they'll get up to."

"I like shenanigans!" Lottie protests.

"*No*. Now, back to the pub window with ye; I see the chef bringing out haddock and chips. That's all the excitement you'll get tonight."

As Agnes hurries the girls back to the pub, she looks back over her shoulder at me and winks.

Bless you, Agnes.

We continue down High Street until we reach the Roman Museum. It's housed in a beautiful old Regency building that used to belong to the Van Wimple family. Cuthbert Van Wimple used it to store his collection of ancient artifacts – mainly from Ancient Rome, but also from Egypt, Greece, and Turkey. When Cuthbert's descendants foisted the estate onto my family, they donated the building and all the ancient 'junk' as they called it to the village for a museum. The museum is quite popular because of the eclectic mix of artifacts. Twenty years ago the council was able to give it a £1.2 million upgrade with a glass and steel extension for more exhibition space and to host events. It's this part of the building where Alice's party is taking place.

We circle around to the rear and climb the ramp, surrounded by glittering lanterns. People spill out of the glass doors, holding glasses of something green and disgusting look- ing. A waiter at the door dressed in a white loincloth holds out a platter to me. Pax grabs seven meatballs on sticks and hands one to me. He stuffs the rest in his mouth, toothpicks and all, until he sees Edward glaring at him, then he proceeds to pull the toothpicks out with his pinkie quirked to the side.

"This place is wild," I whisper.

"Describe it to me," Ambrose says.

"Allow me," Edward says. "The room is filled with museum display cases, lit from above and packed with all manner of ancient junk. And around these cases are squeezed at least a hundred young people, most of them wearing their bedsheets. The music comes not from a band of minstrels but from a single guy with a table and a large spinning disc. One woman has snakes entwined in her hair. I hope they're fake. I see many swords made of strange and useless materials. That man's sword is actually drooping. Why if he wishes to see a real man's sword, I shall oblige him..."

I didn't even know there were this many young people in Grimdale. Alice has always been popular, but I thought that kind of popularity faded once you're no longer at school. I remember that she read at Oxford, so some of these people must be her uni friends.

I feel a stab of something that's half jealousy, half empathy. I never went to uni because I didn't know what I wanted to do with my life apart from travel. I still don't. But Alice was always the smart girl, dux of the school, top of every class, leader of every school club and committee. And this bright girl with her whole life ahead of her is back here for the same reason as me – because her dad is sick, and he needs her.

Only Alice's dad is actually *here*. He's standing in the corner with a glass of orange juice and a dazed expression on his face. Whereas mine is galavanting around Europe like he doesn't actually have Parkinson's. And I miss him so bad that it *hurts*.

"Bree? I'm so happy you could come."

I turn to see Alice standing beside a plinth containing a towering cake shaped like the Colosseum. She's dressed as Queen Cleopatra in a flowing white linen dress, a collar of pretty glass beads, and a beaded headdress with a snake in the middle. Her dark eyes are rimmed in kohl. She looks *amazing*.

"I must see this costume of yours. Turn around," Alice commands in that clipped, demanding tone of hers. Alice's voice used to always set my teeth on edge, but I'm starting to wonder if the way she talks *isn't* a derisive voice she reserves for people she hates, but just the way she is.

I turn obediently, showing off Mina's stencilled message. Alice cracks up laughing. My heart flips.

I never thought I get Alice Agincourt to laugh *with* me, not at me.

"Your costumes are brilliant," she says. "I'm so glad you came. Here, you have to try the Mint Julius Caesar."

She grabs two of the slime-green cocktails off a waiter's tray and shoves them into Pax and my hands. I take a sip through the green straw and immediately wish I hadn't.

"Well, that's...um..." I search for a polite term.

"It tastes like Druid scrotum," Pax says.

Another barking laugh from Alice. "Yeah, it's a bit of a failure, but the rest of the party is awesome."

"We're happy to be here," I say, and I genuinely mean it. "I hope it's okay that I brought a date. I don't think I've officially introduced you. Alice, this is Pax. Pax, this is Alice, the birthday girl."

"Nice to meet you, Pax." Alice looks him over with a bemused expression as she holds out her hand.

"Salvē." Pax grabs her forearm. I wince. Edward appears over his shoulder and whispers something in Pax's ear. Pax squares his jaw as he realizes that he got the handshake wrong, so he pulls Alice into one of his patented, spine-crushing bear hugs.

"It's so good to meet you!" Pax cries. "And no hard feelings about the duck pond! I was damp, you were damp. We are friends now, yes?"

"I...can't...breathe..." Alice wheezes.

"Let her go now, Roman," Edward coaches. "You don't want things to get awkward."

No, we definitely wouldn't want that.

Pax sets Alice back on the floor and straightens her headdress. He then gets down on one knee. "I will serve you, as I serve all friends of Bree."

"Um, sure." Alice looks a bit miffed. Behind her, a couple of her guy friends see Pax, and they get down on their knees, too.

"We serve you, O illustrious queen Alice," they intone, bowing repeatedly. Pax grins at me, and I can't help but grin back.

Are we actually going to pull this off?

"Arise, servants," Alice waves her empty glass at them. "And refill my vessel."

The men rush off to the bar to fulfill her whim. Alice extends her hand to Pax, which is probably a tactical error since he pulls her into another soul-squashing hug.

"Are you okay?" I ask as he lets her go and she staggers back, dazed.

"I'm fine," Alice breathes. "If you'll excuse me, I'm going to go sit down until my spine twists back the right way around again."

"Thank you for behaving super normally," I say sarcastically. Pax beams at what he thinks is praise. He's never had much skill for sarcasm.

"Are you *certain* we can trust this Alice?" Pax stares at his cocktail. "I wouldn't feed this drink to my enemies."

I spy a potted plant in the corner – the poor defenseless roots are already swimming in green liquid. I tip mine into the pot, and Pax adds his. Hopefully, the plant is the only victim of tonight's cocktails. "Come on, let's go to the bar and get a real drink."

The bar is set up on a display case containing a massive Egyptian sarcophagus decorated in gold and lapis lazuli. Edward appears at Pax's shoulder again, wincing as a guy in a plastic centurion helmet walks through him. He leans in close as Pax peruses the drinks selection.

He really is taking his job as Pax's etiquette trainer seriously.

"We have an open bar tonight. What will you have?" the bartender asks him. Pax eyes the handle of beer that the guy next to him has just accepted.

"Civilised men drink wine," Edward reminds him.

"Yes, wine!" Pax bangs his fist on the glass. "In my army days, we had a daily ration of a wine called *posca*, which was so sour we had to sweeten it with honey or hold our noses while we drank it."

"They don't have that swill here," Edward whispers. "They offer only fancy wines."

"Oh, I didn't mean to say that." Pax's face lights up as the bartender stares at him quizzically. "I love fancy wine. I know all about fancy wine. I'll have a cup of your finest Falernian wine."

"Falernian?" the bartender frowns. "Is that like a Riesling?"

"We'll have two glasses of Sav," I say, saving Pax before the situation escalates. The bartender looks relieved. He sets two wine glasses on the case in front of us and pours a small serving of wine into each. I grab them both and hand one to Pax. He stares at the glass in horror.

"What is this?"

"It's wine."

"This is not wine." Pax frowns into the glass. "It is cold. And it has not been mixed with water. And where are the grape pips? What fun is drinking wine if you can't spit grape pips at your friends?"

"I assure you that drinking wine is its own reward." Edward makes an apologetic face at me. "Sorry, Brianna. We hadn't quite got to wine yet. I'm still working on getting him to fold napkins into the shapes of various barnyard animals."

"Very useful," I whisper back.

Pax is still inspecting his wine. "And how do I get my face into this glass?"

"Um...you don't?" I hold the glass by the stem. "You tip your head back and drink it like this."

I demonstrate. The wine tastes cool and refreshing and delicious. Edward watches me with a twinkle of admiration in his dark eyes.

Pax puckers his lips, tips his head back, and somehow manages to slosh wine down the front of his yoga tank.

"Do it like a *gentleman,*" Edward instructs him.

Pax goes for another sip. This time, he sticks his pinkie out.

"Much better," Edward murmurs.

I can't help it. I burst into giggles. All around us, the party surges as the DJ switches to a Sam Smith remix that gets the crowd pumping.

"This music is enchanting." Beside me, Ambrose sways gently. "Would you like to dance?"

"I'd love that," I say truthfully.

Pax crowds in beside me, not holding my hand but instead using his battering ram of a body to ensure no one walks through Ambrose or Edward as we strut onto the floor. Around us, people giggle as they see my and Pax's costumes. My veins bubble with joy. *I can't believe we get to be here. We get to be a part of this.*

We find a corner near a Roman statue of the war god Mars, on the left of the DJ booth. It's less crowded here – not so many people to accidentally walk through ghosts. I take Ambrose by the hand.

To my surprise, Ambrose's fingers close around mine. His other hand settles possessively into the small of my back, and he manages to spin me wildly in a circle.

"I was quite the dancer when I was alive," he says with a

mischievous twinkle in his eye as he spins me again, then dips me, his ghostly hands holding me tight thanks to the moldavite in my purse. "I can feel the music in my veins."

"And what's great about dancing with a ghost is that we can't trip over each other's feet," I say as I misstep and kick my foot right through his shin. It must have hurt Ambrose, but he doesn't react. His eyes are closed, dark lashes tangled together. A lock of hair escapes from his ponytail and drapes over his face, and I don't think he's ever looked more beautiful to me.

His dance doesn't exactly fit the crunchy industrial music the DJ is spinning, but Ambrose makes it work. Once again, I catch a glimmer of what it would have been like to travel with this man, who could bend and shape himself to fit in anywhere, with anyone. We would have had so much fun together...

"Are you trying to make the woman sick with all that twirling and skipping?" Edward scoffs. "That's not how I dance. *This* is how one treats a lady on the dance floor."

Before I can protest, Edward has inserted himself between me and Ambrose. He whirls me around so my back is against his naked chest. One hand wraps around my waist, holding me in place, while the other strokes languidly over my cheek, my neck. He grinds his hips in time to the pounding beat, and the reckless, craven part of me arches back and grinds against him.

"This isn't how you danced in the seventeenth century!" I glare at Edward over my shoulder, even as my body opens up for him and a dark, wanton ache pulses in my stomach. "You were all minstrels and hey nonny nonny."

"I didn't say this was how everyone dances." Edward's lips brush the bare skin on my neck as his hands wander down my body. He palms my breasts, teasing my nipples through the fabric until I gasp. "I said that this is how *I* dance."

"No," Pax elbows Edward and Ambrose out of the way. He grabs my hands in his and starts stomping the floor with his feet. "*This* is how you dance. And then you throw your woman over your shoulder and take her back to your tent and ravish her."

I burst out laughing as Pax leads me in a ridiculous Roman jig and Edward stares daggers at him. All three of them are completely ridiculous. But everyone on the dance floor looks ridiculous. No one is paying any attention to weird Bree and her invisible friends.

"I don't understand," Pax frowns at the DJ as the song winds down. "Where is the music coming from? I don't see any nubile slave girls with lutes and bells around their ankles."

"See, the thing is, we don't have slaves any longer. Instead, we use this wonderful invention called the Spotify playlist," I grin as I spin him around.

The song switches to a drum and bass version of a Sisters of Mercy song. *This must be Dani's influence.* I pump my fist in the air and get *fucking down,* throwing my hair around as I bounce on my heels. Pax copies me, but only manages to look like a chicken pecking at the air. Ambrose spins in slow circles, moving his hands in expressive ways. And Edward is swaying, his hands roaming over my body in a way that makes heat skip over my skin.

I'm having *fun.*

I'm actually having *fun.*

So this is what it feels like to be normal? I'll take more of it, please.

Pax lifts me up and spins me in a circle, so fast the faces in the room blur together. The only faces that rise over the crowd are my two ghosts. Edward smiles at me with gentlemanly charm as he spins Ambrose around in languid circles.

Pax lets me down, scooping me into his arms and crushing his lips to mine. The kiss steals my breath.

When I pull back, a couple of people wolf-whistle. My

cheeks flush with heat, but before I have time to think, I'm back in Edward's clutches, his trim, god-like body fitting so perfectly around mine.

"Just wait until we get you home tonight," Edward whispers as his hands skim my thighs. "Perhaps the four of us may dance some more."

My mouth falls open in surprise. "You mean that you're ready to come back—"

Edward spins me into Ambrose's arms, and I lose myself in my adventurer's touch as his hands grip my neck, his lips crushing mine in a hot, passionate kiss. Behind me, Pax bites my neck, his hands indecently roaming over my tight Lycra.

I'm so caught up in their touches, I don't even notice there are other people in the room. That is until Pax spins me around, and a pair of piercing dark eyes catch me from across the room.

Dani.

She raises a wine glass to her lips and sips. Her eyes don't leave my face. My stomach churns. I pull away from Pax. *Are we making a spectacle?*

Dani's lips curl ever so slightly into a tight smile. *She's trying.*

And so should I.

"Wait here," I whisper. "I have to do something."

Pax whirls around and sees Dani. He narrows his eyes. "I should come with you," he says. "You may need me to protect you."

"I'll be fine. You get another drink for Edward and Ambrose to sniff. I promise I'll be right back."

I lean up and peck him on the cheek, letting my lips linger for a moment before pulling away.

I push through the crowd. I recognize a couple of faces from high school. Kelly glares at me from a sofa in the corner, but tonight I don't have a thought to spare for her.

I reach Dani and lean against the display case next to her. It's filled with giant stone phalluses. Because Romans.

"I see that Pax hasn't stabbed anyone yet." Dani leans against the case, her fingers wrapped around the stem of one of the horrific cocktails. She's wearing a deep purple drapey Grecian-style dress that looks amazing on her.

"Edward and Ambrose are proving a stabilizing influence. They're here too. I hope that's okay?"

"I can't exactly kick them out," Dani says.

"I guess not. But apart from crushing your girlfriend's spine with his hug, Pax has been behaving himself. Edward's etiquette lessons are paying off."

"Yes, I've never been happier knowing that the success of Alice's party is in the hands of a long-dead royal prince who died after drinking all the absinthe and falling out a window."

"You're right." I groan. "This is going to be a complete disaster."

I meet Dani's eyes. I hold my breath.

The silence stretches between us.

"Hey, as long as he doesn't have a sword down his trousers, what harm can he do?" Dani says, Listen, Bree, I wanted to say—"

"No, I'm the one who should—"

We both crack up laughing. Dani takes my hand and squeezes it. "I guess we said everything we had to say the other day. Thank you so much for making an effort. I'm really happy you're here tonight. I saw you dancing out there. You looked like you were having lots of fun."

"I was." I beam. "I am. I know it's crazy, Dani. I know that Pax is not meant for our world. But to hold him and touch him and kiss him...What if I can figure out how I did it? What if I can bring all three of them back?"

"What then?" Dani tilts her head. She looks genuinely curious. "Do you date three guys at once? Does death mean nothing anymore? Do you put me out of a job?"

She says it lightly, but I can tell the question is serious.

"I don't know. I don't know what any of this means. The only thing I do know is..." I swallow. "I think that I'm falling—"

The terrifying thought I'm about to voice is drowned out by a commotion on the other side of the room.

A swoop of Lycra.

Pax.

Oh, ghost-balls.

I dive into the crowd, Dani right behind me. Pax has shoved some poor guy in a purple toga up against one of the display cases. His hands are wrapped around the terrified dude's throat.

"Pax, you must unhand him," Edward urges him. "Brianna is here. She will sort everything out."

"Pax, *please*," Ambrose begs. He swings his cane at Pax's legs but somehow misses and hits one of the waiters, who topples over and smashes into one of the display cases, sending drinks flying everywhere.

"What's going on?" I cry, grabbing Pax's forearm and tugging it uselessly. It was like trying to move a tree with a teaspoon.

"This foul creature dares to infiltrate this symposium," Pax growls, his hands. "He *dares* to wear the colors of the emperors."

"Pax," I try to use my most soothing voice, even though I'm *shaking* with terror. I have to get Pax to calm down before he kills this guy. "What are you talking about? He's wearing a costume. Remember, we talked about this."

Pax takes one beefy hand off the guy's throat and reaches for me. I think that I've reached him, but instead, he curls his hand into a fist and smashes the display case. Someone screams. An alarm starts to wail. Pax roots around inside the display, heedless to the glass sticking out of his forearm. He grabs an ancient gladius from its cushion and presses it to the guy's throat.

"Pax, *stop.*"

"You absurd Roman!" Edward wails. "You're ruining *everything.*"

I wrap my arms around Pax's forearm, putting all my body weight into dragging him off. But he's too huge and too determined. Bloodlust stains his pale blue eyes. I can tell that I've lost him. This was a mistake, bringing him here with all these people wearing his culture as costumes, all these artifacts that are so much more to him than objects in cages.

He's stuck in a place between worlds, between the living and the dead. And I can't reach him.

"Only Druids wear their hair like that," Pax growls. "He's an enemy, a soldier of the monster. I won't let them take you from me, the way they took my men."

"He's not a Druid, Pax," Dani says gently, coming up beside me. "His name is Brent. He's a software engineer. That hairstyle is called a man bun."

"Hmmmph, nothing manly about it."

Dani's eyes burn into me, begging me to sort this out. But there's nothing I can do. It crashes into me then – the futility of my hope.

I've been trying to make Pax into someone he's not. But this is who he is – the warrior born of blood and violence.

He doesn't belong here.

And neither do I.

"Please," Brent chokes out. "Call the cops. Get him off me. Please..."

"What are you saying about me, Druid?" Pax roars.

I rest my head against his arm, tears falling down my face. "Pax, *please...*"

"Pax!" Ambrose yells.

Several people stagger back.

"What was that?"

Ambrose never, *ever* raises his voice. But he'd yelled so loudly that it penetrated into the Living world. The shock of it wakes Pax up from his stupor. He shakes his head as he turns to face Ambrose. Ambrose raises his stick, maybe to slap Pax's knuckles, maybe to gesticulate at him.

"You can't do this, Pax. Look at Bree. You're upsetting her—"

Ambrose's cane catches on another waiter's tray, sending the drinks flying. A scream tears through the room.

I whirl around. My heart sinks as I see Alice.

Her beautiful white dress is covered in sticky green alcohol. She screeches again as she totters in her heels. She reaches out to grab hold of something to prevent her from toppling over. Unfortunately, the only thing arm's distance away is the towering Colosseum cake.

SPLAT.

"No." Alice cries as her hand sinks through the cake, knocking over the stands that hold up the different layers.

As she collapses into it, the top layer slides off its plate and lands on her head.

The room falls silent, except for the wailing alarm.

Icing drips down Alice's face.

The alarm wails.

Pax drops Brent, who scrambles under the broken display case and hides amongst his friends.

Ambrose freezes. "What did I do?" he breathes.

"Nothing, Ambrose. Nothing at all," Edward says as his eyes meet mine, those dark orbs reflecting my own horror.

Pax drops the priceless ancient sword on the floor. "Bree, I..."

Alice's eyes fall on Pax, and then me. All the friendliness that's built between us shatters into rage. "Bree." She spits my name between gritted teeth. Icing drips from her chin. "I would appreciate it if you and your boyfriend left."

I say weakly. "It was an accident. Pax thought—"

"Just *go,* Bree." Dani moves to help Alice. She glares up at me, and there's nothing of my old friend in her eyes.

Tears streak down my cheeks. I look over at Pax, then Edward, then Ambrose.

I turn on my heel and flee.

32

BREE

The minute my feet hit the concrete ramp outside, I know that I can never run fast enough to get away from this horror. The voices rise up behind me, the hum of their disdain coalescing into a hive, buzzing under my skin.

Freak. Psycho. Isn't she the one who used to have all those invisible friends?

My feet churn, but it feels like I'm running through syrup. My heart hammers as if I've already run a marathon. I have – I've spent the last seven years running from *this exact thing*, and I thought I was safe. I thought I could finally relax, could finally have a normal life, but of course, I'm wrong.

It's all my fault. I let them in. I let myself develop feelings for them. I let myself *hope*.

"Bree, please, don't run away," Ambrose cries out from behind me.

"Don't come after me," I sob as my sneakers slide over the uneven cobbles of Main Street. "I don't want to talk to you."

"Bree, I am sorry that I hurt the Druid." Pax's boots clomp on the cobbles as he chases after me.

"You need not concern yourself, Brianna," Edward calls. "Why, at my parties, someone falling into the cake was the beginning of a great night."

Their voices rise inside me, and suddenly all the fear and all the pain I've been shoving down since I got back to Grimdale coalesces into a white-hot ball of *rage*.

I whirl around. The three of them pull up, not expecting me to face them. Ambrose falls into Edward, knocking him through a post box.

"I *told* you how important this night was to me." I ball my hands into fists. Angry tears burn trails down my face. "I *told* you that if anything went wrong tonight, I'd lose Dani as a friend forever."

"But—"

"No buts. This is the *same shit* all over again. You're doing the same thing that you did back in high school."

"It wasn't Pax's fault," Ambrose says. "He doesn't understand."

"You're right. It's *not* Pax's fault. He's a two-thousand-year-old warrior who's been thrust into a world completely foreign from the one he knows. He doesn't understand how to act, how to dress, how to *be*. All of this is my fault. I actually believed that we could pull this off. I thought that you guys wanted to be with me, even if it meant being in my time, with my rules, but tonight has made it clear to me that we can't ever make this work. I'm from a completely different world from you."

"We don't care about that," Edward floats toward me. "All we need is you. All we want is for you to smile."

"But *I* care. And I don't know how to feel any different. I don't want you to have to change everything about yourselves to be with me, but I also don't want to be an outsider in my own life. I'm so tired of being pulled in a million directions." I sniff.

"I feel like I'm splitting down the middle. I...I care about the three of you so deeply, but I don't know if it's enough."

"What are you saying?" Pax cries.

"I'm saying that...I don't know if I can do this."

The tears come thick and fast now. Their silver cords swirl around each other, tugging at my chest until I'm gasping for breath.

Ambrose steps forward, his hand outstretched to me. Edward grabs his shoulder, holding him back.

My prince's eyes meet mine, and all those things he told me in the attic dance between us. *He's been trying to save me from this, but I'm not a kid anymore. He can't protect me from the cold, bitter truth.*

"I have been a burden to people my entire life," Edward says bleakly. "I will not be a burden to you, Brianna. I will respect your wish."

"You are going to let Bree run away?" Pax growls. "I will *not.* Bree, I will tie you down if I have to. I have waited thousands of years for you. I will not lose you again."

"It's too late, Pax," I sniff. "You've all lost me tonight. We're just too different."

"*No.*" Ambrose shakes his head so hard that his hair comes loose of its knot and spills over his shoulders. He's so beautiful in the starlight, his cheekbones almost sharp enough to sever the connection between us forever. "It doesn't have to be like this. We can figure this out."

"That's not what Brianna wants." Edward places his hand on Ambrose's shoulder. "She wants us to leave her alone again. Isn't that right?"

"Bree?" Ambrose's voice stutters.

It takes everything I have to turn away from them.

"Bree, please—"

"Let her go," Edward says, his words flat, devoid of emotion.

"This isn't over," Pax calls out as I take my first, shaky step away from them. "We waited a lifetime for you to realize you were meant for us, Bree Mortimer. Several lifetimes. We will wait for you forever."

I don't want you to wait.

I want you to set me free.

My lungs gasp for air as I run toward home. I pass the gloom-draped gates of the cemetery. I think about hurling myself onto the steps of Edward's mausoleum, where the shroud of death will protect me from their presence. But that place reminds me too much of what the men I care for truly are – dead.

Dead, and beyond me. Because whatever magic brought Pax back to life, it can't bridge the gap between us.

Grimwood Manor stands sentinel on the hill, the security light blazing like a beacon against the gloomy light. I scramble up the driveway and shove my way into the house, flicking on lights as I go.

Grimwood is my refuge, but I know it won't be long until they come looking for me. Pax and Ambrose aren't ready to give up.

And I'm not ready to face them. I know that if I have to see their faces, that if Edward touches my cheek or Ambrose presses his forehead against mine, that if Pax takes me in his arms and crushes me against his bulk, I'll be gone to them.

I need space. I need to *think.*

So I head to the one place where I know they won't go after me.

The attic.

33

PAX

"How could you do this?" Edward turns to me, his see-through face blazing with anger.

My veins sizzle with the need for vengeance. I whirl to face that insolent, self-righteous prince who has never lifted a finger to protect Bree in all the years he's irritated me with his existence. "Me? I did nothing wrong."

The blaring horn from the party behind us seems to suggest otherwise. I don't know why they placed a perfectly serviceable gladius on display if they didn't expect people to use it.

Maybe this is what Bree is talking about. I don't understand this new world. Nothing is the way I remember it. Nothing tastes or feels the way I expect it to. My forearm throbs with pain from the glass embedded in it.

Everything I do seems to upset Bree or make her life harder.

"We had *one rule* for this party, Pax." Edward glares at me. He's *shaking* with anger. This is the most Roman I've ever seen him. "One rule: *do not get into a fight.* Can you seriously not go two hours without getting into an altercation?"

"Bree's really upset," Ambrose sounds terrified. "The last time she sounded like this..."

He doesn't need to finish his sentence. Edward and I exchange a look. We all know what happened last time.

We lost her, our Bree, and we had to live in the attic.

"Things are different now," I say brightly, trying to make myself believe it. "Bree is ours. She belongs to us. I told her that I love her. She knows that we would never hurt her—"

"You're such a simpleton. Just because we gave her a few orgasms doesn't mean that she loves us," Edward says, his dark eyes lit with blazing flecks of gold. "And we *did* hurt her."

"It was dangerous, Pax. Did you ever stop to think that drawing attention to yourself like that might alert the Ripper about Bree's powers?" Ambrose says. "If the Ripper figures out that you're a ghost brought back to life, then it won't take much to realize Bree is the one with the resurrection magic."

My hand flies to my belt, but I'm not wearing a belt, and my sword is back at home. I curse these stupid yoga pants, which may feel buttery soft against my skin but are useless when it counts.

I curse all pants and leggings and trousers. Why couldn't the twenty-first century be *simple?*

"I'll talk to her," I growl as I pick pieces of glass out of my forearm. I don't want them to hate me. Bree hating me is bad enough. "I'll make it better."

I take a step in the direction of Grimwood. Edward thrusts out his hand. It goes through my chest, making my skin tingle with cold. He shudders at the pain of touching me. "You stay far away from her," he hisses. "You've done enough damage."

"At least I have been here for her," I yell. "I taught her to defend herself. I have worn these barbarian clothes and submitted myself to your deplorable lessons in manners, all for her. But what about you? You've barely even been in the same room with her for weeks. You don't care about her. Everything you do is for yourself."

"You cannot say those things to me," Edward yells back. "You...*you*..."

A couple walking down the street toward us crosses over to the other side of the road and makes a run for the pub. I remember that they cannot see Ambrose and Edward – to them, it must appear that I am yelling at thin air.

This is what it's been like for Bree.

"Please, both of you," Ambrose's voice wobbles. "Let us not fight. We have all done things to hurt Bree and make this situation worse. But—"

"Yes, Ambrose, we have," Edward sneers. "But you pressuring Bree to use her magic is nothing compared to Pax ruining the party. And he won't stop at that." Edward glares at me, his gaze full of hate. "You've been given the greatest gift – a chance to live again with the girl we all want – and you're determined to ruin it."

I thought all I ever wanted to do was be alive again, to feel Bree. But now that my wish came true, I realize that it's a lie. Pax the centurion died that day on the battlefield. What I am now is a shadow of an era long past.

I'm a relic, as dead to Bree's world as my dusty old bones in a box in a lab.

Bree is better off without me.

She'd be better off if I never came back to life.

I turn on my heel and run.

"Don't you run away!" Edward yells after me. "I'm not done berating you yet."

I run faster than I've ever run before, faster than the time I got drunk and accidentally missed the bugle and had to race halfway across Gaul to catch up with my legion.

I run to the duck pond on the village green and retrieve my sword from beneath the bench where I hid it earlier, in case the

Ripper showed up at the party. I didn't know they would have swords on hand.

I sprint up Grimwood Crescent, stopping outside the towering iron gates of Grimdale Cemetery.

The gates are locked. I swing my fist and the rusty lock breaks in my hand. *Ow.* I shake my fist. *That stings a little.*

I am still getting used to feeling pain again. The physical pain – such as the sting of the glass in my skin – I can tolerate, but the hollow, empty feeling I've had ever since Bree started crying...that I'll never be used to.

That is the kind of pain that will kill a man.

I slip inside the cemetery. I've never been inside, not since this land was a battlefield. I wander through the graves, my mind whirring, the hollow hurt in my chest growing and gnawing at me until I can't breathe.

I know exactly what I have to do.

It is the right choice. The honorable choice.

I just need the courage to go through with it.

Edward's mausoleum towers over the rest of the cemetery. Judging by the size of the thing, you'd think he was an emperor who had won many battles and impregnated many queens. The last part is probably true.

Edward hates that mausoleum. He can't even bear to glance in its direction.

Right now, I hate Edward, so I sit on the marble steps, gazing up at the angels. These Britons have such strange ideas about death. They should have adopted the Roman ways.

I heard Edward tell Ambrose once that suicide is a coward's way out. How ridiculous! Killing yourself may save your name or your family from dishonor. Wives who follow their husbands into the underworld are venerated, and men who knock themselves off before they become old and infirm are given a hero's funeral.

What will I be?

I rest my sword across my knees.

Can I even die a second time? Can I do it properly? I know that Bree will find me here. She will give me a proper funeral. She will be sad, but she will understand that I did this because I love her. I do not want her to suffer anymore. She has Edward and Ambrose. They are much better for her than I am. At least they cannot mess up her life in the real world as I have done.

If I am to die, let me die as a Roman.

I kick off the offending yoga pants. A real Roman will not journey to Hades in such barbarous garb.

I pick up a loose stone from beside the tomb and scrape my sword along the length of it, enjoying the satisfying hum of the blade as I give it a nice, sharp edge.

My sword. It will be an honour to die by this blade that has fought so valiantly for Rome, and for Bree.

I will fight for her still, even in death.

I am no good to Bree as a Living. But the monster, this Jack the Ripper, he is like me. If he cannot be killed in this world, then he can be killed in Hades. And that is where I intend to meet him in battle.

I will do what I was born to do.

My blade is sharp now. I stand. One last time, I perform the motions of my sword training, the drills I have practiced for thousands of years. I used to run through these drills with my men, enjoying their company as we imagined victory on the battlefield. Before they were cut down on this very ground where I stand.

Now, for the last time, I perform them alone.

The one purpose I have in my afterlife was to protect Bree. She needs me to protect her now. From the Ripper and from myself. From the chaos that I will rain down upon her life.

I'm not supposed to be in this world.

It's time for me to leave.

I fall to one knee, my sword in my hands. I raise my head to the heavens, and utter one final prayer to the gods – to Jupiter and Mars and Venus, that they will watch over Bree when I cannot.

"Goodbye, my Bree. I will rain down your vengeance on that monster. One day, I shall see you in Elysium."

I raise the sword.

I kiss the blade.

A single tear rolls down my cheek.

I...

A movement catches in the corner of my eye.

There, behind that weeping angel statue – the flap of a black cape, the bobbing of one of those silly top hats that Ambrose likes.

My sword hovers in front of me. I am unsure now. I did not wish to do this with an audience.

"Go away," I yell. "I wish to die alone."

"Yesssssss," a voice slithers over my skin. It is like no voice I've ever heard before. It does not sound human, but like grave dirt falling through your fingers, like bones clacking together. "You shhhhhall."

I stand. I know who is watching me from behind that stone angel.

The monster steps in front of me and raises his own weapon. A blade thinner and shorter than mine but just as deadly. Blood-red smoke curls along its serrated surface.

"Hello, little centurion," it rasps.

34

BREE

I yank open the third-story closet, revealing the narrow stairs that rise up into the gloom. Originally, when the house was first built, this staircase was part of the network of servants' passageways leading between the floors and rooms of the house. I flick on the switch and a single grimy lightbulb flickers to life, basically only adding to the creepy shadows.

I press my hand against the back of the closet for balance and start up the dusty stairs. I can see the outlines of my footprints from the last time I climbed up here, when I found Edward wallowing in the gloom. Hopefully, he won't think to look for me in the attic.

Dust closes in my throat, and I briefly wonder what the hell I'm doing. I'm running away again – exactly the thing I promised myself I wouldn't do.

But now that I've started up the staircase, I can't stop.

My head bumps against the trapdoor. I push against it, and it flings open and lands on the floor inside, kicking up another cloud of dust that has me sinking to my knees and coughing.

I give the dust a few moments to settle, then haul my body through the hole. I click on the single dim lightbulb.

During Edward's time, the attic was divided into several rooms that served as servants' quarters for the house's thirteen staff members. When Ambrose stayed in the house, the staff had dwindled to three and they lived on the bottom floor of the western wing, and the Van Wimple family had the walls torn out so they could use the attic for storage of Cuthbert's artifacts and excavation journals. And then the house came to my family and we continued the madness.

The attic is a whole floor filled with wardrobes and boxes and discarded bric-a-brac from different eras of the house. As a kid, I played up here sometimes, pulling old, moth-eaten clothing out of the trunks to use as costumes for staging plays. Edward tried to teach me to dance wearing an enormous hoop skirt. Although he definitely didn't dance the way he did tonight...

No, don't think about it.

I step into a corner of the room, recognizing the dusty stack of ball games and the old dollhouse my dad made for me.

My old toys.

I peer behind the dollhouse, my eyes drawn by a flash of bright red. My heart hammers against my ribs as I recognize...

My bicycle.

I push out the breath I was holding. I touch the handlebars. My fingers ring the little bell.

It's my bicycle.

The frame is still bent from when I took that fall. This was once my favorite toy, but then it became a wreck. A piece of junk that reminds me of the worst day of my life. The day when I became Bree the Ghost Whisperer.

But is it really the worst day of my life? For most of my life, the ghosts have been my friends. And now...they're something more...

And I banished my three best friends to live in this attic, where broken, unwanted things go.

My tears fall thick and fast now. I slump to the floor, my back against the dollhouse, and I let the tears fall.

"I don't know how to do this," I whisper into the darkness.

I love them.

I will never admit it, but the word is the one way to describe the broken, haunted feeling in my heart.

I love them. But I don't know how to love them and still be a part of the world. I don't know how to stop being torn apart by what I wish was real and what I want so badly—

SQUEAK?

I whirl around, my sadness turning to horror at the idea of being overwhelmed by rats...only to see a silhouette hanging upside-down in the window.

A bat.

Not just any bat, I realize. Ozzy, the bat my father named. The critter who has the ghosts in such a tizz that they can't even talk about him.

"Hey, Ozzy." I get to my feet and move slowly around one of the trunks, trying to get closer. The bat lazily unfolds one tiny wing and peers at me with two huge, round eyes, through which I can see the moon's light from behind him.

"Hey...you're a ghost." I can make out sparkling stars through his dark wings.

The bat flips forward and lands on his little feet on the windowsill. He hops along and unfurls his wings, cocking his head to the side as if to say, "Ta-da!"

"And you're adorable," I smile. "I don't know why the ghosts are so afraid of you."

The bat opens his mouth, revealing teeny, tiny fangs.

I brace myself for some kind of sadistic mischief.

Ozzy lets out an almighty yawn and collapses, folding his wings around himself.

I cry out as the little critter drops from the window onto my shoulder. Ozzy's tiny claws feel along my collarbone as he climbs down my arm.

I cry again as he wraps its tiny ghost bat wings around my hand, cupping me in its warm, furry, ghosty body. *He's such a cutie.*

Light shimmers across the surface of Ozzy's wings, and a silver cord winds around and around my arm, tingling where it touches my skin. It's thinner than the ghosts' cords, but no less bright. And then, the cord starts to unravel, twisting and turning in the air, spiraling through the clutter as it fills the attic, wrapping over the rafters and under the piano and around and around my body and—

Suddenly, I'm in a different place.

No. Not quite.

I'm in the *same* place, but the attic shimmers and trans-forms wherever the silver cord touches – the furniture moves around a little, the dust loses a layer, and the pale moonlight outside the grubby windows turns into a blazing sun.

"I can't believe I'm staying here instead of my beautiful boudoir," a familiar voice grumbles behind me.

I whirl around. Edward, Pax, and Ambrose stand in the middle of the clutter, wrapped in the silvery light. They don't acknowledge me. Edward peers down at me with that haughty gaze of his and doesn't flinch.

They can't see me.

It's not them. They're a projection, I think. A memory, the way I keep seeing flashes of the ghost's lives when I get too close to them. I'm seeing a memory that Ozzy wants to show me.

"I think it's lovely," Ambrose says as he pretends to gaze around the room. He plasters a smile on his face. "Airy, lots of space. Plenty of new corners to explore."

"I can beat you at many sword fights here." Pax elbows Edward in the gut.

"Excellent. I'm rooming with a couple of comedians who have no taste for the finer things," Edward says tersely. "I guess I'll take the dingy corner with the curtain of spiderwebs."

"I call the interior of that old steamer trunk," Ambrose says gleefully.

"I will not need a cot. I will spend my nights at the foot of Bree's bed, guarding her from danger."

"No, Pax." Edward sighs. "I explained this. You can't do that. Brianna wants us out of her life. *Forever*. That means no guarding here."

Pax's whole face falls. Even though I know this isn't real, it still breaks my heart. "But who will protect her while she's sleeping?"

"Maybe he could still guard her?" Ambrose offers, always the peacemaker. "If Pax stands outside her window where she can't see him, and he promises to never speak with her, then he should be able to maintain his post. I feel better knowing that he's watching out for her."

"Fine, but *absolutely no talking* to Brianna," Edward says. "We made a promise, and if I can't break it, then neither will you."

"I'm sure that when Bree calms down a little, she will miss us," Ambrose says brightly. "She'll ask us to come back. We need to give her a little space, is all."

But I never did.

In the two years that we lived under the same roof but didn't talk, they hid in this attic and waited for me to want them again. But I never asked for them to come back, even though I thought about it so many times. Even though I missed them terribly.

I thought I'd banished them forever. I didn't know they were right there this whole time.

Always watching over me.

I burst out of the vision, my breath coming out in ragged gasps.

Something moves out of the corner of my eye. I yelp and crawl back, not wanting to confront another shitty thing I've done.

But it's not another memory. It's Edward in the here and now, hovering above the trapdoor. His pouty lips are crooked with worry.

"My apologies, Brianna. I didn't mean to—"

His words cut off with a strangled cry as he notices Ozzy. "Get away from her, you furry sky-demon!"

"Squeak?" says Ozzy indignantly.

Edward lunges for Ozzy, who flaps away and lands on the piano. He flies through the wood, but seems to get stuck halfway through, one leg trapped inside, and the rest of him outside as he deals with the effects of being partially able to touch things. Ozzy squeaks angrily as he hops up and down.

"I'm sorry, little fella." I reach over to lift the lid and free him.

"No!" Edward flies past me and gets there first. His eyes are wild as he shoves the bat through the piano and sits on the lid. Ozzy shakes his tiny claws at Edward, who yelps and covers his face, but he doesn't get off the piano.

Ozzy swoops back over to land on my hand again.

"You didn't have to do that. I could have freed him, since you're afraid of the big, bad bat." I pat Ozzy's head, and he makes the most adorable little purring noise. "Ozzy's not so bad. What did he do to you to make you so afraid of him?"

Edward shudders. "You don't want to know."

"Oh, I really do."

"No. You don't." His eyes dart from Ozzy to the piano and back.

I decide not to get into a game of 'yes I do' with him. "You managed to go a whole ninety minutes before you came to look for me," I say, not sure if I'm angry or grateful. "That has to be a record."

"We would not have disturbed you if it weren't important. Ambrose and I have been looking everywhere for you. Well, I looked, because Ambrose is useless. If he were my manservant, I'd have had him flogged by now."

"No matter how flippant you are, I'm not ready to talk about the party." I can't think about Dani's hard, angry face without feeling sick, especially with the memory now reeling inside me.

I hurt everyone who cares about me.

"Good." Edward slides off the piano and floats gingerly toward me. "Let's agree that we shall never again speak of this evening, and leave it at that. But I need to tell you something else. Pax is missing."

35

BREE

Pax is missing?

It doesn't make sense. Pax would never go off on his own at night. He has to be here, guarding the house from monsters, standing at the foot of the bed. My centurion.

That's what he's done every night for since I was a kid.

So how can he just be...gone?

What if the monster got him? What if he's being ripped to shreds right now?

And I told him...I told him...

Tears well in the corners of my eyes as I think of all the terrible things I said, but I push them down. This is not the time to fall apart.

"We have to find Pax," I say to Edward.

"I was afraid you'd say that." He screws up his face. "We have other options. We could leave him to his fate. This house is crowded enough as it is, and the air will be much cleaner without his Roman flatulence—"

"Edward, I'm not joking around. Pax could be in trouble."

"I know." Edward floats back down the staircase. I place Ozzy down on the windowsill and follow Edward, flicking out

343

the lights as I go. Ambrose is at the bottom, his expression drawn. The same thought has occurred to him.

"Pax didn't just disappear," I say. "You've checked the whole house?"

Ambrose nods.

"Well, what happened after the party? Where did the three of you go after I—"

After I ran away. Again.

Ambrose and Edward exchange a look, which is quite hard to do considering Ambrose can't see. Panic rises in my chest. I place my hands on my hips. "What happened after the party?"

"We had a disagreement," Ambrose says, staring at his shoes.

"A fight," Edward says. "It was a fight."

"Edward was *vicious,*" Ambrose says glumly.

"We didn't come to blows."

"We didn't have to," Ambrose's long lashes tangle together. "Our words cut him deeper than a blade ever could."

I stare down at my chest, where Pax's silver cord still extends. Alarm bells ring in my head when I see how dim it is, the vibrant blue light barely visible. "What did you fight about?"

"About you." Edward stares at his feet.

"About the fact that we failed you."

"We drove you away again."

"We should never have let you see us," Ambrose's lip wobbles. "That was my fault. I should have been more careful—"

"No, the blame lies with me." Edward's voice sounds far away. "I reminded Pax that you were better off when he was a ghost. And he stomped off somewhere."

Ghost-balls.

"You can't say things like that to Pax. He doesn't think the same way we do. He always does his duty, and he believes that his duty is to protect me. And if he thinks that he's put me in danger, then..."

Then he won't want to keep on living.

Then the Ripper isn't the only danger we face tonight.

I can't let this happen. I *won't*.

Ambrose's face collapses. He has the same thought I do. "Oh, no. We have to find him."

I press my hand against my chest, trying to calm my racing heart. *Think, Bree. Think.* "Okay, where would you go if you were a bloodthirsty, depressed Roman centurion and thinking of sacrificing yourself?"

"I'd want to drown in a vat of beer," Edward declares.

"I'd want to be slain in a mighty battle," Ambrose suggests.

I'd want to die alongside my comrades.

"I think he's gone into the cemetery," I say, grabbing my coat. "We need to—"

"Excuse me, Ms. Mortimer. But I don't think you'll be going anywhere."

I whirl around. There, on the landing, blocking the top of the stairs, is Father Bryne.

36

BREE

"G-G-Good evening, Father," I stammer. "I'm terribly sorry. I thought you were out at the pub. I didn't wake you with our—er, *my* yelling, did I? I had to get something from the attic and I, um, stubbed my toe and—"

"You didn't stub your toe." Father Bryne takes a step toward me. I notice he's wearing his black cassock, which seems an odd thing to wear for karaoke night at the Goat. The black gown flowing around his legs and his long, pointed cross give him a surprisingly menacing air. He tilts his head to the side. "Who *are* you talking to, Bree?"

He doesn't say it as if he's curious. He says it as if he already knows the answer.

"I talk to myself," I murmur. "I've done it ever since I was a kid. Ask anyone in town, they'll tell you."

"Oh, I have. I've asked all around about you. Bree Mortimer, the little girl who survived a bicycle accident that split your head open – an accident that no one should have survived. The strange little girl with invisible friends and a vivid imagination. The lovely young woman with the boyfriend who appears to be a Roman soldier brought back from the dead. You weren't

talking to yourself. You're talking to the ghost of a Victorian gentleman and the dandy with the glass shard in his posterior."

"Excuse me," Edward's voice flares. "That's hardly the way to address your prince, Catholic! I'll have you burned as a heathen!"

My blood runs cold. "You...you can see them?"

Father Bryne smiles, but there is no mirth in it. "I can. They are not as clear to me, I think, as they are to you. I have worked my entire life to suppress my curse. I do not wish to see these abominations."

"You see ghosts." The news is so strange, so impossible, I don't know what to do with it. I'm not thinking clearly. I don't have time for this. I need to find Pax and yet...

My feet won't move.

I *need* to know.

"I see ghosts," Father Bryne's eyes sweep over me. "I came to Grimdale to look for you, Bree. From your reaction, I'm guessing you have never met another who shares your power."

Beside me, Edward growls low in his throat. He and Ambrose move closer, and Ambrose takes up a pugilist's stance. I don't get their animosity. If Father Bryne knows about my powers, then he might be able to help us stop the monster.

"No, I..." I can't think of what I want to say. This is too much to take in. "I wondered if maybe Vera did, but then she was killed. And we—that is, I—found another woman who had the power, Penny Hatterly, but she was killed, too. Someone is hunting down people like us, Father. Whatever we are. And we have to stop it—"

"You are a Lazarus."

"Bree." Ambrose's fingers brush mine. "We don't have time for this. We have to find Pax."

I barely hear him. Pax's string tugs urgently at my chest, but I'm drawn to the priest, to his calm, kind voice, to the certainty that here is someone who understands everything that I've gone through.

"Lazarus – like the saint?"

"Yes. We are the children of Lazarus, carriers of his blood – blood that has been anointed by Christ himself. We have the power to cross the line between the living and the dead. Over the centuries, we have sought each other out to encourage those with this gift, this *curse,* to follow the path of light. But there are some who falter and fall, and they are too dangerous to remain."

"What do you mean?"

Father Bryne holds up his cross around his neck. Once again, I notice that it's not quite the same as a normal cross. It has extra barbs on the sides.

"Do you know what this is?"

"A cross?"

"It is the cross of Lazarus, the symbol of the ancient Order of the Noble Death." He drops the cross in front of his cassock. "There are few of us left now. We are the righteous sons and daughters of Lazarus. Each of us in the order is touched by the hand of Christ, gifted with the power of resurrection. I have come to offer you a place in our illustrious order."

"There's an Order? Like, you're wizards?" I'm so confused by this, and by the way Edward and Ambrose move in around me as if to protect me.

"Yes. The Order of the Noble Death travels the earth doing God's work, performing resurrection miracles that glorify His name, and doing what needs to be done to maintain the sanctity of death. You told me that you have always been searching for your place in the world, yes? Well, your place is with the Order of the Noble Death. We will take you to our monastery in Italy, and we will educate you on how to use your powers to glorify the Lord."

"But..." To be with other people like me. To not be alone. Father Bryne offers me the one thing I've always wanted. But I'd have to leave Grimdale to join some holy order? And what about the ghosts? "What do you mean, maintaining the sanctity of death?"

Father Bryne clasps his hands over his cross. He looks crestfallen. "Some of our siblings do not share our righteous path. They choose to use their powers to glorify themselves. And so, to keep order, we must hunt out these rogue Lazarii and put them down."

"Put them down? But..." My heart thuds. "*You* killed Vera and Penny. *You're* Jack the Ripper."

"Heavens no. I would never dream of doing such a grisly, unholy thing to a vessel of God's spirit," Father Bryne says. "My soul must remain pure, or I cannot ascend to the kingdom of heaven as Lazarus eventually did. But we must have order, so if we find Lazarii who do not wish to join us, we raise soldiers from the dead who have the skills to destroy the infidels."

"Bree," Edward whispers. "I really think we should be going now."

Yes, I scream, but I cannot use my mouth. Fear struggles up my spine. But still, I cannot move. I look into Father Bryne's eyes as he mutters something in Latin. Red smoke curls through his fingers where he clasps his cross.

He's doing something to me.

Pax, where are you?

I wish that my Roman would burst through the wall, sword waving, and break whatever spell Father Bryne has placed on me. But that's just the problem. I've always relied on Pax to watch out for me.

Now he's the one who needs saving.

"That is why I am here tonight. You have raised a soul from the dead without God's consent. That's very impressive. It takes a tremendous amount of skill and power to perform that ritual, and it's usually not possible for one so young. I have been studying your friend Pax ever since I arrived in Grimdale. At first, I couldn't be certain he was resurrected and not simply an oafish young man, but after seeing him on the street this evening, arguing with the two ghosts, I now know that he is an unholy abomination."

"He is nothing of the sort," Edward spits out. "The only person allowed to insult Pax is *me*."

Father Bryne shoots Edward an amused glance. "Brave words for a ghost, but no Lazarus can be allowed to use this power outside of the order. And I am here to see that you join us or accept God's wrath."

"She'll never join you," Ambrose cries. He tries to shake my arm, but I'm still frozen. "Bree, answer me. What's wrong?"

"You understand, don't you?" Father Bryne says, squeezing his cross tighter. "These men you love are not of our world. God has said that they should die, and your sacred duty is to help them to pass over, not to allow them to remain on earth or return to their bodies. What you have done here is wrong, and I must make the world right again."

"As opposed to bringing a Victorian serial killer to life?" Edward shoots back. "That's totally fine and dandy?"

"I really am sorry, Bree. You are a bright girl with potential, and we would gratefully welcome you into our bosom. What is your decision?"

He snaps his fingers and suddenly my jaw works again. My eyes dart to Edward, his pouty mouth all twisted with fear, and Ambrose, his dark hair fallen out and wild about his face.

"I'll never join you," I snap.

"Very well. God has granted you free will. But if you will not join the Order of the Noble Death, then I must ensure the world is safe from your powers."

My jaw still works, but it's the only part of me that can move. *Ghost-balls, I'm going to die and I can't move a finger to help myself.*

Father Bryne twists the cross in his fingers and mutters something in Latin. The cross glows, and a thread untangles from its center and stretches out. It's like the cords I see in the guys, but instead of being silver, it's a pulsing, bloody red.

"He will be here shortly," he says. "He is dealing with your friend."

"You won't hurt Pax." Edward draws himself up. "I won't allow it. And whatever you've done to Brianna, you must stop it right now."

Father Bryne chuckles. "Do you think you can hurt me, spirit?"

Edward's eyes dance with mischief. I can't think what he possibly has planned, but then I see that he's moved the priest closer to the wall of the landing, near the light switch.

Oh, Edward...

"Your Lord sayeth, 'let there be light," Edward grins as he shoves his hand into the light switch. All the lights in the house flicker. "Does this mean you worship me now? I *am* a god between the sheets, and now, I am filled with heavenly light."

He's right. A faint glow circles Edward's body, pulsing in time with the flickering lights.

"What—" Father Bryne backs away, his hands raised, the cross dangling between his fingers, spilling red mist all around.

Edward slams out his hand, touching Father Bryne's forehead.

CRACK.

There's a sizzle.

The lights flicker again.

Father Bryne staggers back. His foot sails off the top step and he loses his balance, toppling heavily down the stairs.

Whatever magic holds my limbs dissipates. I slump forward into Ambrose's waiting arms. He helps me right myself, and I thread his arm through mine as I race down the stairs. Edward slinks after us, blowing on his fingers like they're the barrel of a gun.

We reach the bottom just as Father Bryne staggers to his feet. His hair sticks out from all angles. There's a huge round singe mark on his forehead, and the hem of his cassock is smoking.

"What in the devil's name was that?" he growls at Edward. "You...you're a ghost. You shouldn't be able to do that."

Edward waves his fingers. "That was me looking out for the woman I love. And if you come any closer you'll get another zap in a rather uncomfortable place."

"You see?" Father Bryne turns to me, his lips curled back into a haughty grimace. "You see how easily this power corrupts? You have given these ghosts abilities beyond what they should have. They can affect the human world. That's dark, demonic magic. You have corrupted your powers for evil—"

My hands ball into fists. "If this is corruption, then what are you?"

But there's no point admonishing him. Father Bryne *believes*. He will never see anything wrong with what he's doing. And he's coming for me again, dragging his feet across the foyer as he grasps for his cross.

I don't know what to do.

I search around for a weapon. Cuthbert Van Wimple's old rifle hangs on the wall, but it's not exactly going to be loaded. I could bludgeon the priest with the hatstand, or topple that suit of armour on him, or...

Something scratches inside the fireplace. Edward stares intently at it, and then his features brighten. It's the expression he gets whenever he finds the perfect rhyming couplet. He places his hand on Ambrose's arm. The two of them move away from me and advance upon the priest, driving him back toward the fireplace.

"You will not harm her," Edward growls, low and menacing. He actually sounds...like Pax.

"We have powers you cannot fathom." Ambrose swipes his cane in front of him. It catches on a lampshade, knocking it to the floor.

"Get back, foul spirits!" Father Bryne clutches his cross. "You're not supposed to be able to do that!"

The red rope curls from the cross, creeping toward my ghosts, wrapping around them. Edward's eyes grow wide with fear.

"Bree?" Ambrose cries. "I feel...I feel strange."

"Cold," Edward murmurs. "So cold."

"Back to the land of the dead with you!" Father Bryne screams.

I gasp as the silver cords around my heart tighten so hard that I can't breathe. They pull taut, humming with power as Father Bryne's death magic stretches them to breaking point...

He's *hurting* them.

He's trying to force them to cross over.

He's going to take them away from me.

I don't know how I know, but I *feel* what I need to do to save them.

I place my hand over my heart, feeling the silver cords that extend from it into Edward and Ambrose, and I *give*.

I push the magic in my veins into those cords. They unravel, circling and circling until they choke out the red. And Ambrose and Edward push through the warring magic and keep moving toward him. Ambrose storms through the furniture, heedless to the pain he must be feeling. He raps his cane on the ground, and the sound reverberates through the tall space.

Rap. Rap. Rap.

Father Bryne backs right up against the fireplace. His eyes flick to the front and down, toward Grimdale Cemetery. "You may hurt me, but mine is the kingdom of heaven. Your Roman friend will not be so lucky when my Ripper is finished with him —argh!"

Something small and black topples out of the chimney and flies at the priest's face.

"Get him, Ozzy!" Edward cries.

Father Bryne tears at the black shape covering his face, but the tiny bat holds on tight, squeaking with defiance as he digs his claws into the priest's skin.

"Get it off! Get it off!" Father Bryne moans as he crashes through the room, trying to get the bat off. But of course, Ozzy is a ghost, so the priest's hands keep falling right through him.

"You cannot be serious," Edward drawls, inspecting his nails. "I'm not touching that thing."

"It would be rude to disrupt Ozzy," Ambrose adds as he backs away toward the wall, trying to stay out of Father Bryne's path.

"Argh!" Father Bryne cries as he manages to tear the bat from his face, bringing a thick clump of hair and skin with him. He hurls Ozzy across the room. Ozzy squeals as he hits Ambrose square in the chest.

"Oof!" Ambrose reels in shock and staggers backward, slamming into the wall holding Cuthbert's rifle.

The gun clatters from the wall and drops into Ambrose's hands. His eyes are wide with terror as his fingers close around the barrel—

BANG.

The entire room falls silent. The gunshot sucks all the air from the house.

Father Bryne drops to his knees, then falls forward on the floor. Ozzy scoots out from beneath him just in time and swoops up to hang upside down from the safety of the chandelier.

SQUEAK, he proclaims happily.

"I guess..." Ambrose says shakily. "I guess the gun was loaded, after all."

I run to Father Bryne's side, but it's too late. He's not moving or screaming. There's a hole in his chest the size of a squirrel's home. His eyes are glazed over.

A pool of dark blood spreads around his body, staining my great-grandmother's Persian rug.

"Is he okay?" Ambrose asks shakily. "Did I...did I stop him?"

You sure did.

First things first. I check the priest's body, but I see no sign of a silver cord connecting us, or that his ghost has hung around. Good.

The cross around his neck is no longer emitting the red tendrils. When Father Bryne died, that must have severed his connection to Jack the Ripper.

I tear the cross from around his neck. I'm not sure why I do this, but I know it's important. The metal feels unnaturally warm in my fingers. I shove it in my pocket.

Fuck, what do I do? I have a priest bleeding out on the floor. But I don't have time to deal with that now. *We need to get to Pax.*

"The cemetery," I manage to choke out.

"You think Pax is in the cemetery?" Edward asks.

"Before Grimdale, before all of us, that was where Pax laid down his life for his soldiers. He would want to die with them."

37

BREE

I reach for Ambrose and take his shaking fingers in mine. "Thank you." I kiss his cheek. "You saved me. You saved all of us."

"I did?" His smile could light the whole world. "I was so afraid, Bree. I thought he was going to hurt you."

"But I'm okay, thanks to you and Cuthbert's ridiculous sense of humor."

"We have no time for sentiment," Edward snaps. "We must find Pax."

Together, the three of us step over the body of Father Bryne and crash through the front door. We pick our way through the maze of statues and lawn art in my father's garden, around the zodiac fountain, down the side of the house to the path that cuts through the forest to my secret hole in the cemetery fence.

Edward races ahead of us. I've never seen my insouciant prince move so fast. By the time Ambrose and I reach the hole in the fence, Edward is out of sight, heading toward the center of the cemetery.

Toward his mausoleum.

Edward hasn't been near that grave, ever. He can't even look at it across the garden without going all funny. After everything he told me, I can't blame him. But now he moves with all the determination of a ghost on a mission. He disappears behind a cherub. A moment later, I hear him cry out.

"Brianna, you need to stay back."

I yank Ambrose behind a weeping angel statue and stop short when I see a sight that turns my blood to ice.

Pax lies on the ground, blood gushing from a wound in his side. Over him stands the dark shadow of a man in a cape, a pair of impeccably tailored trousers with shiny black shoes and white spats, with a top hat pulled so low over his eyes that it casts his whole face in shadow.

No, not a man.

A monster out of time.

Jack the Ripper.

The Ripper's cape flaps in the breeze, falling open to reveal... nothing. Red smoke curls from where his body *should* be. Whatever he is, it's not human. Not like my Pax.

Pax lifts his head and sees me. His pale eyes swim with pain. "Bree," he chokes out, raising a bloodied hand. "Stay back. I will vanquish him."

The Ripper looks up at me and smiles. His teeth gleam from the shadow of his face. He has no eyes but dark, empty sockets from which more red smoke falls.

"Thank you for freeing me," he whispers, his breath a hiss of cold air. "Now, I have no master containing my desires."

Jack the Ripper raises a knife over his head. Red tendrils swirl around it. With a cry like the clattering of ghostly hooves, he swings the knife down, straight into Pax's heart.

TO BE CONTINUED

How can Pax survive a mortal wound? Will Bree finally discover who she truly is? Will Ozzy kick the ghosts out of Grimwood and claim the manor for himself? Find out in book 3, *Ghoul as a Cucumber.*

http://books2read.com/grimdale3

What do you get when you cross a cursed bookshop, three hot fictional men, and a punk rock heroine nursing a broken heart? Read book one of the Nevermore Bookshop Mysteries – A Dead and Stormy Night – to get the story of Mina and her book boyfriends.
http://books2read.com/adeadandstormynight

(Turn the page for a sizzling excerpt).

Can't get enough of Bree and her boys? Read a free bonus scene from before Bree left on her travels, as well as her playlist, along with other bonus scenes and extra stories when you sign up for the Steffanie Holmes newsletter.

http://www.steffanieholmes.com/newsletter

FROM THE AUTHOR

And with that evil cliff-hanger, book 2 is done!

I hope you're enjoying Bree's story. This has been such a fun series to write. I'm a bit obsessed with ghosts and hauntings (if you're a member of my newsletter, you'll know this), so it's been wild to create this world where ghosts aren't scary apparitions, but rather they're just like you and me...except hotter and stubbier.

Our three ghosts are all fictional – they don't exist historically, although the details about their costumes and memories are as real as I can make them.

Pax's name means 'peace' in Latin. It's not a traditional Roman name, but I thought it was too fun not to use. He uses the word 'verpa', which is a vulgar Latin word for penis. And his insult – vappa! – means scum! (It refers to wine that's gone sour). His views on Druids are his own.

Ambrose is based on one of my own personal heroes – the Victorian adventurer, James Holman. Holman became mysteriously blind in his early 20s, and when this curtailed his naval career he first put himself through medical school and then set off on a series of adventures across the world. He was known as the 'Blind Traveller'.

Using a cane to rap on the ground, Holman was able to learn about the spaces around him through echolocation. He would walk holding a rope, which was then tethered to a carriage, so that he remained on the road. He wrote books about his travels using the frame with strings that Ambrose describes.

Holman's books were at first well-received, but he then became a bit of a novelty and wasn't taken seriously as an adventurer. People even said that he couldn't really be blind. He rode elephants in Ceylon, fought the slave trade in Fernando Po Island, helped chart the Australian outback, and was captured in Siberia by the Tsar's men on suspicion of being a spy. He was not killed, though, but ejected to the frontier of Poland.

His final manuscript – an autobiography encompassing all his travels – was never published and likely did not survive. He died in obscurity and is buried in London's Highgate Cemetery – the very place for which Grimdale Cemetery is based. Jason Roberts wrote a wonderful biography of Holman called *A Sense of the World* and I highly recommend it.

You might not know this, but I'm legally blind. Unlike Ambrose, Mina, and Holman, my eyesight didn't disappear one day or fade over time. I was born with the genetic condition *achromatopsia*, which means my eyes lack the millions of cone cells required to recognise colours and perceive depth. I'm completely colour blind, light sensitive with poor depth perception, I squint and blink all the time, and struggle to make eye contact. I'm so short-sighted I'm considered legally blind.

I love being able to write stories where people like me get to have adventures, save the world, and discover that they can be sexy and have their happily ever after.

Oh, and one fun fact for you – Bree and Pax's "yoga" costumes for Alice's party are inspired by my wonderful and hilarious friend Shane, who showed up to my 18th birthday toga party in a lycra catsuit and sweat band and immediately started stretching.

There are so many people who've supported me and believed in me, even when I struggled to believe in myself. My family – my Mum and Dad and sister Belinda.

A special shoutout to my writer fam – Angel Lawson, Bea Paige, Daniela Romero, Eden O'Neill, Rachel Jonas, AK Rose, and EM Moore. You have been one of the greatest joys in my life over the last two years.

To my found family, the bogans – my brothers and sisters of metal. I apologise for the volume of our shenanigans that end up in my books.

Always, to my cantankerous drummer husband, who is everything. Every hero I write is a piece of you and what you mean to me.

And lastly, to you, my readers, for going on this journey with me. I love you more than words can say.

A portion of the royalties from the sale of this book are donated to Parkinson's New Zealand. Thank you for the work you do!

Every week I send out a newsletter to fans – it features a spooky story about a real-life haunting or strange criminal case that has inspired one of my books, as well as news about upcoming releases and a free book of bonus scenes called *Cabinet of Curiosities*. To get on the mailing list all you gotta do is head to my website: http://www.steffanieholmes.com/newsletter

I'm so happy you enjoyed this story! I'd love it if you wanted to leave a review on Amazon or Goodreads. It will help other readers to find their next read.

Thank you, thank you! I love you heaps! Until next time.

EXCERPT
A DEAD AND STORMY NIGHT

Uncover the secrets of Nevermore Bookshop in book 1, *A Dead and Stormy Night*

http://books2read.com/adeadandstormynight

Wanted: Assistant/shelf stacker/general dogsbody to work in secondhand bookshop. Must be fluent in classical literature, detest electronic books and all who indulge them, and have experience answering inane customer questions for eight hours straight. Cannot be allergic to dust or cats – if I had to choose between you and the cat, you will lose. Hard work, terrible pay. Apply within at Nevermore Bookshop.

Yikes. I closed the Argleton community app and shoved my phone into my pocket. *The person who wrote that ad really doesn't want to hire an assistant.*

Unfortunately, he or she hadn't counted on me, Wilhelmina Wilde, recently-failed fashion designer, owner of two wonky eyes, and pathetic excuse for a human. I was landing this assistant job, whether Grumpy-Cat-Obsessed-Underpaying-Ad-Writer wanted me or not.

I had no options left.

I peered up at the towering Victorian brick facade of Nevermore Bookshop – number 221 Butcher Street, Argleton, in Barsetshire – with a mixture of nostalgia and dread. I'd spent most of my childhood in a darkened corner of this shop, and now if I played my cards right I'd get to see it from the other side of the counter. It was the one shining beacon in my dark world of shite.

I don't remember it looking so... foreboding.

Apart from the faded *Nevermore Bookshop* written in gothic type over the entrance, the facade bore no clue that I stood in front of one of the largest secondhand bookshops in England. A ramshackle Georgian house facade with Victorian additions rose four stories from the street, looking more like a creepy orphanage from a gothic novel than a repository of fine literature. Trees bent their bare branches across the darkened windows and wisteria crept over grimy brickwork, shrouding the building in a thick skin of foliage. Cobwebs entwined in the lattice and draped over the windowsills. There didn't appear to be a single light on inside.

Weeds choked the two flower pots flanking the door, which had once been glazed a bright blue but were since stained in brown and white streaks from overzealous birds. A pigeon cooed ominously from the gutter above the door, threatening me with an unwelcome deposit. Twin dormer windows in the attic glared over the narrow cobbled street like evil eyes, and a narrow balcony of black wrought iron on the second story the teeth. A hexagonal turret jutted from the south-western corner, where it might once have caught sun before Butcher Street had built up around it.

When I used to hang out as a kid, the first two floors were

given over to the shop – a rabbit warren of narrow corridors and pokey rooms, every wall and table covered in books. The previous owner – a kindly blind old man named Mr. Simson – lived on the remaining two floors, but for all I knew, the new owner used that space as an opium den or a meat smoker.

At least the flaccid British sun peeked through the grey clouds, which meant I could make out these finer details of the facade. The buildings on either side of it were cloaked in the creeping black shadow that now followed me everywhere. I squinted at the chalkboard sign on the street, hoping for some clue as to the new owner's personality, but all it had on it were some wonky lines that looked like chickens' feet.

This place is even more drab than I remember. It could use a little TLC.

That makes two of us. I squinted at my reflection in the darkened shop window, but I could barely make out the basic shape of my body. At least I knew I looked fierce when I left the house, in my Vivienne Westwood pleated skirt (scored on eBay for twenty-five quid), vintage ruffled shirt, men's cravat from a weird goth shop at Camden market, and my old school blazer with an enamel pin on the collar that read, 'Jane Austen is my Homegirl.' Combined with my favorite Docs and a pair of thick-framed glasses, I'd nailed the 'boss-bitch librarian' look.

That is, if you ignored the fact that I pushed my nose up against the glass to see my reflection, and twisted my head in order to see all the details of my outfit because of the creeping darkness in the corners of my eyes.

Please, Isis and Astarte and any other goddess listening, let me get this job. I can't deal with any more rejection.

I smoothed my hair, sucked in a breath, pushed open the creaking shop door, and stepped back in time.

As the shop bell tinkled and the smell of musty paper filled my nostrils, I became nine years old again – the weird outcast kid whose mother was banned from school events after swindling the chair of the PTA with a Forex trading mastermind program that was really just a CD-rom of my mother comparing currency trading to doing the laundry. (It was his own fault for getting swindled. Who even uses CDs anymore?)

As soon as the school bell rang I'd sprint into town, duck through this same door and escape into another world. I'd curl up in the cracking leather armchair in the World History room with a huge stack of books and read until my mother finished her shift and came to collect me. Books became my friends – characters like Jane Eyre and Dorian Grey the perfect substitutes for the kids who were horrible to me. When I was older and the guys at school sneered at me and fawned over my best friend, I fell into books again – this time to fall in love with the bad boys, the intelligent boys, the boys filled with anger and lust and pain. Dark horses and anti heroes like Heathcliff and Sherlock Holmes, and melancholy authors like Edgar Allan Poe spoke directly to my soul.

Mr. Simson barely said a word to me, but he never seemed to mind the fact that I read every book in the shop but couldn't afford to buy any. Sometimes he'd even let me riffle through the boxes of rejects before he sent them away for recycling. People would come into the store and try to sell Mr. Simson stacks of airport books – James Patterson and John Grisham paperbacks that no one buys secondhand. When he refused their generous bounty, they'd creep back at night and shove the volumes one by one through the mail slot, so Mr. Simson always had stacks of them lying around. I would smuggle the books home to our housing estate – If Mum caught me reading she'd lecture about how men didn't like smart girls and we'd have a big row – and read them under the covers at night or hidden in my textbooks during class.

It was in Nevermore Bookshop where I first discovered punk

music. I found a box of battered 1970 zines in the Popular Music section, and I lost myself in faded photographs of bored teenagers with bleached mohawks. None of them fit in, and they didn't give a shit. I was in love.

The memories flooded back as I stepped into the gloomy interior. My boot landed on a thick carpet in the wide entrance hall, flanked on either side by tall shelves crammed with books. A small line of taxidermy rodents peered down at me from tiny wooden shields nailed along the moldings. *I don't remember those.* The new owner sure had strange taste in interior decor. But then, he had written that acerbic job ad...

I ran my fingers along the spines of the books, moving carefully to avoid tripping over the stacks of paperbacks littering the floor. Must and mothballs and leather and old paper caressed my nostrils. The air practically *sweated* books.

"Hello?" I called, coughing as dust tickled the back of my throat. *Was the bookshop always this dusty?*

Hello, beautiful. A voice croaked from behind me. I whirled around, a retort poised on my lips. But no one was in the doorway. I twisted my head to peer into the corners of the room, but I couldn't penetrate the shadows.

Where did that voice come from?

"Hello?" I called out. *The first thing I'm going to do if I get the job is brighten this place up a bit.*

Something rustled in the dark corner above the door. I glanced up. My eyes resolved the shape of an enormous black bird perched on the top of the bookshelf. At first I assumed it was stuffed, but it unfurled a long wing and flapped it in my face.

"Argh!" I flung my arm up, slamming my elbow into a stack of books, which toppled to the ground. The raven croaked with satisfaction and folded its wing away.

What in Astarte's name is a raven doing in here? It'll poop over the books. I wonder if it's roosting in the roof somewhere? We'll have to find that if we want to chase it out...

"Croak," said the raven with an accusatory tone, as though it had heard my thoughts.

"I guess you kind of suit the place." I glared at the bird as I bent down and fumbled for the books. "A raven in Nevermore Bookshop. Once upon a midnight dreary——"

"Croak." The raven's yellow eyes glowed. Something in that croak sounded like a warning.

"Fine. Fine. I didn't come here to quote poetry to a bird." I stood up and rubbed my throbbing elbow. "I want to talk to the boss. Do you know where I might find him?"

As if it understood the question, the raven dropped off the shelf, swooped past me, and flew around the corner, disappearing through an archway on the left. I followed it into what would have once been a drawing room and was now a jumble of mismatched shelves and junkstore furniture. In the middle of the room were two heavy oak tables – one holding a large globe, the other a taxidermy armadillo. Books stacked so high it looked as though the armadillo was building itself a border wall. Old cinema chairs and beanbags under the window formed a reading area, and the large lawyer's desk that had served as Mr. Simson's counter still took pride of place beside the grand fireplace, although the brass plaque on the front now read "Mr. Earnshaw."

The raven swooped around me and perched on the desk lamp, its talons clicking against the metal. It took me a few moments to register the man hunched over the desk – the dark, wavy hair that spilled over his shoulders obscured his face, and his black clothes faded into the wood behind him.

"We're closed." A gruff voice boomed from inside the hair.

"Your sign still says open."

"Well, flip it over for me on the way out," the voice managed to sound both exasperated and uninterested.

"Um, sure. Mr. Earnshaw, was it?" I waved. He didn't even look up from his paper. "I saw the job ad you posted on the Argleton app, and I wanted to—"

"App?" The head snapped up. Eyes of black fire regarded me with suspicion from beneath a pair of thick eyebrows, deep set in a dark-skinned face of such remarkable beauty I sucked in a breath.

The new proprietor was younger than I expected him to be – Mr. Simson had been an old man even when I was a girl – and far too handsome to be working in a bookshop. His exotic features and sharp cheekbones belonged on the cover of a fashion magazine. The defiant tilt of his chin and twitch of his haughty lips concealed a storm raging inside him.

Danger rolled off him in waves. Danger... and desire.

Thick muscles bulged at the seams of his shirt. He'd rolled the sleeves up to his elbows, one thick forearm graced with the tattoo of a barren, gnarled tree and some words in cursive script below.

Even though he was an Adonis, this Mr. Earnshaw also looked like a complete wanker. He scrunched up that perfectly-sculpted nose, his lips curling back into a sneer. "What the devil is an app?"

What kind of weird question is that? "Um... you know, an application for your phone, so you can get the bus timetable or talk to your mates or—"

"Don't talk to me about *phones*," Earnshaw snapped. "People spend too much time on their phones."

Right. I'd forgotten the part in the job ad about hating ebooks. *This guy must be one of those weirdos who eschews technology.* "Oh, I agree. I mean, phones should only be used for calling people. And checking social media. That's it. I would never read on mine," I blubbered, shoving my phone behind my back. "I mean, studies have shown it can cause long-term eye damage and—"

"No matter how long you keep talking, it's not going to change the fact that we're closed. What do you *want?*"

"I'm applying for the assistant's job." I fumbled in my purse for the envelope I'd carefully sealed, trying to avoid accidentally showing him the ereader tucked behind my makeup case. "I've got my resume in here for you with all my qualifications and—"

"I don't need that. If you want the job, tell me why I should hire you."

"Right, well..." This was the weirdest interview I've ever been to. Earnshaw's eyes stabbed right through me, turning my insides to mush. I opened my mouth, but then he blinked, long black lashes tangling together over those eyes – they were like black holes, gobbling whole universes for lunch. A shiver started at the base of my neck and rocketed down my spine, not stopping until it caressed me between my legs.

Now I wanted the job more than ever, just so I could stare at this specimen all day. Bloody hell, I always did have a thing for surly bad boys. I blamed Emily Brontë. The brutish and untamable Heathcliff ruined me for nice guys.

"If your answer is to gape at me like a bespawling lubberwort," he growled, "then you can take the job and shove it where the sun don't shine—"

"That's *not* my answer." My cheeks flared with heat. *Who even is this guy? Adonis or not, how'd he get off talking to customers and potential employees like that? No wonder the place is deserted.* "I was just collecting my thoughts. You should hire me because I'm a hard worker. I'm punctual. I have some retail experience, as well as design expertise so I can do graphics and window displays—"

"I don't care. Why do you want to work *here?* No one wants to work here. That was the whole *point* of the ad."

I racked my brain for an answer to that question. *What does he want from me?* "Um... I guess because I used to hang out in the bookshop all the time as a kid. I know where all the books go and I've personally helped Mr. Simson fix that till on at least two occasions." I pointed to the ancient contraption the raven was pecking.

Earnshaw glared at me, his eyes flicking over my face as though searching for something. He didn't say a thing. The silence stretched between us until even the raven got bored of hunting for worms in the credit card machine and stared at me, too.

Is he waiting for more?

"And... um, I have all sorts of useful skills." I scrambled for anything that might endear me to this strong-chinned man. "I have a fashion degree, so that's probably not useful. But I am a Millennial, so I can do the store's social media. I could build a website—"

You can see it, can't you? That strange voice said. *It's obvious. She's the one he told you about.*

Earnshaw grunted. I narrowed my eyes at him. *Does he hear it, too?*

Just hire her already, that voice said again. *She's pretty.*

"Hey!" I glanced over my shoulder, looking for the owner of the voice so I could kick them in the nuts. But there was no one else in the room.

Was it Earnshaw? But the voice didn't sound like him, and judging by the way he was still staring at me, he already thought I was nuts. *Maybe he didn't hear the voice after all?*

Besides, the voice sounded like it came from *inside* my head.

Please, don't tell me that on top of everything else, I'm now hallucinating voices—

I like her, the voice interrupted. *I bet she'll bring me treats. Berries, smoked salmon, maybe even a hard-boiled egg.*

I peered over my shoulder again. *Are they hiding in the hallway? Behind the beanbag stack?* "Who's there?"

Earnshaw's head whipped up. "Who are you talking to?"

"You didn't hear that? Someone prattling on about salmon and eggs."

Earnshaw's eyes narrowed. He reached out and clamped an enormous hand around the raven's beak. "You didn't leave the door open, did you? We're supposed to be *closed.*"

"No. I..." My shoulders sagged. *Who am I kidding? This is hopeless.* "I guess I'll just be going now. Thank you for your time and—"

"You start tomorrow," Earnshaw glowered. "We open at nine. Be here at eight-thirty, but don't let anyone else in. If you're late, the bird gets your paycheck."

TO BE CONTINUED

Uncover the secrets of Nevermore Bookshop in book 1, *A Dead and Stormy Night*

http://books2read.com/adeadandstormynight

AGATHA CHRISTIE MEET BLACK BOOKS

What do you get when you cross a cursed bookshop, three hot fictional men, and a punk rock heroine nursing a broken heart?

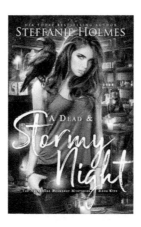

After being fired from her fashion internship in New York City, Mina Wilde decides it's time to reevaluate her life. She returns to the quaint English village where she grew up to take a job at the local bookshop, hoping that being surrounded by great literature will help her heal from a devastating blow.

But Mina soon discovers her life is stranger than fiction – a mysterious curse on the bookshop brings fictional characters to life in lust-worthy bodies. Mina finds herself babysitting Poe's raven, making hot dogs for Heathcliff, and getting IT help from James Moriarty, all while trying not to fall for the three broken men who should only exist within her imagination.

When Mina's ex-best friend shows up dead with a knife in her back, she's the chief suspect. She'll have to solve the murder if she wants to clear her name. Will her fictional boyfriends be able to keep her out of prison?

The Nevermore Bookshop Mysteries are what you get when all your book boyfriends come to life. Join a brooding antihero, a master criminal, a cheeky raven, and a heroine with a big heart (and an even bigger book collection) in this brand new steamy reverse harem paranormal mystery series by *USA Today* best-selling author Steffanie Holmes.

READ NOW:
books2read.com/adeadandstormynight

OTHER BOOKS BY STEFFANIE HOLMES

Nevermore Bookshop Mysteries

A Dead and Stormy Night

Of Mice and Murder

Pride and Premeditation

How Heathcliff Stole Christmas

Memoirs of a Garroter

Prose and Cons

A Novel Way to Die

Much Ado About Murder

Crime and Publishing

Plot and Bothered

Grimdale Graveyard Mysteries

What do you do when three hot AF, possessive ghosts want to jump your bones? Find out in this spooky, kooky paranormal romance series set in the same world as Nevermore Bookshop.

You're So Dead To Me

If You've Got It, Haunt It

Ghoul as a Cucumber

Not a Mourning Person

Kings of Miskatonic Prep

Shunned

Initiated

Possessed

Ignited

Stonehurst Prep

My Stolen Life

My Secret Heart

My Broken Crown

My Savage Kingdom

Stonehurst Prep Elite

Poison Ivy

Poison Flower

Poison Kiss

DARK ACADEMIA

Pretty Girls Make Graves

Brutal Boys Cry Blood

Manderley Academy

Ghosted

Haunted

Spirited

Briarwood Witches

Earth and Embers

Fire and Fable

Water and Woe

Wind and Whispers

Spirit and Sorrow

Crookshollow Gothic Romance

Art of Cunning (Alex & Ryan)

Art of the Hunt (Alex & Ryan)

Art of Temptation (Alex & Ryan)

The Man in Black (Elinor & Eric)

Watcher (Belinda & Cole)

Reaper (Belinda & Cole)

Wolves of Crookshollow

Digging the Wolf (Anna & Luke)

Writing the Wolf (Rosa & Caleb)

Inking the Wolf (Bianca & Robbie)

Wedding the Wolf (Willow & Irvine)

Want to be informed when the next Steffanie Holmes paranormal romance story goes live? Sign up for the newsletter at www.steffanieholmes.com/ newsletter to get the scoop, and score a free collection of bonus scenes and stories to enjoy!

About the Author

Steffanie Holmes is the *USA Today* bestselling author of the paranormal, gothic, dark, and fantastical. Her books feature clever, witty heroines, secret societies, creepy old mansions and alpha males who *always* get what they want.

Legally-blind since birth, Steffanie received the 2017 Attitude Award for Artistic Achievement. She was also a finalist for a 2018 Women of Influence award.

Steff is the creator of *Rage Against the Manuscript* – a resource of free content, books, and courses to help writers tell their story, find their readers, and build a badass writing career.

Steffanie lives in New Zealand with her husband, a horde of cantankerous cats, and their medieval sword collection.

STEFFANIE HOLMES NEWSLETTER

Grab a free copy of *Cabinet of Curiosities* – a Steffanie Holmes compendium of short stories and bonus scenes – when you sign up for updates with the Steffanie Holmes newsletter.

http://www.steffanieholmes.com/newsletter

Come hang with Steffanie
www.steffanieholmes.com
hello@steffanieholmes.com